C   B

"You permit that I join you?"

Antonia tried to hide her lack of enthusiasm. Jaime de Almeida was not her choice of breakfast companion. But she rang the service bell on the table as he continued.

"Permit me to offer my condolences on your recent bereavement. However, you must be reflecting on how fortunate you are at this bleak juncture in your life to find another mother so comfortably situated."

Antonia stared at him incredulously. "I don't care for your inference, Señor de Almeida. You obviously harbor dark suspicions about my motives in accepting Diana's invitation."

"I make no secret that I fear for Diana. I would do much to protect her from further hurt." His black eyes held her inexorably. "You would do well to remember that, Miss Grant."

Catherine George was born in Wales, and
following her marriage to an engineer, lived eight
years in Brazil at a gold-mine site, an experience she
would later draw upon for her books. It was not until
she and her husband returned to England and bought
a village post office and general store that she
submitted her first book at her husband's
encouragement. Now her husband helps manage their
household so that Catherine can devote more time to
her writing. They have two children, a daughter and a
son, who share their mother's love of language and
writing.

Books by Catherine George

HARLEQUIN ROMANCE

HARLEQUIN PRESENTS

Don't miss any of our special offers. Write to us at the
following address for information on our newest releases.

Harlequin Reader Service
901 Fuhrmann Blvd., P.O. Box 1397, Buffalo, NY 14240
Canadian address: P.O. Box 603,
Fort Erie, Ont. L2A 5X3

Man of Iron
Catherine George

Harlequin Books

TORONTO • NEW YORK • LONDON
AMSTERDAM • PARIS • SYDNEY • HAMBURG
STOCKHOLM • ATHENS • TOKYO • MILAN

Original hardcover edition published in 1987
by Mills & Boon Limited

ISBN 0-373-02924-1

Harlequin Romance first edition August 1988

Copyright © 1987 by Catherine George.
All rights reserved. Except for use in any review, the reproduction or utilization
of this work in whole or in part in any form by any electronic, mechanical or
other means, now known or hereafter invented, including xerography,
photocopying and recording, or in any information storage or retrieval system,
is forbidden without the permission of the publisher, Harlequin Enterprises
Limited, 225 Duncan Mill Road, Don Mills, Ontario, Canada M3B 3K9.

All the characters in this book have no existence outside the imagination of
the author and have no relation whatsoever to anyone bearing the same name
or names. They are not even distantly inspired by any individual known or
unknown to the author, and all incidents are pure invention.

® are Trademarks registered in the United States Patent and Trademark Office
and in other countries.

Printed in U.S.A.

CHAPTER ONE

THE office was very quiet, and smelt of leather and the dust dancing in a shaft of sunlight from the tall window. The young solicitor behind the desk watched his client uneasily, heartily wishing his father had delegated this particular interview to someone else as he saw the letter in the girl's hand shaking slightly, and the tears she tried to hide as she followed the familiar handwriting on the page. Normally she was a glowing, attractive girl, but the combination of grief and the black dress she was wearing had drained all the life from her olive skin and fair hair. He was accustomed to seeing the latter curling freely about her face and shoulders, but today it was pulled back severely with a black ribbon, in a way which emphasised her pallor and drew attention to the red, swollen lids concealing her eyes.

At last she folded the pages with painstaking care before returning them to their envelope, giving herself breathing space to get her emotions under control. Paul Deeping waited in silent sympathy while she took a handkerchief from her handbag and dried her eyes. After a while she looked up at him, smiling valiantly in apology.

'Sorry, Paul. I'm not usually such a watering can. It was just the shock of seeing Mother's handwriting like that. She writes exactly as she talks—talked, I mean.'

'Personally I think a few tears might do you good, Antonia,' he said. 'My parents were very worried over your iron calm at the funeral yesterday.'

'I've tried to do all my crying in private.'

Paul Deeping's eyes were kind. 'Are you upset by what you've just learned from your mother's letter?'

Antonia straightened in her chair. 'Not upset, exactly. I've known all along I was adopted, of course, or "chosen"

5

as Mother preferred to put it, but I was always under the impression nothing was known about my—my origins. It's rather a shock to find Mother actually *was* on the scene when I was born, after all. *And* in the very bedroom I've slept in all my life.' Antonia shook her head, frowning. 'It's hard to take in. Oh, I know I've just found out that one of Mother's student lodgers actually gave birth to me, but that doesn't mean much for the moment.'

'That's only natural. Janet Grant was the only mother you've ever known, Antonia—and a jolly splendid one at that.'

Antonia nodded in vigorous agreement, her hazel-gold eyes bright with tears again. She blinked them away and smiled. 'Absolutely true, Paul. Of course we had arguments now and then, and sometimes she laid down the law a bit much—but she was always ready with a wisecrack and a laugh, even on top of storming away about the state of my bedroom or the noise from my record player.'

Paul eyed her uneasily. 'I take it Mrs Grant hasn't said much about finances?'

'No. Her letter's more concerned with the young student who came back from a holiday abroad to find herself pregnant, and then got turned out of the house by her parents when they were told the glad news.' Antonia grimaced in disgust. 'Can you imagine people doing that?'

He coughed drily. 'You must remember that the young lady's parents were elderly and very strait-laced. In any event, she fled back to the only haven she knew, which was the house where she'd lodged with your parents for two years previously. I believe they were very fond of her.'

Antonia sighed. 'Mother says that after I was born the girl dropped out of her language course at the university and went off to London. At which point Mother calls a halt. She feels—felt—the rest of the story is up to—to my natural mother.' She looked at Paul Deeping in appeal. 'Could you just let me know her name? It would simplify things.'

He nodded slowly. 'Very well—her maiden name was Moore, but I can tell you nothing more because the lady in question is leaving all decisions to you. If you decide you want to make her acquaintance I have permission to reveal her identity. If not, she wishes to remain anonymous.'

'I see.' Antonia pushed a stray tendril of hair away from her forehead, her eyes thoughtful. 'I wonder why she imagines I might *not* want to meet her?'

Paul Deeping leaned back in his chair, obviously searching for the right words. 'Remember, Antonia, she's of a different generation. It was more of a stigma at the time to be single and pregnant, and from what I understand she suffered deeply over having to give you away. The Grants adopted you legally, of course, but you were five days old before your real mother was strong enough to leave, which must have made it hard for her to part with you. Probably she felt as though she was abandoning you.'

Antonia nodded slowly. 'And she thinks I might feel the same way.'

'Exactly. Now, to facts and figures.' He drew a large file towards him and began to put her in the picture. Janet Grant's struggle to make ends meet after her husband had died was a familiar story to Antonia, who had always tried to help by working in various jobs through her vacations. It came as no surprise to learn that the family home was heavily mortgaged, and that even after the sale of house and contents she would be lucky to break even. 'There is, however, still a small sum in the account set up for your education,' went on Paul Deeping.

Antonia looked up quickly in surprise. 'Really? How did Mother manage that?'

'She didn't, actually. Your natural mother, Miss Moore, made certain conditions when you were born. The names you should be given, the right to contribute to your education as soon as she was capable of earning enough money to do so . . . Also she was adamant that you should remain ignorant of her existence while Mrs Grant was alive.'

'So now I know how I went to such an expensive school!'

He nodded, then went on to explain that in due course

Miss Moore's parents had died, leaving a modest legacy to their erring daughter. Too proud to use it for herself, she had set it aside for her own daughter, augmenting it from time to time with sums saved from her own earnings.

'What did she do for a living?' asked Antonia curiously.

'I'm not at liberty to say.'

'But she's married?'

'Yes. But any further information must be for the lady herself to supply when, or if, you meet her.' Paul looked uncomfortable. 'My father said I must stress that unless you find work fairly soon your position is difficult. You have enough to live on for a while, but once the house is sold you'll have to find rent as well as food, since the very fact you have such a sum in your name, modest though it is, renders you ineligible for assistance from the State.'

Antonia was very thoughtful on the bus journey home, feeling distinctly dazed by all the new facts ingested in one fell swoop. Yesterday there had been all the grief and strain of the funeral, then today, almost before she had time to draw breath, she had made the astounding discovery that she possessed another mother. One, what was more, who had been in the background all the time, contributing anonymous financial help.

'She would have been welcome to visit you, of course, in the guise of an old friend of mine,' Janet Grant had written, 'but considered this unfair to me. I wouldn't have minded sharing you—I think. But that's easy to say, since I was never put to the test.'

Antonia read the letter again once she was home. It told her so much and yet so tantalisingly little, leaving her wanting to know more. It seemed that Janet Grant had kept her promise about the facts of Antonia's birth until she realised how short a time was left, and only then, a few short weeks earlier, had entrusted Deeping & Son with the letter for her beloved child. It gave merely the bare facts leading up to her adoption of the unfortunate young student's baby; the rest of the letter had been by way of the farewell she had been unable to put into words during those final days before she'd died, and Antonia re-read the loving farewell message, humorous even to the last, and forced herself to face the fact that Janet Grant was gone for ever. Antonia Luisa Grant, give or take a few adoptive relatives, was on her own.

Slowly she went upstairs to take off the ugly black dress, and ran herself a hot bath so she could think. It was a family joke that her thought processes functioned better when she lay relaxed in hot, scented water, and she had endured many a maternal scolding for lingering too long in the bathroom. Antonia's eyes softened as she leaned her head against the back of the tub. Janet Grant had been a great one for scolding, though seldom without the leavening twinkle in her eye. She was probably up there in heaven right this minute, sorting out the Angel Gabriel! Antonia's little chuckle ended in a sob, and she tried hard to make her mind blank, but it was no use. She had been existing in some kind of vacuum since her mother's death, but now it was gone. She could feel again, and it hurt. But no amount of tears would bring her back. Antonia sighed as she thought of the way her life had changed so dramatically in the past few weeks.

The summer had been hectic. Apart from the cramming for finals and the nerve-racking labour of the actual examinations, there had been an endless round of parties, Ladies' Day at Ascot and a win on a horse, the Summer Ball in college, followed a day or two later by the terrifying call from Janet's sister, asking Antonia to go home at once because her mother was ill. Antonia was familiar with her mother's erratic blood pressure, which had a tendency to rocket, and needed constant medication to regulate it. But, widowed when Antonia was five, Janet Grant had been overworked for a long time, and finally she suffered a stroke.

When Antonia arrived on the scene as quickly as humanly possible, Janet was lying against her pillows looking old and tired, her face slightly twisted, but otherwise her usual cheerful self. Hiding her fear, Antonia

took charge at once, playfully bossy as she assumed
responsibility for speeding the departing lodgers. She tidied
the house and did the cooking, and for almost a month
persuaded herself life could go on as normal. Then Janet
had asked Antonia to sit by her bed last thing one night,
and told her a letter was with Deeping & Son should
anything happen. Antonia had held her mother tight for a
long time before Janet patted her shoulder and sent her off
to bed. During the night Janet suffered a massive, fatal
stroke, and Antonia was alone—or as alone as it was
possible to be in a household taken over immediately by
Janet's sisters and various other relations.

Antonia came to several conclusions while the bath
water slowly cooled. First, the house must be put up for sale
right away. It had been a lively, welcoming place in the
past, but the warmth of the house had obviously emanated
from her mother, who had been the heart of it. Now that
loving heartbeat was stilled Antonia found the deadly quiet
hard to bear.

Also, she acknowledged, she was very curious to meet
this other, unknown mother of hers, so much so that in some
measure the mere discovery of her existence went a little
way towards blunting the sharpest edge of her own grief. A
strong feeling of disloyalty troubled Antonia at first, until
she eventually realised that Janet Grant had died happier
in the knowledge that her daughter would have someone
else to turn to in her loneliness.

Antonia dressed and ran downstairs to ring Paul
Deeping, telling him she had given the matter some
thought, as he had advised, and that she would like to meet
her real mother, if only to thank her for the financial help
Antonia had unknowingly received all her life. Paul
promised to set things in motion, and to contact her the next
day as soon as he had some news for her.

Feeling a little better, Antonia made herself some coffee,
suddenly at a loss as to what to do with herself. She wished
now she hadn't been so adamant to relatives and friends
alike that she needed a few days on her own. Her mother,

she knew only too well, would have been dead against the idea, *and* the black dress. Life was for living in Janet Grant's opinion, and during those last few days she had made her outlook very clear to her daughter. Even her final message in her letter had been to wish Antonia a wonderful life. Tomorrow, Antonia decided, she would ring up Jane, her room-mate in college, and look up some of her old schoolfriends locally, and, even more important, start the hunt for a job and some kind of flat or bedsitter.

It was quite late in the evening when the doorbell rang. Antonia looked at her watch and frowned. After a pause, while she hoped whoever it was would go away, a second peal on the bell brought her to her feet. Reluctantly she went to the front door and opened it the small distance allowed by the safety chain, then stood staring in astonishment at the man standing on the doorstep. Not only was he the most handsome man she had ever seen in her life; but he was also a complete stranger. Below curling black hair his face was as classically perfect as a Greek statue, and Antonia watched, fascinated, as his mouth curved in a smile of great warmth that lit his dark, thickly fringed eyes as they met hers.

'You are Miss Grant?' he asked, with a faint trace of some foreign accent.

Antonia simply nodded, rendered momentarily speechless by the mere sight of him.

'I was given your address by Mr Paul Deeping,' the man went on, to Antonia's surprise. 'I fear I should have waited until tomorrow, as he said, but I was impatient to meet you.'

'You were?' she said faintly.

His smile widened, and he made a little gesture of appeal with slim, expressive hands. 'Would you allow me to come inside, please, Miss Grant?'

'You say Mr Deeping sent you?' she asked.

'No,' he answered ruefully. 'He did not *send* me. I was to see you tomorrow at his office, but on impulse I came here tonight——'

'Would you mind telling me who you are?'

'Of course! Forgive me, I should have done so at once. I am Mario de Almeida.' He smiled again as Antonia looked blank. 'I am, I think—how do you say?—your stepbrother.'

Antonia stared at him, dumbfounded. 'My stepbrother!' Then the telephone rang and she glanced back at it, then again at the man outside, wondering what to do.

'I will wait here outside until you have spoken on the telephone,' said Mario de Almeida, and stepped back with a graceful little bow. Antonia left the door ajar on the chain, not liking to shut it in his face, and picked up the telephone from the hall table. To her great relief it was Paul Deeping, asking her to visit his office the following morning to meet a relative of her mother's.

'Too late, Paul. If you mean Mr de Almeida, he's here already on the doorstep. I was just trying to decide whether I should let him in or not.'

Paul chuckled. 'Sensible girl. But don't worry. Mario de Almeida's the son of the man your natural mother eventually married. He's flown over to the UK as her representative in this rather delicate little matter.'

'Flown from where?'

'Brazil, Antonia. Perhaps it's a good thing for you to get acquainted informally this evening, but tell Mr de Almeida that I still want to see you both in the morning at eleven. Now go and let him in—I expect he's finding our March evening a bit chilly!'

Mario de Almeida's white teeth were quite audibly chattering by the time Antonia, reassured as to his authenticity, let him in the house at last. She led him into the sitting-room and knelt to turn on the gas fire, very conscious that dark eyes were examining her with great interest.

'Thank you so much,' he said, rubbing his hands together as the warmth began to reach him. 'Your country is beautiful, but the climate is a little—bracing is right?'

'Absolutely.' Antonia smiled at him for the first time, and his expressive eyes registered the fact with appreciation. 'I'm sorry I kept you outside for so long, Mr de Almeida, but now I'm on my own here I feel a bit wary about opening the door to strangers.' She made a frantic mental inventory of the food in the house. 'May I offer you something to eat?'

'Thank you, no. I have dined already—you eat very early in England.'

'Do we?'

'Compared with Brazil, most definitely.'

'Then would you care for a drink? I have Scotch, or some sherry?' Antonia was on sure ground on this, since both were left over from the funeral.

Mario de Almeida nodded, smiling. 'A small whisky would be most welcome.' He shivered again slightly. 'To keep out the cold, I think you say.'

'You've obviously never been here in winter!' Antonia smiled at him again, then went off to fetch the drinks, making a sprinting detour for the bathroom to inspect her appearance. There was no make-up on her face, but her eyes had lost their pink, swollen look, and her skin looked normal again, glowing above the yellow of her sweatshirt. There was no opportunity to do anything to herself at this stage, beyond releasing her hair from its elastic band and brushing it so it fell in its usual curly profusion to her shoulders. A pity she hadn't known about this gorgeous surprise visitor in advance, she thought with resignation, for she could have done something to her face, if nothing else. Not that it mattered, she told herself impatiently, then smiled as she wondered what Janet's comment on Mario de Almeida would have been. Pithy as usual, no doubt!

The handsome Brazilian sprang to his feet as Antonia returned to the sitting-room with a loaded tray, relieving her of it with ceremony.

'Thank you.' Antonia gestured to the small table beside her and he set the tray down, insisting on making the drinks himself. He took his own whisky neat, but took care to mix Antonia's scant amount of spirit with the required generous top-up of ginger ale she liked. Afterwards he sat down and regarded her gravely over his glass.

'Firstly, Miss Grant, I come to offer my sincere condolences on your bereavement,' he said gently.

'Thank you, Mr de Almeida.'

'Also I apologise if I intrude upon your grief.'

'You don't,' she assured him candidly. 'To tell the truth I was feeling very lonely before you came. Entirely my fault—I insisted I wanted to be on my own for a bit when friends and relatives asked me to stay. Unfortunately, now I am on my own I'm not nearly so enamoured of my own company as I expected. The house is so quiet.' She shrugged apologetically. 'It's usually so noisy here, you see. Mother always took in students as lodgers and quite often they stayed on during vacations as well, particularly those from overseas. But this last batch were all third years, doing their finals, and now everyone's gone.'

He nodded understandingly. 'You must be very lonely. It is not right for a young girl to live alone here. You are vulnerable.'

'Ah, but I didn't let you in the house right away!'

'I was pleased you did not. I never imagined you would be alone, you understand. I believed some female relative, at least, would be here in the house with you at such a time.'

'I see.' Antonia eyed him questioningly, unable to restrain her curiosity any longer. 'Mr de Almeida——'

'Could it not be Mario,' he said swiftly, 'since we are to be relatives?'

She smiled shyly. 'All right—Mario. To be frank, I'm very curious to know just exactly how we *are* related!'

His eyes were velvet soft with sympathy. 'What you really desire, I think, is to know why I am here instead of Diana.'

'Diana?'

Mario nodded. 'My *madrasta*—stepmother—and your natural mother, Miss Diana Moore, as she was when you were born. Senhora Diana de Almeida as she is now.'

Antonia stared at him, her mind working overtime. Did this mean she had a stepfather, too, a whole distant family she knew nothing about? And, to her intense disappointment, she realised abruptly, this newly discovered mother of hers was way out of reach, thousands of miles away in Brazil.

Mario leaned forward, smiling in reassurance. 'My father, Francisco de Almeida, married Diana after meeting her in the British Embassy in Rio more than twelve years ago. He had been *viúvo*—widower—for many years. She came to live with us in the state of Minas Gerais, but alas my father died after they had been married for only seven years. My family is in mining. The land around us is rich in iron ore, you understand, and my brother and I carry on the family business. I travel much to the States, but Jaime stays more in Brazil, and Diana lives now at Lagoa del Rey, which used to be the family's weekend retreat. She prefers to remain there in seclusion; at least until Marisa grows older and needs further education.'

'Marisa?'

He smiled. 'You have a little sister of five years, who, with wondrous timing, developed *varicela*, so Diana was not able to leave her to fly to England.' He grimaced. 'Chicken-pox at such a time! Jaime—well, Jaime could not get away, so I came in Diana's place. Her emissary, I think you say?'

'I see.' Antonia rose to top up Mario's glass. 'And as emissary, as you put it, what exactly is your purpose in contacting me?'

'I did not know until this evening whether I would be allowed to contact you at all. Diana said I must go home without seeing you if you had no wish to meet her. I think she feared this very much; that you would want nothing to do with her.' Mario thanked her for the whisky and looked up into her eyes. 'Mr Deeping assures me that you do. Is he right?'

Antonia nodded, and sat down again. 'Yes, he is. I would very much like to meet her—some time, that is. I naturally thought she lived here, in this country, you see. I'm afraid it's out of the question for me to travel to Brazil.'

His dark eyebrows lifted. 'Why? You have finished in the college, and Mr Deeping says you have no job yet.

What prevents you?' His eyes narrowed. 'Is it some man, perhaps? Someone you cannot bear to leave?'

Antonia flushed. 'No, nothing like that.' Her eyes slid away from his in embarrassment. 'It's very hard to put into words.'

'Then perhaps I am permitted to do it for you.' Mario de Almeida smiled gently. 'You mean you have no money.'

The flush in Antonia's cheeks grew hectic. 'Not exactly. I'm not penniless, and I'm perfectly capable of supporting myself once I find a job. But I'm afraid a trip to Brazil is utterly out of the question.'

'You do not want to come? Lagoa del Rey is very beautiful.'

Antonia nodded sadly. 'I'm sure it is, and I would like to come, very much, and I also want to meet Diana. But until I'm better placed financially it just isn't possible.'

'Before you make up your mind perhaps you should read this.' Mario reached into his inner pocket and drew out a long envelope, which bore the single name 'Antonia' in unfamiliar, flowing handwriting. He handed it over, and Antonia opened it with care. Inside she found an airline ticket, and a note which said:

Dear Antonia,

If you are reading this I know you will already have agreed to meet me. I have taken the liberty of buying you the enclosed ticket in the hope that you will use it to fly back with Mario, who will bring you here to Lagoa del Rey. Since the moment you were born it has been my constant wish to have you with me again, even though I would never have intruded on your relationship with Janet while she lived. I loved her too; she was a pearl among women, and I only wish I could have been there with you at her funeral.

I'm certain a change of scene at this time would be good for you, and I know for a fact that Janet wanted you to come. She said so many times in her letters, but I always felt it would be unfair, both to her and to you.

Now, however, I very much hope that you will come to visit me, Antonia, for as long as you wish. A warm welcome awaits you.

The letter was signed, simply, 'Diana'.

'Will you come?' asked Mario, as Antonia finished reading.

'I don't know,' she said slowly. 'I need time to think it over. So many things have happened all at once my brain is having difficulty taking everything in.'

'You came as a great surprise to *us* also, little sister,' he said. 'Diana never told my father about you, and she informed Jaime and me only a few days ago when she received the news that Mrs Grant had died.'

'Was I a shock to you?'

Mario rose to his feet and pulled her up from her chair, smiling down at her. 'Not a shock, Antonia. A very charming surprise.' And he bent and kissed her cheek. She drew back, startled, and his eyes danced. 'Is a brotherly kiss not allowed, *querida*?'

'But you're not really my brother,' she pointed out.

Mario cast his eyes up piously, then grinned at her. 'No, I'm not, *graças a Deus!*'

CHAPTER TWO

Antonia felt excitement knot inside her as the aeroplane began its descent through majestic mountain peaks towards the airport at Boa Vista. She looked nervously at Mario, to find him watching the changing expressions on her face as different emotions warred inside her. He smiled at her reassuringly and took one of her hands in his.

'Not long now, *cara*. Almost there. How do you feel?'

'Tense!'

'Relax, *menina, calma do Brasil*. You have nothing to

worry about. Diana, as I've told you many times, is *muito simpática*—a very lovely lady.'

'I'm sure she is. But——' Antonia breathed in deeply. 'It's just that it's all so sudden, and everything happened so quickly.'

Which was true. The moment Paul Deeping had been sure Antonia really did want to fly to Brazil, and convinced his father of the same thing, he acted with a rapidity that had left his young client dazed. Her aunts were informed about Diana, and pressed into service with preparing the house for sale. Aunt Marion, Janet's younger sister, had been openly relieved, and said so in no uncertain terms. With a family of three herself there was little she could do personally for Antonia, neither could Beatrice who had an invalid husband. The electrifying news of Antonia's natural mother came as a considerable relief to them both, and with brisk kindness they helped Antonia to get ready for her trip, assuring her of a temporary bed with either of them when she got back, until she found a place of her own once the house was sold.

Mario de Almeida made a tremendous impression on both women, and on some of Antonia's friends, when they came to an impromptu get-together to wish her *bon voyage*. Jane, in particular, was loud in her admiration.

'Are there any more at home like you?' had been her frank response to Mario's greeting, and totally unembarrassed he had admitted to a brother.

'But Jaime is not much like me,' he said, smiling serenely.

Antonia was relieved. Two men as good-looking as Mario would be a bit much to have around at the same time! But even without the startling good looks Mario would still have been an attractive man, because of the warmth and kindness of his personality. For the short period before they left for Brazil Mario had taken it on himself to make sure his new stepsister had little time to herself for grieving. He drove her to out-of-the-way inns to dine where no one was likely to know her and exclaim over Janet Grant's daughter living it up so soon after her

mother's death. Apart from this Mario rather surprised
Antonia by informing her it would not be proper for him to
spend time alone with her in the house, since she was a
young lady without chaperon. Amused, and secretly very
touched by his attitude, Antonia went out with him as he
wished, and was grateful.

Paul Deeping had provided Antonia with money from
the account Diana had set up for her, and she spent some of
it on clothes for herself, a doll for Marisa, and a cashmere
sweater for Diana, having been informed that the evenings
at Lagoa del Rey could be chilly in the cold season. Now at
last, after the transatlantic flight to Rio, they were on the
plane to Boa Vista, and the moment of truth was at hand.
As the plane descended towards the runway Antonia knew
a moment of sheer, unadulterated panic, wondering wildly
what she was doing here, and what on earth had possessed
her to come. What if she and Diana loathed each other on
sight? Just because an accident of nature had made them
mother and daughter it didn't necessarily follow that they
would even like each other. And, much as she tried to
dismiss it, another spectre haunted Antonia, to add to her
stress: the question of who her father had been. Could it
have been some waiter in whatever resort Diana had spent
that fateful holiday abroad twenty-two years ago?

'Carinha,' said Mario, interrupting her train of thought.
'Do not look so terrified, I beg you. No one will eat you, I
promise.' He leaned close suddenly as the plane bumped
along the tarmac. 'Though I confess it is sometimes a great
temptation to nibble on this so alluring little ear of yours.'

Instantly Antonia felt better, and she pulled away,
laughing. Clever Mario to know exactly how to rout the
blues bedevilling her! Then there was no more time for
introspection as they left the plane for the bright sunshine
outside, and went through the usual routine with luggage
inside the airport building. Antonia looked at Mario
questioningly as he shepherded her through the people
thronging the building.

'Will Diana be here to meet us?'

He shook his head, craning his neck to look above the crowd. 'No, *cara*. She does not wish her first meeting with her daughter to take place in an airport. Ah, *bom*, there is Sabino.' He waved a hand vigorously, and a smiling, dark-skinned man pushed towards them.

'*Como vai*, Senhor Mario?' Sabino inclined his head towards Antonia. '*Senora*,' he added pleasantly.

Antonia smiled at him in return, and in a remarkably short time they were outside again in the sunshine, where a large estate car awaited them. The luggage was stowed away in the back and Antonia installed on the front seat between Mario and Sabino. Mario's arm behind her provided warmth and stability in this new exotic world of mountain peaks and brilliant green vegetation lining the road that stretched out before them in the hot, yellow light as they set off in the direction of Lagoa del Rey, which Mario informed her was roughly fifty kilometres away.

'And not all of them on a main highway like this,' he warned her, smiling, and pointed out the city of Boa Vista in the distance, a frieze of geometrical shapes, chalk-white against the unbelievable blue of the sky. Antonia sat silent, her eyes wide as she drank in everything around her while Mario, after a swift word of apology in English, conducted a brief conversation with Sabino, asking questions in gunfire-rapid Portuguese interspersed with much laughter.

'All is well at Lagoa del Rey,' he reported to Antonia presently. 'Marisa is recovered from the *varicela* and is her usual exhausting self. Diana, too, is well, and the whole household awaits your arrival with much anticipation.'

Antonia took a deep breath. 'Do I look all right, Mario?'

He laughed indulgently. 'According to Sabino you are *muito bonita*—very pretty—and I agree with all my heart. Stop worrying, *chica*, you look perfect.'

Antonia doubted that, but at least she was confident that her green cotton jersey dress had survived the journey remarkably well, and that the colour was good with her olive skin and light eyes and hair. Nerves still affected her stomach muscles, but her interest in the spectacular

mountainous scenery they were driving through eased her
tension gradually. Eventually they turned off on a rougher
minor road that swooped around hillsides and stretched out
between peaks like a tightrope now and then before it
began to descend gradually, the red, dusty road levelling
out as a great expanse of water came into view, glistening
like a great sapphire in the rust-red setting of the
surrounding slopes and peaks.

'Lagoa del Rey,' announced Mario, intent on her
reaction as she saw the great lake for the first time.
Antonia's eyes opened wide as she caught sight of the house
on the hillside beyond the lake. It was much larger than she
had ever imagined, and infinitely more beautiful, with red-
tiled roofs and glimpses of white walls screened by glossy
green hibiscus hedges starred with blossom. Sabino brought
the car to a halt at a small jetty at the water's edge, where a
small, power-driven boat lay waiting. Mario jumped down,
then held up his arms to Antonia to deposit her on the
wooden planks of the jetty, and help her into the boat, with
a voluble stream of thanks to Sabino, who drove off on the
road which encircled the great lake.

'It's a long way to the house by road,' said Mario,
grinning at the expression on Antonia's dazed face. 'This is
the short cut.' And with the grace and panache with which
he seemed to accomplish everything he did, he started the
engine and with a roar they were off across the broad blue
expanse. The breeze of their passage swept her hair from
her face as the boat sped like an arrow along the gold path
painted on the water by the setting sun. Antonia was
dazzled and exhilarated, and suddenly very glad she was
here. This was adventure! She marvelled at the thought
that only a short time ago she had been grief-stricken and
bereft, whereas now she had been granted the good fortune
to visit this magnificent country and spend a holiday here,
and she would do her utmost to like Diana, and everyone
else, however much effort it took. If only Mother could see
her now! Antonia swallowed, then smiled to herself at the
thought of Janet's reaction to all this. She would have loved

it—and so shall I, vowed Antonia silently.

Mario cut the engine as they reached a jetty at the foot of
the steep, winding track which led up to the house. He leapt
out to secure the boat, then helped Antonia out with care,
keeping her hand in his as they walked up the path, which
went on for longer than she had expected before they
arrived at double iron gates wreathed in yellow blossom,
and a smiling, dark-skinned man, very like Sabino, let them
through into the terraced garden. He was Geraldo, Sabino's
brother, explained Mario, after exchanging voluble
greetings with the man. Mario urged Antonia up towards
the long, low house crowning the beautiful, flower-filled
garden. At any other time she would have been interested
in the profusion of exotic shrubs and trees among the more
familiar roses and zinnias, but for now her entire attention
was centred on the fair girl hurrying down the steps from
the veranda with a small, dark-haired child trailing behind
her.

Mario's eyes lit up and he left Antonia to run the last few
yards to embrace the blonde girl with enthusiasm, then
turned, beaming with his arm round the slender waist of
the young woman as he beckoned Antonia towards them.

'Come, little sister,' he said exuberantly, 'let me present
you. Senhora Diana de Almeida, Miss Antonia Luisa
Grant.'

Antonia only just managed to prevent her jaw dropping
as she gazed at the other woman in surprise. *This* was
Diana? For a long, silent moment they all stood frozen in
tableau, then Diana de Almeida detached herself from
Mario's grasp and moved forward, smiling, holding out her
hand in welcome.

'Hello, Antonia,' she said without drama. 'I can't tell you
how glad I am to see you.'

Antonia took the hand and smiled uncertainly. 'Hello.'
She shrugged helplessly. 'I just don't know what to say.'

'There aren't any rules for this type of situation, are
there?' Diana held on to Antonia's hand, just looking at her,
a warmth in her large grey eyes that went a long way

towards dispelling the awkwardness of the moment. She
was so much younger than Antonia had expected that her
appearance was a definite shock. The heavy ash-blonde
hair, skilfully cut to curve inwards at her jawline, and her
unlined, porcelain-fair skin gave her the look of a woman at
least ten years younger than sheer arithmetic indicated she
must be. For several moments the two women just looked at
each other, while Mario looked on with unconcealed
delight, until a small figure broke the spell by butting him
violently, and a mutinous voice let forth a flood of
Portuguese.

Diana released Antonia's hand and turned to bring the
child forward. 'Speak English, please, Marisa,' she said, but
the small brown face beneath a mop of dark curls looked
rebellious.

'*Porquê?*' said Marisa rudely.

'Because Antonia is our guest, and you must make her
welcome. She does not speak Portuguese,' said Mario
conciliatingly.

'And Antonia is your new sister,' Diana said firmly. 'I've
already told you all about her, so say how do you do
properly.'

'Hello, Marisa.' Antonia smiled down at the child
warmly. 'It's very nice of you to let me come and visit you.'

Marisa clutched Diana's hand possessively and scowled,
refusing to answer.

'Forgive her,' said Diana calmly. 'She's just had chicken-
pox, and her temperament has suffered accordingly.' She
looked down at Marisa without pleasure. 'However,
chicken-pox is no excuse for bad manners, Marisa de
Almeida, so I think you had better go and lie down on your
bed. Perhaps tomorrow you will feel more civilised.'

The big, dark eyes filled with tears as the child flew to
Mario and clutched his arm. '*Mario, não quero deitar agora
mesmo. Quero meu presente de Inglaterra!*'

'Marisa!' Diana's voice was gentle but inexorable, and
Mario bent to kiss the child swiftly, shaking his head at her
in disapproval.

'Do what *Mamãe* says, *pequena*. You shall have your present from England tomorrow!'

'I want it now!' The child stamped her foot, sending a baleful glare at Antonia, who was beginning to feel very uncomfortable.

Diana gave her a swift glance of apology, then thrust her rebellious little daughter towards a dusky-skinned girl in a gingham dress and white apron, hovering near the house. 'Zelia will take you to bed, Marisa, and I'll be along to see you in a little while.'

'I won't, I won't *go*!' screamed Marisa, and abruptly lay on her back on the grass, drumming her heels in a frenzy, sobbing loudly while the maid cast a look of anguished indecision at Diana.

'Let me take her,' offered Mario, but Diana stood firm.

'No, Mario, she must do as she's told——'

'I won't! I won't!' screamed the child, and another girl, dressed like Zelia, came running from the house to see what was the matter, breaking into a voluble discussion with the other maid, obviously arguing as to the best way to cope with the distraught child. Mario joined in, trying to raise the rigid, resisting little girl to her feet, and Diana bent to help him, her pretty face determined and angry.

Antonia stood apart, forgotten, feeling very much the outsider, trying not to feel hurt by the attitude of this child who, amazingly, was her half-sister. Eventually Mario's persuasion won the day as he cajoled Marisa into a calmer frame of mind, and at last the child scrambled to her feet, holding up her arms to him in entreaty. Diana relaxed, the maids melted into the background, and as Mario murmured a flood of soothing Portuguese into Marisa's ears the child hid her head on his broad shoulder. Above her tangled damp curls Mario smiled reassuringly at his stepmother.

'I shall take her to bed, *Madrasta*, do not upset yourself—stay with Antonia. Take her in the house and reassure her that we de Almeidas do not conduct all our affairs in public in the garden.'

Diana turned to Antonia in apology, her grey eyes rueful. 'I'm terribly sorry, Antonia. I wouldn't blame you in the least if you turned tail to catch the next plane back to London—but forgive us, please. I assure you we're not usually so inhospitable. Marisa, I think, we shall leave until tomorrow, when hopefully she will be more civilised.'

As Mario carried off Marisa, with the two maids in tow, Antonia quelled a sudden longing to be back in Bristol where she belonged and followed Diana up the steps to the veranda which encircled the house. It was obviously used as an extra room, Antonia saw, furnished with rattan chairs and chintz-coverered cushions, with small glass-topped tables scattered about and toys abandoned on the polished boards of the floor. The hot pink of bougainvillaea blossom cascaded down a trellis screening part of the veranda from the sun, and several pairs of glass double doors led at intervals into the rest of the house. 'We tend to congregate here,' went on Diana, 'except for the depths of the cold season, but the more formal reception-rooms are over on the far side.' She opened a pair of doors, and ushered Antonia through them. Antonia, almost dazed with fatigue by this time, gained a vague impression of numbers of doors and corridors leading to left and right until Diana showed her into a large, high-ceilinged room with white walls and furniture made from some unfamiliar, beautiful wood.

Antonia smiled with pleasure. 'What a charming room.' She turned to Diana rather awkwardly. 'I haven't thanked you properly yet for inviting me here.'

Diana sat down on the bed, smiling whimsically. 'I wasn't at all sure you'd want to come. But I was so worried about you, Antonia. Janet wrote to me some time ago saying her health was deteriorating——'

'You and Mother wrote to each other?'

'Yes. I sent my letters to Mr Deeping's office, of course, but Janet and I kept up a correspondence over the past twenty years; a fairly regular progress-report on you, I'm afraid, Antonia.' Her delicate face looked troubled. 'I hope you don't mind too much.'

Antonia shook her head, smiling faintly. 'And I thought I knew my mother so well——' She stopped short in dismay. 'I'm sorry, I don't mean to be tactless, but it's a bit difficult——'

'Don't apologise,' said Diana swiftly. 'Janet Grant was the only mother you've ever known. How else could you refer to her? I loved Janet dearly myself—you must miss her badly.'

'I do.' Antonia said forlornly, suddenly feeling very tired. 'She left a letter for me with Mr Deeping, telling me just a little about you, just that you were once one of her lodgers, really. She said the rest was for you to tell me.'

'Then you know she wanted very much for us to meet?'

'Yes.'

'I was afraid you'd want nothing to do with me.' Diana looked away.

Antonia hesitated, trying to find the right words. 'It *is* difficult for me to come to terms with the fact *you* are my mother, to be honest, but only because it's still very new to me, and, well—because you're so young! It's absolutely nothing to do with the fact that you had me adopted and went away. It seems to have been the only thing you *could* have done since Mother said your parents weren't exactly supportive.'

Diana smiled wryly. 'They didn't turn me out in the snow, precisely, but they were utterly disgusted with me, so I just walked out and threw myself on Janet's mercy. Which, as you know, was infinite.' She sighed. 'I'm not really all that young, though. Forty-two, to be exact. A good age to have a daughter of twenty-one, but a bit past it for coping with a lively little bag of tricks like Marisa, I can tell you. I do apologise for her horrendous tantrum. She's not usually as bad as that.'

'I suppose she's jealous. It's only natural.'

'It was quite a job to explain about you.' Diana grimaced. 'I sweated tears of blood over telling Jaime and Mario, let alone trying to get a five-year-old used to the fact that she has a brand new grown-up sister she's never heard of before.'

'I hope your stepsons' reactions were more tolerant than your daughter's,' said Antonia with feeling.

'Mario's were predictable. He was utterly harrowed by my shabby little story, and only too delighted to take my place when Marisa's chicken-pox made it impossible for me to fly over for you myself.' Diana met Antonia's eyes squarely. 'Jaime—well, Jaime was the same as always; a tower of strength at all times, but not always very communicative about his feelings.'

'You mean he disapproved of my coming here?'

'No, no, I wouldn't say that. I think perhaps he feels you should have been consulted about your wishes a bit later, when your emotions were less involved.'

'Perhaps he thinks my only motives for coming are my lack of money, job, and shortly even a place to live. Three powerful reasons for wanting to come and stay with you.' Antonia returned Diana's look without evasion. 'I came, Diana, not only because I felt horribly lonely without Mother, but also because I genuinely wanted to meet *you*. I had no idea about all this——' She waved a hand about her. 'It never occurred to me that you lived in such a fantastic house, or had money. The picture in my mind was of a poor unfortunate student who got herself in such a mess.'

'Which isn't far wrong even now.' Diana's smile was wry. 'Only twice in my life have I managed to get pregnant. The first time I was single and too young. On the second occasion I was married right enough, but too old. As you can see, Marisa gets her dire sense of timing directly from me. You must admit she did a great job of wrecking the big reunion scene between you and me, Antonia.'

'Perhaps it's just as well. If it had been a film I suppose I'd have thrown myself into your arms and cried "Mother" in broken tones as I laid my head on your shoulder,' said Antonia, grinning, 'but somehow I don't think either you or I are suited to soap opera. Anyway, to be honest, I was so astounded at first sight of you I was speechless.'

'It was the same for me.' Diana stood up and touched a hand to Antonia's cheek fleetingly.

'Wasn't I what you expected?'

'Oh, yes! Janet's sent me a photograph or two over the years. But they were no preparation for the impact of your looks in the flesh. You're the living image of your father—at least, as he was twenty-two years ago.'

Antonia's eyes were eloquent with unspoken questions, and Diana nodded. 'Yes. I'll tell you about him some time soon, I promise, but now I think you should have a rest before dinner, while I see if Marisa is in more penitent mood.'

'Mario seemed to know exactly how to deal with her,' commented Antonia.

'He and Jaime take the place of the father she's never known. Francisco died before she was born, you see. I achieved the daughter he wanted too late.' Diana smiled crookedly. 'My wretched timing again! But now, Antonia, I insist you rest. You look shattered. I see Sabino's already brought your luggage, but don't try to unpack. One of the maids will do that later.' Suddenly she put her arms around Antonia and hugged her hard. 'Welcome to Lagoa del Rey, Antonia.' Then she went quickly from the room.

Antonia stood still for a moment, then went to investigate a door in the far wall, finding a bathroom with brass taps and white porcelain and an enormous supply of fluffy white towels. Minutes later she was stretched out between the crisp white sheets, under a thick woven cotton spread, relaxed and drowsy as she realised the first difficult hurdle had been cleared with ease. Marisa's tantrum was irrelevant. What really mattered was the first confrontation with Diana, and it had been no ordeal at all. So far Marisa had been the only shadow on the welcome given her at Lagoa del Rey, thought Antonia sleepily. Of course, there was still Jaime de Almeida to come—and if he were only half as charming as his brother, she would count herself more than content!

CHAPTER THREE

WHEN Antonia woke, light was filtering through the rose-printed curtains drawn across the windows. She sat up, blinking sleepily, and discovered a laden tray on the table beside her. On investigation it proved to be a cold dinner, untouched. She bit her lip in dismay, jumped out of bed and flew to the bathroom, embarrassed at having slept for so long. As she washed her face and tugged at her tangled curls she consoled herself that she had a fair chance of being early for breakfast, at least. Not bothering with make-up, she rummaged in a suitcase for a pair of stonewashed denims and a yellow shirt, pulled on espadrilles and looked uncertainly at the tray. She ought to take it somwhere, but where? She opened the door and looked outside into a deserted corridor with gleaming wood floors, aware of faint noises in the distance. Antonia collected the tray and bore it off in what she hoped was a kitchenwards direction, a wonderful smell of fresh coffee soon confirming that she was right.

She elbowed open a swing door and found herself in a big, marble-floored kitchen lively with activity. The two young girls of the evening before were busily flitting to and fro under the direction of a tall, statuesque black woman in the familiar print dress and snowy apron. Antonia coughed a little to announce her presence, and three pairs of black eyes swivelled in her direction, wide with surprise and curiosity; then one of the girls hurried to take the tray, as all three chorused '*Bom dia*', and beamed in welcome.

Antonia smiled back and lifted her hands expressively. 'Good morning,' she ventured. There was much nodding of heads and gestures intended to convey concern because the food on the tray was untouched, then the majestic black woman, unmistakably in command, pointed to each of the maids in turn and said 'Zelia, Pascoa.' She pointed a finger at her own heroic bosom and said regally, 'Maria de Nascimento.'

Antonia smiled warmly and touched a hand to her own chest. 'I'm Antonia,' she said, and there was more nodding and beaming, then a stream of quickfire instructions from the cook to the girls, one of whom immediately set about loading a fresh tray, while the other beckoned Antonia to follow her through a long, formal dining-room out on to the veranda glimpsed only briefly the night before. Now it was orderly and immaculate with upright rattan chairs drawn up to a table laid for breakfast.

Zelia indicated shyly that Antonia should seat herself, saying, '*Café de manhã num momento* Dona Antonia.'

Antonia blinked a little at her new title as the girl went off, then chose a chair which gave her an uninterrupted view of the terraced garden, through palms and tall eucalyptus trees which rustled slightly in the breeze from the lake gleaming far below in a great curving expanse of gilt-tipped ripples under the quickly rising sun. She sighed with pleasure as she breathed in the pure air, aware of dogs barking in the distance and a cockerel crowing somewhere near at hand as her eyes feasted on the panorama spread out before her. Mario had never even hinted at the beauty and sheer splendour of Lagoa del Rey. Probably to him, used to it all his life, it was just home, as the house in Bristol was to her.

Antonia turned from the view as Pascoa arrived with a tray and swiftly set a coffee pot beside her, followed by a crystal jug of fruit juice, a toast rack and several covered dishes. The girl smiled and withdrew, leaving Antonia to investigate, finding hot, crusty rolls, scrambled eggs and crisp, smoked bacon, all of which she dispatched with speedy appreciation. Afterwards she drank two cups of coffee and eventually began to wonder where everyone was. It was early, she knew, but with the time difference had no way of telling exactly how early it was, since her watch was still functioning at Greenwich Mean Time. Suddenly the dogs in the distance began barking again and the sound of hoofbeats carried through the clear, still air.

Antonia heard male voices raised in laughter, then footsteps on the path below and the jingling of spurs. Next moment a man took the veranda steps two at a time and stopped dead as he reached the top, staring at her. He was taller than Mario and his well worn khaki shirt and trousers made no difference to the air of authority he wore like a cloak. His likeness to his brother was instantly recognisable, but this man was built on a larger scale, and the features that were so classically perfect on Mario were blunter, harder, and very much more imperious on the face of Jaime de Almeida. His black eyes were examining her with clinical detachment, Antonia noted with misgiving, and held somewhat less welcome than those of the jealous Marisa the evening before. He strolled across the veranda towards her, the spurs on his dusty riding boots jangling as he stripped off his gloves and bowed slightly.

'*Bom dia.* I am Jaime de Almeida. You, of course, are Miss Antonia Grant—the so surprising long-lost daughter of Diana.'

'How do you do?' said Antonia quietly.

'I much regret I was not here in time to welcome you last night, Miss Grant. I was detained in Boa Vista and by the time I arrived for dinner you had already gone to bed.'

There was precious little apology in his eyes, or in his voice, Antonia noted, her spirits sinking. 'I'm afraid jet-lag overtook me, Senhor de Almeida. I must have slept the clock round.' She smiled politely. 'I'm not sure what time it is even now.'

Jaime de Almeida glanced at his watch. 'Not yet quite seven. You are early for breakfast, *sem dúvida*. The rest of the household is still asleep. You permit that I join you?'

Antonia tried to hide her lack of enthusiasm for the suggestion, and rang the silver handbell as her companion requested. At once Pascoa appeared and cleared away the used dishes while her master gave his instructions regarding breakfast.

'And what do you think of Lagoa del Rey, now you are

sufficiently awake to see it properly?' he asked.

'It's superlatively beautiful.' Antonia shrugged expressively. 'I had no idea it would be like this. Mario said very little about it in advance.'

'Perhaps other things preoccupied him more when alone in your company.' The note in the hard, faintly accented voice brought Antonia's head up sharply. His face, so like Mario's and yet so different, wore a faintly derisory expression she resented. And his eyes, she decided, were nothing at all like his brother's. Mario had velvet, expressive eyes. The pair now studying her so dispassionately were hard and gleamed like slivers of jet beneath half-closed lids. Jaime de Almeida's springing black hair was ruffled from his early-morning ride, and his turned-back shirt-sleeves revealed sinewy brown forearms and hands more muscular, though no less well shaped than those of his brother, Antonia conceded grudgingly.

Pascoa returned with Jaime's breakfast before Antonia could form a reply to his remark, and in the little burst of activity that followed, she rose, bent on escape.

'Do not desert me, Miss Grant,' said Jaime de Almeida blandly, once the girl had gone. 'Marisa is sleeping late this morning, I imagine. She had a disturbed night, which means Diana slept very little also, otherwise, I have no doubt, she would be here at this moment to fuss over you.'

Antonia stood undecided for a moment, then sat down, trying to hide her urge to bolt. 'May I pour coffee for you?' she asked punctiliously.

'If you would be so kind.'

Antonia refilled her own cup at the same time and sat sipping in silence while her companion attacked his meal with zest.

'You are very silent,' he remarked after a time.

'I'm sorry. Not everyone cares for conversation first thing in the morning.'

'But for me it is not first thing. I have been out of my bed for more than an hour.' The iron-hard eyes held hers deliberately. 'My brother has been extravagant with his praise of you in his telephone calls, Miss Grant.'

Antonia's eyes narrowed. 'That's very nice of him. Mario is—kind.'

'You think I am not?'

'I have no idea. How could I? I don't know you well enough to judge.'

'Yet I fear you have passed judgement, I think,' he said mockingly. 'I sense that I have been weighed in the balance with Mario and found wanting. Is that not an English saying?'

'Yes.'

'And am I not right?'

'We have another saying, too, to the effect that comparisons are odious.' Antonia looked him squarely in the eye.

Jaime de Almeida smiled sardonically, then sobered. 'Permit me to offer my condolences on your recent bereavement, Miss Grant. I sympathise with you in your loss, but you must forgive me for reflecting on how very fortunate it is for you to discover a comfortably situated, long-lost mother at such a bleak juncture in your life. Therefore I rejoice with you in your gain—at finding your natural mother so very well placed to cushion your grief, materially speaking,' he added.

Antonia stared at him incredulously. 'I don't care for your implication, Senhor de Almeida. You obviously harbour dark suspicions about my motives in accepting Diana's invitation to come here.'

'I make no secret of the fact that I fear for Diana. That she will be hurt.' The black eyes held hers inexorably. 'I would do much to protect her from further hurt. She has suffered much in her life. How much I discovered only recently. I love Diana. Remember it well, if your intention is to get what you can out of her as quickly as possible, then rush back to England with your spoils. I will personally obstruct any such plan, I promise you. Mario may have succumbed without a struggle to the blandishment of those beautiful eyes of yours, *querida*, but I am made of sterner stuff, as I think you say.'

Antonia could hardly believe what she was hearing. The golden morning was tarnished and spoiled by Jaime de Almeida's insinuations, which only served to confirm her first reaction to Diana's invitation, she thought bitterly. She should never have come here, laid herself open to insult like this. She had been a naïve little fool to think everyone would understand her reasons for wanting to meet Diana. She contemplated her companion's watchful face dispassionately, reflecting that since Lagoa del Rey bore such a remarkable resemblance to her idea of the Garden of Eden, it was only to be expected that it should possess its very own serpent in the formidable person of Jaime de Almeida!

Antonia stood up, and politely he followed suit, his eyes on her rigid face. 'Since I am a guest in your house, Senhor de Almeida,' she began coldly, 'and dependent, for as short a time as I can possibly manage, on your hospitality, good manners prevent me from answering you in the way I would dearly like——'

'Don't let that stop you,' said a voice from the dining-room doorway, and both Jaime and Antonia turned quickly to see Diana watching them as she leaned there gracefully, looking a little tired, but exquisitely groomed in white trousers and ink-blue shirt.

'Diana——' Jaime started towards her, but she held up an admonitory hand.

'I didn't intend to eavesdrop,' she said, her grey eyes very cool as they rested on his set, grim face. 'But once having begun I became riveted.' She looked from Jaime to Antonia and sighed. 'I had hoped so much you two would be friends.'

'I wish only to guard you from hurt,' he said quickly.

'And you think I won't be hurt by your attempt to make Antonia leave at the first possible opportunity?' Her voice was gently cutting, and Jaime de Almeida flinched. 'I apologise for my family, Antonia—first Marisa last night, now Jaime this morning.' Diana shrugged her slender shoulders. 'Marisa, at least is too young to know better. She

was just plain jealous.' She eyed Jaime's taut figure
pensively. 'My stepson here is too complex a personality for
me to analyse *his* motivation. But please, Antonia, don't
allow your feelings about Lagoa del Rey to be influenced
by the lack of enthusiasm from some quarters. Marisa will
come round soon enough.'

Antonia turned to look at the silent man. 'And you,
Senhor de Almeida? Will *you* become accustomed to
someone you look on as a parasite living under your roof?'

Jaime de Almeida's face was expressionless. 'It is not *my*
roof, Miss Grant, therefore your presence itself will not
affect me in the slightest. My father left Lagoa del Rey to
Diana. Mario and I own the land and the mineral rights,
also the lake itself is mine. But I live in a house on the
outskirts of Boa Vista, and Mario in an apartment in the
city centre. Diana is truly the *dona da casa* here. My brother
and I are only visitors in her house.'

Diana put a hand on his arm. 'Hardly that, Jaime.'

His hard face softened as he looked down at her.
'*Desculpe-me*, Diana. Forgive me for causing you distress. I
shall leave you alone with—your daughter now, and try to
drag Mario from his bed to drive over to Campo d'Ouro
with me to see Luc Fonseca.'

'Will you be back to dinner, Jaime?'

At the note of appeal in Diana's voice his face softened,
and he nodded, then looked across at Antonia. 'Miss Grant,
I make my apologies to you also. It is not my custom to be
discourteous to Diana's guests.'

Antonia remained silent, her face perfectly blank, and
Diana looked thoughtfully from one unsmiling face to the
other.

'Antonia is not a guest, Jaime,' she said gently. 'She is my
daughter.'

'You must forgive me if it takes time to adjust to the fact,'
Jaime said stiffly, then kissed her cheek. '*Até logo*, Diana.' He
looked up at Antonia. 'I shall see you at dinner, Miss
Grant.'

Since the prospect gave Antonia very little pleasure she

made no response, other than another slight nod. Jaime de Almeida turned on his spurred heel and strode into the house without another word, and Diana sat down at the table, her eyes troubled as she looked at Antonia's tense face.

'Come and sit down.' She rang the bell. 'Pascoa shall bring us coffee while Zelia dresses Marisa, then I shall take great pleasure in eating breakfast in the company of both my daughters for the first time.'

Antonia relaxed, and left her post at the veranda rail to sit at the table again. 'Senhor de Almeida has dark suspicions about my motives in coming here, you know.'

'Try to understand, Antonia. Since Francisco died so suddenly five years ago Jaime has taken his responsibilities very seriously, not only towards Marisa and me, but to the company and Mario—everything.' A shadow darkened Diana's eyes. 'He felt his father's death very deeply. As we all did, of course, but for Jaime it was the end of a way of life. While Francisco was alive Jaime had more time for leisure. He worked in the company, of course—he's a highly qualified metallurgist, in fact, but he had more time for socialising and the great love of his life, sailing. He's good—almost Olympic class—but seldom has much time for it these days. This is the first weekend in ages that he's managed to get away to Lagoa del Rey.'

'Because he wanted to vet me, I suppose!'

'Partly. And I kept plaguing him to.' Diana smiled as Pascoa appeared with yet more fresh coffee. 'Ah, *muito brigad'*, *Pascoa. Fala com Maria, por favor. Um ovo cozido para Marisa, e ovos mexidos para mim.*'

'*Sim, senhora.*'

'Sorry about the language barrier, Antonia.' Diana poured coffee for them both. 'I was asking for a boiled egg for Marisa and scrambled ditto for me. How did you manage at breakfast time, since I gather you've already eaten?'

Antonia chuckled. 'I took my uneaten dinner into the kitchen and introduced myself—well, sort of—and in no

time at all I was tucking into bacon and scrambled eggs. I
was starving.'

'I tried to wake you last night for dinner, but you were
dead to the world, so Maria insisted on leaving a tray in
your room in case you woke in the night yearning for
sustenance.' Diana examined her over her cup. 'You look
better this morning. Although after Marisa's personal form
of welcome last night, plus a brush with Jaime in dictatorial
mood this morning, I wouldn't blame you if you wanted to
leave again right now.'

'I'm made of sterner stuff than that!' Antonia grinned
cheerfully. 'After all, I suppose you could say I broke even
as far as welcome was concerned. Two all—you and Mario
versus Marisa and . . .' She hesitated.

'Jaime,' prompted Diana. '"Senhor de Almeida" is much
too much of a mouthful for common use. I'm sure you'll like
him once you get to know him better.'

Antonia looked sceptical. 'Ah, but will he ever get to like
me?'

Diana smiled. 'I don't see how he can help it. You're a
very good-looking girl, Antonia. Your photographs don't
do you justice. By the way, I meant to ask straight away—
how did your finals go?'

'I got a two-one.'

Diana beamed. 'Oh, well done!' She sobered quickly.
'Did Janet know?'

Antonia nodded. 'The results came out the day before she
died. She—she was so pleased.' Her eyes filled with tears.
'Sorry,' she choked, and fumbled for her table napkin.

'Oh, my dear!' Diana sprang up and put her arm round
Antonia's shoulders. 'Don't apologise. How could you not
cry?' The gentle kindness in her voice totally unmanned
Antonia, and she turned her face blindly into Diana's
shoulder and wept, the hurt inflicted by Jaime de Almeida
all mixed up with a sudden upsurge of grief for Janet.

Diana stroked her hair and made soothing, crooning
noises until a small voice said, 'Why is she crying?'

Diana squeezed Antonia's shoulders as they looked up to

see a little figure in red dungarees in the doorway, with Pascoa hovering behind.

'Perhaps it's because you were so horrible to her last night,' suggested Diana. 'Poor Antonia travelled for thousands of miles, for hours and hours in an aeroplane to a strange place where she didn't know anyone, and what happened, Marisa de Almeida? You screamed and shouted at her. Was that a nice thing to do? *I* don't think so, neither does Jaime, nor Mario.'

Marisa's lower lip trembled and she hung her curly head, scuffing her sandal on the floorboards of the veranda. She shot a guilty look up under her eyebrows at Antonia, who managed a watery smile at the little girl in response.

'Well?' demanded Diana relentlessly. 'How would *you* have felt, Marisa?'

The child ran to her mother and burrowed her face against her. 'Sorry,' she mumbled indistinctly. Diana moved her away a little to look down at her with meaning.

'I'm not the one who needs the apology, Marisa.'

A great sigh shook the child and she turned to look at Antonia. 'I'm sorry I made you cry,' she blurted.

Antonia felt horribly guilty, but Diana gave her a conspiratorial look over the child's head. 'Thank you, Marisa. Then I won't cry any more.'

'Good,' said Diana briskly. 'So come and eat your egg, Marisa, and Antonia can watch us.'

'Aren't you hungry?' demanded Marisa.

'I've already had mine,' confessed Antonia. 'I was up early. Shall I cut your toast into soldiers?'

Marisa consented graciously, and Diana watched with pleasure as the fair head bent close to the dark one. 'Isn't it a lovely day?' she said suddenly, and Antonia looked up, smiling.

'Yes. A truly lovely day.'

'I do not agree,' said a male voice bitterly, and Mario emerged from the house, yawning and heavy-eyed. He kissed Diana and ruffled Marisa's hair, smiling warmly at Antonia. 'My sadist of a brother insists I crew for him today in that boat of his, but I refused. I yearn for more sleep.'

Diana smiled at him with sympathy. 'Have some breakfast first, then go back to bed.'

'*Não, 'brigado.* Pascoa brought coffee and toast to my room.' Mario yawned again, and looked injured. 'I am not allowed to rest, Diana. Since I will not sail I must accompany Jaime to Campo d'Ouro to talk with Luc Fonseca about water supplies instead. My brother is not a human being—he is a machine!' With a comic look of martyrdom on his handsome face Mario went off, after giving his little stepsister a farewell kiss.

Diana laughed affectionately. 'Don't be taken in, Antonia. Mario's just as keen on sailing as Jaime. Tomorrow he'll be the first up and raring to get the *Esperança* on the lake.'

'Is there a yacht club here?'

'Oh, yes. At the far end of the lake. Jaime owns it. I went there quite a bit in the beginning, when Francisco was alive, but not much since then. To be honest, sailing just isn't my thing.'

'I've never tried it,' said Antonia, and looked down at Marisa. 'When you've finished your breakfast, would you like to help me unpack?'

Marisa looked surprised. 'Pascoa does that.'

'I left one bag locked.' Antonia looked questioningly at Diana. 'That won't have upset Pascoa, I hope? I just wanted it left until later.'

'No, of course not.' Diana stood up. 'You two go along while I have a chat with Maria about dinner.'

'I rather hoped you'd come too,' said Antonia diffidently.

Diana looked pleased as she bent to remove fruit juice from her little daughter's face. 'Then we'll all go, shan't we, poppet, since Antonia needs help?'

'I don't think I can remember the way back to my room,' said Antonia. 'I wonder if you'd show me where it is, Marisa?'

The little girl looked at her pityingly, then nodded and ran on ahead importantly to show the way. Diana squeezed

Antonia's hand appreciatively as they followed.

'Well done!'

Antonia's bedroom was immaculate when they reached it, her clothes ironed neatly and put away in the wardrobe and chest. She was impressed as she unlocked the zipped bag left at the foot of the bed, and said so ruefully. 'I shall get very lazy and spoiled by all this attention, you know!'

Diana shook her head indulgently. 'I don't think so, somehow.'

'How must I help?' asked Marisa curiously.

Antonia drew her down beside the bag. 'I want you to look in there and see if you find anything wrapped in paper with coloured balloons all over it.'

Marisa rummaged eagerly, taking out several packages before she found the right one, which was larger than the rest and took up all the base of the bag. It had a very large label with 'MARISA' printed on it in huge capitals, and she squeaked in excitement.

'*Olha—Mamãe—meu nome!*'

'I know it's your name,' said Diana, 'but remember Antonia doesn't speak Portuguese.'

The child shook her head, puzzled. '*Why* can't you, Antonia? I thought everybody could.'

Antonia shrugged apologetically. 'I'm not as clever as you, I'm afraid. Do you think you could teach me, perhaps?'

Marisa's expressive little face showed astonishment, then delight. She nodded enthusiastically, then her eyes strayed back to the large, brightly wrapped box. 'Is it for me, Antonia?'

'Why don't you get it out and see?'

Marisa needed Antonia's help to pull the box out, and Diana sat on the bed, her eyes very bright as she watched her daughters tearing the paper from a large cardboard box secured with sticky tape which needed much impatient treatment before the little girl could open the lid to reveal the contents. First came a package swathed heavily in tissue paper, which Antonia helped remove from a brown ceramic teddy bear holding a string attached to a pink ceramic balloon. Marisa exlaimed with delight.

'Look, *Mamãe*—he's just like my teddy!'

'Only you put this one on your bedroom wall,' explained Antonia. 'See how his one leg sticks out? That's where you hang your dressing-gown.'

'*Engraçadinha*!' crowed the child, then paused. 'That means funny, Antonia.'

'Really? Thank you, I'll remember that. Now for the next parcel.'

This was a very smart doll with adjustable arms and legs, dressed in jeans and sweatshirt, and a final package, to Marisa's jubilation, yielded up an entire wardrobe of clothes for the doll. Her face scarlet with delight, Marisa spontaneously hugged and kissed Antonia, then rushed off to show her trophies to the maids.

Antonia smiled guiltily at Diana. 'A bit like bribery, I suppose, but it was worth it to see the expression on her face.'

'It was very sweet of you, Antonia, but the real stroke of genius was asking her to teach you Portuguese.'

'She certainly seemed quite struck with the idea.' Antonia bent to pick up another parcel, then offered it to Diana. 'This isn't bribery. Just a little present for having me to stay.'

Diana smoothed the elegant, silver-striped paper then removed it with great care, her eyes suspiciously bright as she drew out a sweater in Cambridge-blue cashmere. 'How lovely, Antonia,' she said huskily, 'and so wonderfully British! Thank you—thank you very much.' And she slid off the bed to kiss her daughter's glowing, olive-tinted cheek for the first time. 'You were very naughty to spend so much money, but I love it. It's my favourite colour.'

'I hoped it might be. Mario told me you were fairer than me, so it seemed like a safe bet.' Antonia smiled as Diana went to the mirror to pull the sweater over her head. 'I hope it's not too big. He was a bit vague about size—said you were something like me.'

'I'm flatter-chested,' said Diana regretfully. 'But this is just perfect—I love it.'

Antonia eyed the remaining two packages without enthusiasm, bitterly regretting the purchase of one of them, at least. It had seemed ill-mannered to bring presents for only Diana and Marisa, but her choice of gift for Mario and the then unknown Jaime had given her some trouble. In the end she had settled for silk scarves as both impersonal and suitable, Mario's in dull gold and Jaime's dark red, but now she fervently wished she hadn't bothered at all. Diana turned away from the mirror and caught her expression.

'For Jaime and Mario, I imagine,' she said, waving at the other parcels.

Antonia nodded wryly. 'I felt Mario deserved some gesture of appreciation for fetching me from England, but frankly I don't much relish giving Jaime anything at all now I've met him. His reception of me wasn't exactly over-warm, to say the least! If I leave him out, of course, I'll look rude, yet if I *do* hand it over he'll have dark suspicions about my motives.'

'Look on the gift as coals of fire,' said Diana serenely. 'Now let's take a walk around the gardens and I'll introduce you to everyone who lives here, not to mention the dogs.'

'Dogs?'

'Dobermann pinschers. Very necessary, I'm afraid, but they need to be introduced to you before we can let you wander outdoors when you want.'

They collected Marisa from the kitchen. The morning air was exhilarating and fresh, and she felt brim-full of energy after her protracted sleep as they made for the far boundary of the property, where there were two small houses and some stables for the horses and mules used for riding, the latter better suited to the wilder parts of the mountainous terrain. Diana clapped her hands in greeting as they reached the houses and Sabino, of the evening before, emerged to welcome them warmly, calling to his wife to come out to meet the guest of Dona Diana. His plump wife, Nazare, was cheerful and talkative and pressed them to coffee and little cakes, which Antonia accepted, at a slight nod from Diana. Then several children were mustered for inspection and eventually Geraldo, Sabino's brother, who was husband to the cook, Maria, it transpired, arrived on the scene with four large Dobermanns. He introduced them with great care to Antonia, and they gave her a very thorough once-over, sniffing and inspecting her before they were let off their leashes to roam free. Marisa was made much of by everyone, including the dogs, and went on at length about the presents Antonia had brought her until Diana put an end to the visit gracefully, and farewells were said before they wandered back through the tiered garden to a terrace overlooking the lake.

'We could have chairs brought out here if you like,' said Diana, 'but the sun gets very fierce by mid-morning, even at this time of the year. The veranda's better, and you won't get burned to a crisp up there.'

Marisa tugged at Antonia's hand eagerly. 'Come and see the pool first,' she pleaded.

Diana nodded. 'That's a good idea. In the meantime I'll have my chat with Maria, and organise some cold drinks by the time you come back.'

Marisa trotted off in front of Antonia, leading her some distance away to the back of the house, facing away from the lake where a large circular pool lay sheltered by the now familiar hibiscus hedges. Edged about with natural boulders and smaller rocks, the pool was fed by a miniature waterfall cascading from a smaller, ornamental pool on the terrace above.

'How gorgeous!' exclaimed Antonia in awe. 'But I didn't think you'd need a pool when you live near such a big lake.'

'Jaime says I mustn't swim in the lake. It has *bichos* in it.'

'*Bichos*?'

Marisa nodded, thinking hard. 'Teeny little worms that make you ill.'

'Oh, dear,' Antonia pulled a face. 'And can you swim?'

'*Pois é*! I mean, of course. Jaime taught me.'

Pois é, thought Antonia, resigned, but she smiled warmly

at the little girl. 'Splendid. We can have a swim together later.'

'Doutor Ferreira says I can't yet 'cos of the chicken-pox.'

'Never mind. We'll make up for it as soon as he says you can.'

'Are you staying until next week?'

'Yes. And for another week after that—if that's all right with you.'

Marisa thought it over. 'OK,' she said happily. 'Let's race back to the veranda.'

Antonia chased the vivid little figure obediently, careful to let her win, and climbed the steps eventually. She flopped into a low, cushioned chair, grateful for the glass of fruit juice she was given. Marisa downed hers, then ran off to find Zelia, eager to resume the fashion show with her new doll, and when Antonia felt recovered Diana took her on a tour of inspection of the house. The main reception room was formally elegant, with tapestry-covered furniture and rose-coloured damask at the windows and several small tables in the same attractive wood as in Antonia's bedroom. It was jacaranda, Diana informed her as she led the way to a smaller, shabbier sitting-room with cushions and books everywhere and a large fireplace where logs could be burned when the family gathered there in colder weather.

'Except that my family is rather small now, apart from weekends,' said Diana, and went on to the bedrooms: a severe, tidy room where Jaime slept, Mario's more cluttered room next to it, then Marisa's bedroom, with pretty white furniture and posters on the walls.

'I sleep in this room,' said Diana, and opened the door of a very big bedroom with heavy carved furniture and an enormous bed. 'I shared it with Francisco, and sometimes I think I should move out of it and sleep somewhere else. But I can never bring myself to do it.'

'You loved him very much?' asked Antonia tentatively.

Diana was silent for a moment, her eyes absent. 'Yes. Yes, I did,' she said slowly. 'More than I ever expected to love anyone after—after you were born.'

Antonia found it difficult to picture this slender, youthful-looking creature married to an elderly man, and she wandered over to the dressing-table, her eyes narrowing as she saw a large photograph of Jaime in formal clothes in pride of place.

'Francisco on our wedding day,' said Diana very quietly. 'He was a very attractive man. It caused something of a sensation when Francisco de Almeida married an unknown young Englishwoman, I can tell you!'

'You mean *that* was—your husband?' Antonia's face displayed her astonishment only too plainly. 'But he looks so young!' And his son's a dead ringer for him, she added silently, glad she hadn't blurted Jaime's name when she saw the photograph.

Diana smiled slyly. 'I do believe, Antonia, that you thought I'd married some stout, elderly sugar daddy for his money.'

Antonia flushed. 'No—not exactly. But Jaime and Mario aren't exactly teenagers. I just assumed their father would be older than the man in the photograph.'

'When I married Francisco I was thirty and he was forty-two. Jaime was twenty-one and Mario sixteen. Their mother, Ana, died when Mario was small.' Diana looked fondly at the smiling man in the photograph. 'Theirs was an arranged marriage when Francisco was barely twenty and Ana even younger. His marriage to me was different. We spent our honeymoon here——' She went bright red. 'Not in this room the entire time, of course,' she added hastily, and Antonia giggled.

'But most of it!'

Diana laughed, and took Antonia by the hand as they left the room. 'Not a suitable topic of conversation for mother and daughter.'

'We're not exactly your average mother and daugher, are we?'

'No,' agreed Diana with feeling. 'That we aren't!'

CHAPTER FOUR

ANTONIA dressed for her first dinner at Lagoa del Rey with
mixed feelings. The thought of dining with Jaime de
Almeida for company was a sobering prospect, and to
match her mood she put on a narrow, dark grey skirt with
matching silk shirt and a modest string of pearls, on the
assumption that she would be expected to wear something
restrained in deference to Janet. If she could possibly help it
Jaime de Almeida should have no cause for censure in that
area, she thought morosely, even if he was so insultingly
suspicious about her reasons for coming here.

Marisa's room was empty when Antonia passed it and
she went on towards the veranda, her steps slowing as she
heard male voices in conversation with Diana through the
open double doors. Antonia hesitated in the deserted hall,
then squared her shoulders and walked out to join the
others. The two men jumped to their feet at the sight of her
and Diana smiled her welcome from her place on a cane
sofa as Marisa came skipping towards Antonia and took her
by the hand, pulling her.

'Come and sit by me, Tonia. I can stay for a little while.'

Grateful to the little girl for breaking the ice, Antonia let
herself be tugged over to sit by Diana, where the child
wriggled between them happily.

'Good evening, Miss Grant,' said Jaime formally. 'What
may I offer you to drink?' He was dressed in superbly cut
black trousers and crisp white shirt, and looked, if
anything, even more formidable than in the riding clothes
of early morning.

'Something non-alcoholic, please,' said Antonia, and
smiled at Mario, who was looking wonderful, as usual, in
white trousers and a blue cotton-knit shirt. His answering
smile was wicked.

'Miss Grant, Jaime?' he commented, eyebrows raised.
'Has Antonia not given you permission to call her by her
first name? And she our sister, too, in a way.'

Jaime handed Antonia her drink, his eyes inscrutable. 'I do not think the thought of such a relationship pleases you, Miss Grant. Am I right?'

Diana broke in impatiently. 'Oh, do unbend, Jaime, *please*. Of course you must call her Antonia, and if she *does* object to the thought of a relationship with you I can't say I really blame her. You haven't been exactly the soul of hospitality so far.'

Antonia took the drink from Jaime's hand, avoiding his eyes as she thanked him politely.

'Forgive me, Antonia,' he said stiffly. 'I would not wish you to think harshly of Brazilian hospitality.'

Antonia regarded him with serene eyes. 'I don't,' she assured him sweetly. 'Almost everyone has been very kind.'

His eyelids flickered slightly at the gently stressed 'almost', and Diana smiled slyly and changed the subject, asking her stepsons about their afternoon in Campo d'Ouro while Antonia helped Marisa dress her doll in its nightclothes.

When Marisa was in bed the others went into dinner, and Jaime assumed the mantle of perfect host. Mario looked on with unconcealed amusement as his brother paid scrupulous attention to Antonia, while Diana skilfully steered the conversation to neutral topics over the meal. Afterwards they returned to the veranda to drink coffee, by which time Antonia felt considerably more relaxed as she chatted easily with Diana, glancing from time to time at the contrast of Jaime's sharp profile with the near perfection of Mario's as the two men leaned against the rail, smoking cigars. Mario caught her eye eventually.

'Do you think you will like Lagoa del Rey, Antonia, now you have had time to explore it a little?'

'How could I help it?' she said simply. 'It's so beautiful here—I never imagined . . .'

'That your mother lived in such a place?' asked Jaime swiftly, turning to look at her.

Antonia returned the look thoughtfully. 'That's not *quite*

what I meant. I was trying to say that I just never imagined such a breathtaking location—not that I had any preconceived idea of where you lived at all,' she added, turning to Diana. 'When the solicitor told me you lived in Brazil I was struck dumb, especially as I'd only just learned about you—and me.' She flushed uncomfortably and Diana put a hand on hers quickly.

'I imagine it was enough of a shock to find you had a spare parent at all, without having to travel six thousand miles to meet her.'

'Precisely!' Antonia smiled gratefully. 'And even then I think I just envisaged a house in a town somewhere, not all this solitude and space—and sheer grandeur, I suppose. The scenery here rather cuts one down to size, doesn't it?'

'Which in your case, little sister, is quite perfect!' said Mario instantly, and grinned as his brother's face went wooden.

'Do not embarrass Antonia with such remarks,' Jaime snapped, scowling at his brother.

Mario swept Antonia a graceful bow. '*Desculpe-me*, little sister.' He winked outrageously. 'I was merely stating an obvious truth.'

'Then thank you for the compliment, Senhor de Almeida!'

Mario rolled his eyes heavenwards. '*Meu Deus*, now *you* are formal, Antonia—do not say you have been affected by Jaime.'

Antonia, despite a laughing disclaimer, *was* affected by Jaime de Almeida, to her intense annoyance, finding his company distinctly disturbing. As the conversation became general she did her best to ignore the tall figure lounging at the veranda rail, but try as she might she failed to resist an occasional glance at him, only to look away again swiftly each time when she found his eyes fixed on her face. It wasn't long before she began to feel very weary after her long day in the new exotic environs of Lagoa del Rey.

'You're one very tired young lady,' said Diana, noticing

the heaviness of Antonia's eyes. 'Time for bed, I think, since you were up even before the lark this morning.'

'Do you always rise so early?' asked Jaime unexpectedly, and Antonia shook her head.

'I'm afraid not. Though here the morning is so beautiful I'm very glad I was up to see it on my first day.'

'If you would care to see more tomorrow morning, perhaps you would like to accompany me on my early-morning ride,' he said casually.

Diana and Mario stared at Jaime in obvious surprise, and Antonia hesitated, very taken aback.

'Of course, if you do not care to——' began Jaime stiffly, but Antonia shook her head vigorously, in no way wishing to reject his unexpected olive branch.

'No, no, it isn't that, I'd love to, but, well—I can't ride. I've never been on a horse in my life.'

Jaime's teeth flashed white in a sudden, disarming smile. 'Then we shall ride mules. You will find it easy, I promise.'

Diana laughed and got up. 'He's telling the truth, I assure you, Antonia. You'll be safe as houses on one of our mules—just like sitting in an armchair.'

Antonia shrugged, smiling. 'Then thank you, Jaime, I'd like to.'

'*Graças a Deus,*' said Mario soulfully. 'Does that mean I am let off a day in the *Esperança?*'

'*Não, senhor!*' retorted his brother. 'We shall return in time for *café de manhã.* There will be the rest of the day for sailing, *sem falta!*'

Mario groaned theatrically, then brightened. 'Will you come to the clubhouse to watch, Antonia?'

Not sure how she'd feel after the proposed mule-ride, Antonia declined regretfully. 'Perhaps I'll have the opportunity later on before I go back.'

'Go back to England?' said Jaime swiftly. 'You do not mean to stay?'

Antonia met his eyes levelly. 'I'm here for a holiday, that's all. When it's over I must go home and get to work.'

Diana took her arm, looking distinctly put out with her

elder stepson. 'Surely you knew that, Jaime!'

'You must have forgotten to tell me, *Madrasta*.' His face was expressionless. 'I was under the impression Antonia had come to make her home with you for a while.'

'If it were up to me she would,' declared Diana, 'but now I think it's time Antonia was in bed—particularly if you intend hauling her out of it again at the crack of dawn!'

Antonia bade the two men a sleepy goodnight, suddenly hardly able to keep her eyes open, and Mario smiled tenderly.

'Sleep well, little sister.'

'But only until seven in the morning,' warned Jaime. 'I will wait for you here, Antonia.'

'Thank you. Goodnight.' She followed Diana to the pretty bedroom which already had a familiar, welcoming atmosphere, as though it considered itself hers.

'Well, Antonia?' asked Diana, as she leaned in the doorway. 'What did you think of your first day at Lagoa del Rey?'

'Highly enjoyable, but rather eventful!' Antonia stretched and yawned unashamedly. 'And I see what you mean by the altitude. I'm dog-tired.'

'Not only from the altitude, I imagine. Probably emotional strain has had a lot to do with it, too.' Diana kissed her daughter's cheek lightly. 'Sleep well—and don't feel you *have* to go riding with Jaime if you don't want to.'

Antonia smiled wryly. 'I think I should, don't you? If only in an attempt to improve diplomatic relations between Jaime and me. Perhaps I can convince him I'm really quite a nice girl, after all.'

Diana laughed softly. 'You're a lot more than that, my love. Forgive me if I embarrass you, but you're all I ever imagined—and more. And now,' she added briskly, 'before I go all mushy on you I'll say goodnight. Sweet dreams—and don't ride too far the first time!'

Because she was afraid of over-sleeping Antonia was awake an hour earlier than necessary, and had plenty of time to look through her small wardrobe for clothes suitable to wear for a mule-ride. Five minutes before the appointed hour she tiptoed through the quiet house to the veranda, dressed in a green wool shirt and fairly elderly green cords and yellow sweater, trying not to make a noise in the sensible walking shoes Janet had always insisted her daughter keep in her wardrobe. Antonia opened the glass doors to find Jaime leaning against the veranda rail, drinking coffee from the tray on the table, and dressed in much the same way as the morning before. He turned at the sound of her footsteps.

'*Bom dia*, Antonia. You are punctual—as is only to be expected. To be early in Brazil is known as "*hora inglês*", English time.'

'Then I'm glad I've upheld my country's reputation,' she said cheerfully. 'Good morning—and another beautiful one, I see.'

Jaime poured coffee for her, then gestured down at the two animals tethered near the foot of the veranda steps. 'Our mounts. Mules are not often very large, so Calçado there, who is our biggest, is kept for my use, to accommodate my legs. More often I go out on horseback.'

Antonia drank the steaming coffee gratefully, eyeing the smaller of the two mules. 'And what is my trusty steed called?'

'Delicado—because it is very gentle.' Jaime smiled faintly. 'Mine is called Calçado because he looks as though he wears boots, *não é*?'

Antonia chuckled. 'So he does! Right then—better not keep Delicado waiting.' She was determined to hide how nervous she was, though to her surprise once Jaime had tossed her up into the big, Western-style saddle she felt reassuringly safe, even when Delicado moved off. The animal's gait was very leisurely, and after a while Antonia began to enjoy herself much more than expected. Jaime, who seemed bent on adhering to his role of punctilious host, took pains to point out various landmarks as they rode inland, away from the lake, and Antonia gazed about her with eager interest as they crossed the road which led to

Campo d'Ouro, and ventured along a path which followed
a stream running down into the lake from the foothills,
Jaime informed her. Along the banks of the stream the trees
grew more densely, forming welcome shade from the sun,
which even at this hour was already bright. Gold rays of
light shone through the branches and picked out the ripples
on the water and once, to Antonia's delight, caught the
iridescent blue-green sheen of several butterflies, fluttering
jewel-bright above the red earth of the track they were
following.

'I just wish I had a camera,' she sighed, 'so I could show
friends how fantastic it is here.'

'If you ask her prettily I am sure Diana will buy one for
you,' said Jaime silkily.

The pleasure drained from Antonia's face. 'I wouldn't
dream of doing such a thing,' she said very quietly, and
glanced at her watch. 'It must be time to turn back. You
intend sailing, I think.'

'There is time yet—unless you mean you particularly
wish to return at once.'

'I think I mean just that.'

Jaime edged his mount alongside and caught Delicado's
reins, holding the animal still. 'You are angry, Antonia.'

Her head went up and she met his eyes proudly. 'I deeply
resent your assumption that I'm out for all I can get as far as
Diana's concerned. I'm sorry you don't like me. There's
nothing I can do about that. But I assure you I'm just here
for a holiday. I came to meet Diana—nothing more,
nothing less.'

'Why do you think I do not—"like" you?' His eyes were
very intent on her flushed, hostile face.

'You've made it very obvious. The contrast with Mario's
reception of me is painful in the extreme.'

'Ah—Mario!' Jaime's smile was sardonic. 'When compared with Mario I must always be the loser, I fear.'

Antonia stared at him with distaste. 'Surely you're not
resentful of Mario because he's——'

'So much more pleasing to the eye than I am?'

'That's not what I was going to say.' Antonia shrugged impatiently. 'I meant that he's kinder, less critical. I wasn't thinking of physical attributes.'

'In brief you find him *muito simpático*, and myself the—how do you say in English? The fly in the ointment?'

They regarded each other steadily, and at last Antonia said slowly, 'Couldn't we call a truce? Just for Diana's sake? I won't be here long; you don't have to see much of me.' She held out her hand. 'Can't we be friends?'

Jaime gathered the reins of both animals in one hand so he could take her hand in his free one, and looked down at her slim fingers for a moment. Then, to Antonia's surprise he raised them to his lips before releasing them. 'I think it will be very difficult for you and me to be friends, Antonia,' he said deliberately.

She flushed hotly and snatched her hand away, and Delicado moved restlessly. Jaime gave the reins into her keeping, and they turned the mules round to begin the ride back to Lagoa del Rey.

'You have a lover in England?' asked Jaime abruptly.

Antonia turned startled eyes on him. 'I don't have a lover anywhere,' she retorted, 'not that it's any concern of yours!'

'I can be forgiven my interest, *não é*? A stepbrother is permitted some concern over his sister's affairs.'

'Since you're no relative of mine, and I don't indulge in affairs, you need have no concern whatsoever.' And I hope you capsize your precious boat on the lake when you go sailing, she thought childishly, before her attention was taken up with controlling her mule, who had decided to put on speed. Jaime cast an amused glance over his shoulder as he led the way. 'Do not be alarmed. Mules have a habit of returning for home at twice the speed of the outward ride. Delicado has his thoughts on *café de manhã*—his breakfast.'

They arrived back at Lagoa del Rey in good time to join the others at breakfast on the veranda, though Antonia excused herself to take a bath first, on the plea of avoiding stiffness. Her real aim was to avoid Jaime over the breakfast table, and she lingered in the soothing hot water so long that when she eventually rejoined Diana and Marisa the two men had left for their day's sailing.

'Did you like riding, Tonia?' asked Marisa, as Antonia sat down to coffee and toast.

'Very much. Only Delicado seemed to think he was racing in the Derby on the way home!'

Diana laughed. 'Mules have minds of their own, I'm afraid, but they're the best mounts for some of the terrain round here.' She cast an eye at Antonia's flushed face. 'And how are diplomatic relations?'

'A bit strained at times, but not completely severed.'

Since Marisa looked full of curiosity her mother changed the subject and asked Antonia if she were content to watch the dinghy racing from the veranda, or whether she would prefer the livelier venue of the yacht club.

'I'd rather stay here with you,' said Antonia with perfect truth, and had the radiance of Diana's smile for reward.

A pleasant morning passed in watching the dinghy races on the lake through binoculars, then the three of them ate a light salad lunch on the veranda, after which Diana insisted Antonia should rest on her bed like Marisa.

'But I'll never sleep tonight!' protested Antonia.

'You will, you know. I'll lay odds on it.'

To her astonishment Antonia slept soundly for two hours, and woke then only because Marisa came running into the room.

'Sleepyhead, sleepyhead,' she chanted. 'Come on, Tonia. Time for tea.'

'OK, OK,' yawned Antonia and slid out of bed. 'All I do here is sleep and eat. I'll get fat.'

Marisa watched with interest as this new big sister resumed her jeans and shirt. She shook her head. 'I don't think so. You're thinner than Isilda. She's bigger than you up there—*and* down there.' She pointed at Antonia's breasts, and touched her own bottom.

'Who's Isilda?' Antonia swung the small hand in hers as they went to join Diana. Marisa shrugged.

'A lady who comes here sometimes. *She* can speak

Portuguese.' She frowned, obviously trying to be fair. 'But I don't think she speaks English very well.'

On this point Antonia found she was soon to judge for herself, since Diana informed her they were to have guests for dinner. 'Jaime rang up a short while ago from the boathouse. Isilda Cardoso's there with her brother Janio, so he thought it a good idea for them to meet you at dinner. I would have preferred just family tonight myself, but I suppose it's a good thing for you to meet people as much as possible.'

'I shan't be here that long, Diana, so you don't have to bother about inviting people on my account,' said Antonia.

Diana looked at her levelly as she handed over a cup of tea. 'Don't you feel you can endure the peace and quiet here for very long?'

'It's not that at all, merely that I must get back fairly quickly to look for a job.'

'You could stay here.'

'And be a parasite?'

'I don't consider living with your mother parasitic exactly!'

'Your stepson seems to.'

Diana held out a plate of little cakes. 'And his opinion matters?'

Antonia took one thoughtfully. 'No. Except that in a way he's right. I can't just live here without contributing anything.'

'My dear girl, I've had to exist for twenty-one years without you. Surely you can spare me more than a week or so now without wanting to pay rent or scrub the floor?' Diana cast a look at Marisa, who was sitting in a corner of the veranda, dressing her doll in swimsuit and snorkel with complete absorption. 'Do you want me to keep quiet about the daughter bit? Introduce you anonymously as a guest?'

'Is that what *you'd* prefer to do?'

'Not in the least. As far as I'm concerned that's who you are and the whole world can know it. But,' Diana looked diffident, 'would you mind if I said you were from a former marriage? I never told Francisco about you, I'm afraid.'

'Wouldn't he have approved?'

'I honestly don't know. But he thought I was very inexperienced and, well, to be melodramatic, pure, I suppose. I could never bring myself to disillusion him.' Diana sighed. 'The money saved for you came from my own earnings and my parents' legacy, so I wasn't dependent on Francisco in that way.'

'And Mother's letters?'

'He thought they were normal correspondence from an old friend. Which they were.' Diana looked unhappy as she sat back in her chair. 'I always meant to tell him, but I never plucked up enough courage.'

'No wonder I was such a shock to Jaime and Mario. A right little surprise package!' Antonia jumped up and touched Diana's hand, smiling down at her. 'By all means use the former marriage story—especially since little Miss M knows about the relationship.'

'You don't mind?'

'Of course I don't.'

Later, when Antonia was getting ready for dinner she wondered how this curvaceous Isilda Cardoso was likely to be dressed—casually, probably, since the dinner invitation was unexpected. After a long soak in the bath she felt fresh and full of energy and more than ready to take on Jaime de Almeida and his bosomy lady friend. She got out a dress in moss-green bias-cut crêpe, cut to cling in some places and swirl fluidly in others, then took more care than usual with her face. Her hair formed its usual aureole about her face, gleaming from the extra brushing she gave it, and just as she slid her feet into plain green pumps Marisa burst into the room, dressed for bed. She skidded to a halt on the polished floor as she saw Antonia, her eyes like saucers.

'*Bonitinha*! That means pretty, Tonia,' she said and sniffed ecstatically. 'You smell nice, too. Can I have some scent?'

'Why not?' Antonia sprayed a little perfume behind Marisa's ear, then bent impulsively to kiss the rosy cheek.

'Do you like me?' demanded Marisa.

Antonia pretended to think it over. 'Why yes, I rather think I do.'

Marisa beamed. 'I like you too—now. I was nasty when you came. I'm sorry.'

'Let's forget all about it, shall we?'

'Yes, please.' Marisa tugged at Antonia's hand. 'Come on, *Mamãe* sent me to fetch you. I can have drinks on the veranda with the visitors until bedtime.'

'Oh, right. Lead on, then.' Antonia was grateful to Diana for sending Marisa to fetch her. It made her entry on to the veranda easier with the small, warm hand tugging at hers as several pairs of eyes turned in her direction. Jaime, Mario, and a slim, dark young man got up at once, while a strikingly attractive girl lounged gracefully in one of the chairs near Diana. A pair of dark, expertly made-up eyes inspected Antonia from top to toe as Mario sprang forward to make the introductions. Janio Cardoso was young, and plainly very eager to make the acquaintance of the visitor.

'*Muito prazer*, Miss Grant,' he said, taking her hand. 'You are a great surprise to us. We did not know Senhora de Almeida had another daughter.'

'Did you not?' said Jaime smoothly, and pulled out a chair for Antonia. 'Surely you have heard us mention her?'

'Not that I can remember,' said Isilda lazily. 'Why have you never visited here before, Miss Grant?'

'She was brought up by her father's family,' said Diana, looking rather strained. 'There were difficulties.'

'Which a recent bereavement has simplified,' said Antonia, and smiled at Diana. 'Besides, I have been studying for a degree at university. I couldn't have come before.'

'Antonia is very clever,' said Mario swiftly. 'She has a degree in English.'

'Also she must be very thirsty,' put in Jaime. 'What may I offer you, Antonia?'

'Wine, please? White, if possible.'

'*Pois é.*' He moved away to a trolley laden with glasses

and bottles, his face mahogany dark against his white shirt after the day on the lake. Mario took the chair next to Antonia's and lifted Marisa on his knee, examining her doll with due attention as she showed it to him happily.

Isilda Cardoso *was* dressed casually, as Antonia had anticipated, but in glove-thin black leather trousers and amber silk shirt, with several rings on her hands to echo gilt-tipped fingers and toes. Just the sort of girlfriend she would have expected Jaime to have, thought Antonia acidly, and accepted a glass of chilled wine from him with a polite smile. Janio sat down near her, his eyes openly admiring as he questioned her about her life in England. Jaime settled himself beside Isilda as Diana excused herself to visit the kitchen, and Antonia did her best to concentrate on Janio's conversation, finding it difficult under the scrutiny of two pairs of black eyes, each trained on her with identical lack of warmth.

Mario broke in after a while to describe the day's racing on the lake, which brought Isilda into the conversation with instant animation, and Antonia sat back and listened as Janio, Isilda and Mario capped each other's stories. Jaime remained unexpectedly silent, his eyes still on Antonia as she tried to follow the rapid, accented conversation of the other three, heavily interspersed with Portuguese by the Cardosos. After a while Antonia could see Marisa's eyes growing heavy, and got up.

'Perhaps I could put Marisa to bed,' she offered, and Mario stood up with the child in his arms.

'I will carry her and you can tuck her in,' he said, but Jaime intervened, taking Marisa from his brother.

'I will take her. Antonia, you may come with me.'

Antonia excused herself to the others and followed Jaime's tall figure into the house, pleased when Diana intercepted them in the hall.

'I'll see to her,' said Diana quickly, but Jaime shook his head.

'You go to our guests, *cara*. Antonia and I can manage one small girl between us.'

Antonia met Diana's surprised eyes and made a little face behind Jaime's back, then followed him to Marisa's room, where he set the child gently on her feet. She muttered something and Antonia bent to catch what she said as she took off Marisa's dressing-gown.

'Bear,' repeated Marisa, yawning widely, and allowed herself to be tucked under the pink quilt. 'Jaime—put my bear on the wall—*faz favor.*'

Jaime de Almeida looked at Antonia, mystified. On tiptoe she went over to the little white dressing-table and silently pointed at the ceramic bear with its balloon. He grinned, his teeth very white in his dark face.

'*Amanhã*—tomorrow, *sem falta, chica.*' He bent to ruffle the dark curls. '*Boa noite, dorme bem.*'

Marisa sighed drowsily, then opened big dark eyes at Antonia. 'Jaime said goodnight, sleep well.'

Antonia smiled and bent down to kiss Marisa's cheek. 'Thank you, poppet. Goodnight.'

When they emerged into the deserted corridor Jaime took Antonia's wrist to detain her. 'I wish to thank you for allowing Diana the privilege of a former marriage.'

The corridor was not overwide and Antonia felt hemmed in as Jaime stood close, wanting to pull her hand away. 'It's nothing. A small return for all Diana's done for me.'

'My father looked on Diana as the most perfect creature in the world, you understand,' he said.

Antonia nodded gravely. 'I do understand. It's why she could never bring herself to tell him about me.'

'I imagine so. Diana has confided nothing about the circumstances of your birth, of course.' Jaime smiled faintly, and Antonia tensed, wary of him in friendly mood. 'Just to learn of your existence at all astounded Mario and myself. But after the first shock faded we were both full of pity for the girl she had been, cast off by her family in her disgrace.'

'Disgrace?'

'Perhaps I mean distress. You must make allowances for

my poor command of your language.'

'You speak excellent English,' said Antonia woodenly, and tried to free her hand.

'I express myself better in Portuguese,' he answered, holding on to her wrist.

'A pity I don't understand it.'

'You could learn.'

Antonia gave him the smile she used as a put-off for unwanted male attention. 'That would be rather pointless, Senhor de Almeida, since I won't be staying long enough to justify the effort.'

His eyes narrowed, and his eyelashes, which were not as long as Mario's but soot-black and very thick just the same, veiled his expression. 'Because of my words this morning?'

'Your words this morning had nothing at all to do with it. I never intended staying longer than two or three weeks at the most. I have my own life at home in England, and I shall go back and get on with it once this very pleasant interlude is over. Unknown to me I've been supported to some extent all my life by Diana, as well as my own mother——' Antonia halted, frowning.

'I know well who you mean,' he said quickly.

She nodded. 'But from now on I have to make my own way in the world.'

'Could you not do that here? Teach English, perhaps?'

She shook her head. 'I don't belong here. You made that very plain this morning.'

Jaime de Almeida's face altered as he looked down at her. 'Perhaps I was mistaken. It is possible I may have made an error of judgement in my first estimate of Diana's daughter.'

'But as far as you're concerned there's still room for doubt.' Antonia smiled at him mockingly. 'Rest easy, Senhor de Almeida. I won't run off with your family silver—too heavy to take back in my luggage. *And* I won't take any money from Diana, either.'

'You have had money from her before.'

'Unknowingly. And it was *her* money, my grandparents'

money—*not* de Almeida money.'

Jaime was quiet for a moment, his thick eyebrows meeting in a frown. 'Antonia—you permit I call you Antonia?'

'Of course—stepbrother.' Her eyes danced suddenly, the ceiling light picking out glints of gold in them. Jaime's face hardened, and he released her hand abruptly.

'I am no brother of yours,' he said, in a tone that curled Antonia's toes in her new green shoes.

A delicate cough interrupted them and Antonia turned away, her cheeks flaming as Diana came towards them, smiling quizzically.

'Dinner is ready, my children—more than ready, according to Maria. Shall we join the others?'

On the surface the dinner party was a very gay, lively occasion. The Cardosos were good guests, contributing witty conversation and taking care to include Antonia, questioning her about her life in England, as well as talking about their own life in Boa Vista. Janio was employed in a minor role in the mining company controlled jointly by the de Almeidas and their American associates, while Isilda designed clothes, and sold them in a boutique she co-owned in the city.

'I have a partner, who is the—the business head,' she explained, with an expressive movement of her long, beautiful hands. She cast an expert eye over Antonia's dress. 'An interesting cut.'

'Thank you.' Antonia smiled politely. 'The style's very popular at home.'

'Home?' said Mario quickly, and smiled at her warmly. 'But you must think of this as home now, *cara*.'

Aware of Diana's carefully expressionless face, Antonia shook her head. 'My *other* home,' she corrected gently. 'Few people are lucky enough to have two.'

Isilda's eyes were watchful, so were Jaime's, and Antonia began to feel as if she were walking through a minefield as she answered questions on how long she was staying, what she would do when she went back to England, when she would visit Lagoa del Rey again. Diana remained quiet, which bothered Antonia as she parried Isilda's curiosity and fended off Janio's unconcealed interest, and after a while she lost her appetite, and began pushing her food around her plate.

'You must eat, *cara*,' said Mario, concerned. 'We shall think you do not like our Brazilian cuisine. Is it the garlic on the *bife* you do not like?'

Antonia assured him with truth that it was not, and attributed her lack of appetite to the altitude, instead of to Jaime's unwavering scrutiny, which was the actual culprit. Isilda seemed all too aware of this, and a hostile glint lit her dark eyes whenever they turned in Antonia's direction. In an effort to convey that she had no designs on Jaime, Antonia began flirting very delicately with Mario, who at least was a familiar face and only too pleased to respond, but it was a relief to move to the lantern-lit semi-darkness of the veranda, where she could drink her coffee in peace and retire from the conversation for a while under cover of her plea of fatigue. Antonia gave a welcoming smile to Mario as he took the vacant place beside her on a sofa, then she stiffened as she realised it was Jaime.

'You are weary, Antonia?' he asked in an undertone. Diana was missing, temporarily, to check on Marisa, and the other three were indulging in a lively exchange on the merits of the Cardosos' new sailing-dinghy.

'A little,' admitted Antonia.

'So many new things to take in. A long journey, a foreign country—new relatives. You can be forgiven for fatigue.'

She felt surprised. 'Thank you. It's a bit wimpish of me, really——'

'Wimpish?'

'Weak-spirited, then.'

Jaime's teeth gleamed fleetingly. 'I do not feel there is much weakness about your spirit, Antonia.'

Diana came back and sat down, smiling. 'Marisa was fast asleep, clutching her new doll, which is now arrayed in a frilly nightie with its hair in curlers.'

'*Engraçad*'!' exclaimed Isilda. 'Was this a present from her sister?'

Mario nodded, smiling. 'Also a china bear to put on the wall.'

'I have been ordered to arrange this,' said Jaime, resigned.

Diana laughed. 'Don't worry—I'll get Sabino to do it tomorrow.'

'*Não, senhora*; I have been given my orders, and must obey!'

'Then Marisa must be the only female successful in ordering *you* about, *caro*!' Isilda gave him her lazy, sensuous smile, and he shrugged, smiling back.

'If they are the right ones, orders from a beautiful woman can be very pleasant to obey, *não é*?'

Mario and Janio laughed, but the look Isilda turned on Jaime was speculative, and Diana changed the subject firmly by telling Isilda about the cashmere sweater.

'Very generous, your big daughter,' commented Isilda, then looked from Jaime to Mario. 'Did you two not receive presents also?'

'Antonia hasn't had the opportunity to hand them over yet,' said Diana quickly, and Antonia was grateful for the dim light which hid her heightened colour as Jaime turned mocking eyes on her face.

'We have no need of presents, Antonia. Your presence among us is gift enough!'

Antonia squirmed inwardly, wishing he'd keep his pleasantries for Isilda, who looked decidedly stormy as Mario crossed to kiss his stepsister's cheek.

'I don't know what the present is,' he said warmly, 'but I shall thank you in advance—I have always yearned for a china teddy bear on my wall to hang my robe!'

In the general laughter that followed the Cardosos rose to leave, and there was a flurry of goodnights and promises to meet again soon.

'We would so much like you to dine with us,' said Isilda

smoothly, and Antonia smiled brightly and said she would love to.

After Mario and Jaime had gone to see the visitors to their car Diana eyed Antonia's face narrowly. 'How about some tea?'

Antonia smiled thankfully. 'Heavenly!'

'Just sit there. I'll get it.' Diana pressed her back down on the sofa and went off to the kitchen with the coffee tray, and for a moment or two Antonia sat limply, watching giant moths courting suicide against the lanterns. Then she got up and leaned on the veranda rail, looking at the stars, which were diamond-bright in a black moonless sky, and seemed twice as large as they did at home. Everything did. The distances were vast, the house was huge, even the roses in the garden were taller than she was. She heard voices as Jaime and Mario returned to the house, and suddenly remembered the presents. Might be as well to get it over with, she thought, and hurried to her room and collected the small packages, taking a look at herself in the mirror. Her eyes burned brightly in a face colourless with fatigue, and she pulled a face at herself and went back hurriedly to join the others.

Jaime was leaning against the blossom-covered trellis smoking a cigar, a brandy glass in his hand, and Mario stood at the table pouring brandy for himself. Diana looked up from the tea tray and smiled as Antonia walked over to Jaime and handed him his gift, then went to Mario with his.

'Just something small,' she said woodenly, and sat down by Diana, grateful for the hot tea as the two men unwrapped the silk scarves. Mario's delight was obvious and immediate, and he bent to kiss Antonia's cheek once more.

'So thoughtful a present deserves two kisses,' he said, smiling, and Antonia returned the smile involuntarily.

Jaime's reaction was predictably less demonstrative. 'How very charming of you, Antonia. And very unexpected.' He crossed and raised Antonia's hand to his lips, kissing her fingers with formal deliberation. *'Muito obrigado*,' he said, looking into her startled eyes, and strolled back to his post at the veranda rail.

Antonia laughed unsteadily. 'I need Marisa here.'

'Marisa—why?' asked Mario, looking from her to his brother.

'As interpreter. She's teaching me to speak Portuguese.'

'But I thought your stay was to be too short to trouble yourself to learn,' Jaime reminded her, and Antonia bit her lips, her colour high again.

'He merely said "thank you",' said Diana swiftly. 'Will you have more tea?'

Antonia accepted gratefully, more for something to do than because she wanted any tea. Jaime's way of expressing his thanks had been indefinably provocative.

Well aware of Antonia's dismay, Diana began an animated conversation about plans for entertaining Antonia during her stay, and Mario joined in readily. Jaime held aloof, lounging relaxed as he watched the others, his eyes on Antonia much of the time.

'I have an idea,' he said unexpectedly after a while. 'I must get back to Boa Vista first thing in the morning, but I shall indulge myself with some time off I think this week, since Antonia's visit must be so brief. Let us give a party next Saturday.'

Diana's eyes opened wide. 'A party? But—but I've never had one here since—since——'

'Since my father died,' he finished for her. 'And I think it is time you did, Diana. Invite the Campo d'Ouro crowd, the Fonsecas and the Treharnes, some of the Americans from Mineração Gerais, people from the Bank of London and South America, the Cardosos, the de Carvalhos——'

'Jaime, stop! How many do you want here, for heaven's sake?' Diana looked alarmed, but Mario's face glowed with enthusiasm.

'*Otimo*, Jaime! Remember the parties here when our father was alive?' He turned to Diana at once in contrition. 'Do not be hurt *cara*, but you know how he loved to entertain.'

'But they were houseparties, Mario. We're a long way from anywhere here, remember. People always stayed the night.'

Jaime shrugged. '*Não tem problema*. We'll have it at my place in town.'

Antonia listened uneasily, not at all sure she cared for the idea. 'Please! You don't have to entertain for my sake.'

Diana squeezed her hand. 'Jaime's right. So is Mario. Francisco loved parties—thank God he did, or I'd never have met him. It was at an Embassy party that he found me, after all.'

'For which we will always be grateful.' Jaime brought his empty glass over to the tray and bent to kiss Diana's cheek. 'I was thoughtless for a moment to suggest you tire yourself with preparations for a party when all you want is the company of your daughters.'

'Oh, Jaime, no. You're never thoughtless!' she protested.

'I will arrange it all. Diva and Joachim seldom have enough to do at Casa Madrugada, anyway. It is time they had something to challenge them,' he said decisively. 'And now I well bid you goodnight, *cara*. Think nothing more about my little *festa*, Diana, except perhaps a new dress for the occasion, and how beautiful both of you ladies will look together.' Jaime turned to Antonia. 'Enjoy your stay. I shall not see you in the morning. Mario and I will be gone before you wake.'

'Goodbye then,' she said quietly.

He lifted her hand to his lips. '*Boa noite, dorme bem*. You remember what that means, without Marisa to translate?'

'Yes. Goodnight, and sleep well.' She smiled serenely, and Mario who had been watching them rather closely, laughed.

'You learn quickly, little sister.' And he, too, raised her hand to his lips. 'I shall see you at the weekend—*fim de semana*.'

'*Fim de semana*,' Antonia repeated. Over Mario's bent head she saw Jaime's face darken, and drew her hand away quickly, then both brothers said goodnight and left

Antonia alone with Diana, limp with reaction.

'There's some tea left if you'd like it,' said Diana.

Antonia shook her head. 'It's sleep I need. You were right. This altitude *does* have an effect.'

'It's been a rather wearing evening, too. You must be tired merely from meeting so many strangers in such a short time.' Diana hesitated. 'Do you mind being paraded publicly at a party?'

Antonia found that aspect of the party the least of her problems, and assured Diana of it sincerely, but made no mention of the matter troubling her more. Isilda Cardoso resented her, that was obvious, and if Jaime went on paying the same unexpected attention to his stepsister at his party it was hardly likely to be a fun occasion. Isilda had a dangerous look about her, like a tigress prowling after her mate, and Antonia had no intention of provoking her any further if possible, particularly when Jaime had been so bloody-minded earlier on. Admittedly he'd warmed towards her later, for some reason, but that didn't make his initial hostility any more acceptable. Antonia yawned suddenly, and got up to help Diana take everything out to the kitchen to leave for Maria in the morning. Afterwards they went round the house together, locking up and chatting in undertones, perfectly comfortable by this time in each other's company. At the door of Antonia's bedroom Diana touched a hand to her daughter's cheek.

'Time you were asleep. Your glow has faded.'

'It'll be back in the morning.' Antonia cast a questioning look at Diana. 'Are Isilda and Jaime actually engaged, by the way?'

Diana's face went blank for an instant, then her eyes danced wickedly. 'You've got it a bit wrong, poppet. It's Mario that Isilda wants. Didn't you see how Jaime was manoeuvring to keep him away from you all evening? Isilda was not at all pleased to learn that Mario's business trip to England included acting as my proxy to bring you here. Your appearance tonight, looking so gorgeous, if I may say so, really took the wind out of her sails.' She chuckled at the aptness of her words.

Antonia shook her head slowly. 'How thick I've been—so *that* was why Jaime was so attentive!'

Diana smiled. 'I don't know that I agree with you there. I'd bet my boots Jaime's behaviour this evening was due to something rather more personal than mere altruism in his efforts to keep Mario away from you, love.'

Antonia flushed. 'Nonsense! Believe me, he was pretty outspoken when we met for the first time, at pains to warn me against any bright ideas on the subject of taking advantage of *you*!'

'He seems to have changed his tune since then.'

'Well, I haven't changed towards *him*. One look at him was enough. He's a chauvinist of the first water, and not my type at all.' Belatedly Antonia remembered Diana was very fond of her stepson. 'I'm sorry. But he was pretty unfriendly, you know.'

'Don't apologise to me, love. At least you can comfort yourself with the thought that you don't have to see him again until next weekend! Goodnight.' Diana kissed Antonia's cheek and went off to bed, leaving her daughter to thoughts which were somewhat chaotic as she undressed.

Jaime de Almeida had annoyed her intensely during their ride in the morning, then stuck to her side all evening for what seemed no good reason since it was Mario the sultry Isilda had her eye on. A good thing Jaime was leaving in the morning, thought Antonia wearily. He was too unsettling by half to have around for any length of time, and she was very pleased she wouldn't be seeing him again until next weekend.

Antonia saw him sooner than that, to her surprise. Something woke her at first light, and she got out of bed, wondering what had disturbed her. She drew back the curtains and, to her astonishment, Jaime stood outside in the small garden outside her own bedroom, dressed in a formal suit and obviously about to depart for Boa Vista. His hand was poised to throw another pebble at the window and she peered at him, half-asleep, pushing the hair from her eyes. He pantomimed opening the window, and she complied, opening the mosquito screens first and then half of the casement window itself.

'Is something wrong?' she whispered.

Jaime shook his head, which looked damp from the shower. 'I wished to speak with you before I left.'

Antonia backed away, suddenly remembering she wasn't exactly suitably dressed for entertaining visitors. 'Surely this isn't the place to do it!'

'I know. Forgive me.' He shrugged gracefully. 'But I could not go away without telling you that I regret my lack of welcome, Antonia. I had reasons for my hostility, none of them admirable. I wish to say I have thought much in the night, and feel that I was mistaken. I thought——'

'I know exactly what you thought—that I'd come to scrounge all I could out of Diana, then leave her high and dry and rush back to England without a backward glance.'

Jaime flinched at the scorn in Antonia's voice. 'Not only that, alas! I was convinced you meant also to trap my brother. His telephone conversations from England were full of how beautiful, how brave you were, so *simpática* in every way, which pleased Diana. It did not please me.'

Antonia's eyes narrowed. 'In short you were even less thrilled with the prospect of me as a sister-in-law than as a stepsister!'

Jaime nodded, his faint smile crooked. '*Perfeitamente*, Antonia. I most certainly do not wish you for my *cunhada*— my sister-in-law.'

'Have no fear,' she assured him kindly. 'I'll admit that at first glance I thought Mario was the answer to a maiden's prayer—which he is. He's the kindest, nicest, and certainly the most beautiful man I've ever met in my life. But he's not for *this* maiden—at least, not in that way.'

There was a very odd look indeed in Jaime's intent black eyes. 'And you are a maiden, *de verdade*, Antonia?'

She went suddenly still, her long, tilted eyes blank. 'Perhaps your excellent vocabulary doesn't include the word virgin, Senhor de Almeida. Because presumably that's what you're getting at.'

'I have made you angry again,' he said swiftly, and moved closer to the window, but Antonia stepped back.

'I think it's time you went——' She stopped, looking over her shoulder as a knock sounded on the door.

Diana came in, dressed in a long cotton robe, and stopped dead, her face astonished as she caught sight of Jaime. 'I heard voices, I thought Marisa must be bothering Antonia.'

'No, it was I,' said Jaime, and sighed heavily. 'I thought I would make apologies to Antonia for my inhospitable reception of her at first, but I went badly wrong. Now I must apologise all over again.'

'Unnecessary.' Antonia looked pointedly at her watch. 'Isn't it time you were off?'

He bowed gracefully. 'You are right.' He blew a kiss at Diana. '*Até logo, cara.*' His eyes met Antonia's. 'Goobdbye for the moment, Antonia.'

'Goodbye. Did you fix the bear on Marisa's wall, by the way?'

In consternation Jaime clapped a hand to his forehead. '*Meu Deus, não!* I shall do it now.'

'You'll wake her up!' protested Diana.

'*Não faz mal*—better that than risk her wrath when I see her next. I promised her, Diana. *Adeus!*' And Jaime de Almeida took to his heels and tore from the little garden like an Olympic sprinter while Antonia watched from the window with Diana, and laughed.

CHAPTER FIVE

LIFE was more peaceful, but no less interesting for the next few days, as Diana initiated Antonia into the ways of the Lagoa del Rey household. Antonia enjoyed riding the aptly named Delicado, and with Geraldo in attendance rode with

Diana and Marisa every morning, sometimes in the afternoon as well. At first they rode only short distances, but gradually, as Antonia grew accustomed to her animal's gait, they explored the local terrain, which had a rugged grandeur that never ceased to amaze her, as did the colours of the rich red earth and green vegetation under the glorious blue of the sky.

They rode past the marina and the modern glass-walled building of the yacht club, which was deserted during the week, almost all the members being weekend sailors. Antonia much admired the expensive craft moored along the shore, and Marisa pointed with pride to the *Esperança*, which belonged to Jaime.

'Jaime and Mario must take you along to the club,' said Diana. 'I gather it's quite lively at weekends.'

But Antonia, for the time being at least, was grateful for the sheer peace and quiet of her stay, not at all bored as Diana feared. The days passed with surprising speed, and in the evenings, when Marisa was in bed, there was a whole lifetime to catch up on as far as Diana was concerned. They talked of Janet a great deal, which was balm to Antonia. It was a joy to have someone to tell about past funny incidents as well as those poignant, painful days before Janet died. And every evening Jaime rang up to see how they were, sometimes Mario as well, and Diana would come back from the telephone bearing messages from both her stepsons to Antonia.

'Preparations for the party are well under way, but it's been postponed until Saturday of next week,' Diana said. 'Apparently some of Jaime's friends are away until then. He's quite pleased about the extra time. He put in a lot of hours while Mario was away in England and intends spending a longer weekend out here this week by way of compensation.'

'If the party's next week it can be my send-off,' said Antonia.

Diana looked stricken. 'You can't go back so soon!

You've only just come. Surely you can spare another week, at least.'

'I ought to see how the house sale is going——'

'Nonsense. Much better to have people going over it with the estate agent while you're not there.'

In the end Antonia allowed herself to be persuaded, and the following afternoon went for a walk by herself while Diana and Marisa were resting. Her skin was darkening rapidly from her hours in the sun, which had bleached lighter streaks here and there among her curling hair, and in sun top and brief pink shorts she wandered down the steep path to the jetty, accompanied by Otto and Hans, two of the Dobermanns, who sat either side of her like panting sentinels as she perched on a boulder on the narrow strip of shingle and feasted her eyes on the wide expanse of water. As she sat there contentedly, enjoying the sunshine, a sailing dinghy came into view, tacking across the lake into the quite stiff breeze blowing. Antonia watched, fascinated, as the lone sailor ducked and dodged as his boom swung back and fore, then the boat made for the shore in a bee line for the jetty. She wondered what to do, not sure whether to walk away before the boat came inshore or wait and see who the sailor was, and what he wanted. Low growls sounded deep inside the dog's throats, and Antonia put an arm around each sleek black neck.

'Good lads,' she said softly, as they laid their ears back. 'You'll protect me, won't you, if this Francis Drake is up to no good?'

The dinghy glided alongside the jetty and the man on board secured his craft to a post before climbing out. He stood his ground several feet away as Otto and Hans each gave a staccato, warning bark. Antonia shaded her eyes against the sun, examining the athletic tanned young man who stood gazing at her. He had close-cut curly black hair and an engaging face, with a crooked nose and wide, smiling mouth. An inflatable waistcoat hung from his shoulders, but otherwise his sole garment was a pair of ragged denim cut-offs.

'*Boa tarde,*' he said, and the dogs growled warningly.

Antonia's Portuguese was equal to everyday greetings by this time, but she said very clearly in English. 'Good afternoon.'

He inclined his head. 'Good afternoon, Miss Antonia.'

Her eyes opened wide. 'You know my name?'

'But yes. Mario has invited me to a party given in your honour next week. He said you were very beautiful. He was wrong.'

Antonia's fingers grasped the Dobermanns' collars as they moved restlessly. 'I'm sorry I fall short of your standards, Senhor——?'

'De Almeida. I am *primo*—cousin to Jaime and Mario. My name is Vasco. And I meant that you are ravishing, not just beautiful.'

Antonia eyed him quizzically. 'And you just happened to be sailing by.'

He grinned. '*Mais ou menos.* I come sometimes to the yacht club in the week. I like to sail alone. But today I catch sight of a vision on the shore and come to investigate—and just see how richly I am rewarded. An encounter with the mysterious new sister of my cousins!' He glanced at the dogs ruefully. 'But you are very well protected.'

Privately Antonia thought it was a very good thing. He might be saying the truth, of course, but she had no proof he was a relative of the de Almeidas. Nevertheless, she couldn't help liking him. He had charm, in a cheeky, offbeat sort of way.

'Perhaps you ought to get back in your boat,' she suggested, her arms beginning to ache with the strain of holding the dogs back. 'Otto and Hans here are getting restive.'

'If I come by at this time tomorrow will you come for a sail, Antonia?' he asked, untying the dinghy. 'Perfectly allowable. I am relative.'

'I might,' she said casually, secretly rather taken with the idea. 'But it depends on what Diana has planned.'

Vasco de Almeida consulted the black, waterproof watch

on his wrist. 'Let us say two o'clock tomorrow, then, if possible. A short sail only—I will bring a life-jacket for you.'

'I can't promise.'

'At least promise one thing,' he said, laughing, as he leapt in the dinghy. 'If you *do* come, leave the dogs behind, *por favor!*'

Antonia chuckled as he hauled on sheets, sails flapped and his boat, the *Paraiso*, glided away across the water. She released the dogs and they bounded to the water's edge, barking furiously, and Vasco raised an arm in acknowledgement. She climbed back up to the house to find Diana coming down through the garden with Marisa.

'Where have you *been*?' demanded the latter indignantly. 'I've been waiting and waiting.'

Antonia laughed and picked her up, whirling her round before setting her down. 'My humble apologies, your highness.' Then, more seriously to Diana, she continued, 'Sorry if you were worried, but I met a man down by the jetty.'

'A man!' Diana began to laugh. 'The very first time you're let out alone and that's what you get up to!'

'I had Otto and Hans with me, don't worry. They were all for seeing him off sharpish, but I hung on to them until he introduced himself.' Antonia explained who the man was as they had tea, and Diana nodded, enlightened, explaining that Vasco de Almeida was the spoilt only son of Francisco's younger brother, who had died shortly after the boy was born.

'Brought up by a doting mother who was wealthy in her own right before she married Jose de Almeida,' Diana added.

Antonia asked what Vasco did, and gurgled when she learned the irrepressible Vasco had his sights set on being a Formula One racing driver, determined to follow in the footsteps of Nelson Piquet and Ayrton Senna.

'I didn't think he was here in the country,' said Diana. 'He's usually hanging round the racing circuits.'

'Apparently Mario met him and invited him to the party.'

'Jaime *will* be pleased; he and Vasco aren't what you'd call soul-mates, exactly.'

'Vasco asked me to go sailing with him tomorrow,' said Antonia.

'Would you like to?'

'The water looked very tempting down there today—I would, rather.'

'There's no reason why not. Vasco's an expert sailor, only don't let him take you out for too long the first time, Antonia. I'd rather Jaime was with you for any serious sailing.'

Later that night, after Marisa was in bed, Diana was very quiet over coffee on the veranda, and eventually Antonia couldn't help asking if something was wrong. Diana shook her head and sighed.

'Not exactly. But you've been here for several days now, and I really can't put it off any longer.'

Antonia looked at her in alarm. 'What do you mean?'

Diana rose. 'Let's go in the study tonight—I think it's a bit chilly.'

When they were settled in the comfortable room, which gave more privacy than the rambling veranda, Diana fixed her daughter with a very direct look. 'First I want to say how much I appreciate your forbearance, Antonia.'

'In what way?'

'For not asking about—about your father.'

Antonia tensed. 'You don't have to tell me, Diana,' she said urgently, 'really you don't. If it's too painful——'

'I haven't spoken about it for well over twenty years, but it's not painful, exactly. After all this time I'm really not entitled to be emotional about it any more. Did Janet ever say anything on the subject?'

Antonia shook her head. 'Only that you went abroad on holiday and came back pregnant.' Something of her misgivings about her parentage must have showed in her eyes, because Diana reached across and touched her hand reassuringly.

'Don't be apprehensive, love. It was nothing so very terrible.' She leaned back in her chair, looking extraordinarily youthful by the soft light of the rose-shaped lamps scattered about the room. It was very easy to visualise the young, inexperienced girl in the little story she told with such surprising detachment, as though it had all happened to someone else.

Diana Moore's subject at university had been Hispanic Studies, and in the vacation of her second year she had gone to live with a family in Spain for a time. Her task had been to improve the English of the younger members of the family during the day, and in return improve her own Spanish with the parents in the evenings. After a time the eldest son of the house had returned from a stay with relatives abroad, and one solitary exchange of looks with the English girl had been enough. That had been that; the *coup de foudre*, the thunderclap of love at first sight.

'We were literally thrown together,' said Diana, her eyes turned inward on the memory of that summer. 'His parents, would you believe, actually enlisted him to show me the town and improve my vocabulary. And he did! Not only did he take me out for a couple of hours every day, but at night he would steal into my room when everyone was asleep, and teach me all the words of love he knew—and not only words.'

The rest of the story was less happy. Eventually his father discovered their love affair and the mother sent the unhappy girl packing post-haste, after informing her coldly that her lover had been betrothed since he was a child to the daughter of a rich local family. The frantic young man was banished at once to his grandparents' house in the Pyrenees, and Diana was put on the next plane for England.

'It must seem very funny to you,' said Diana apologetically, 'in these days of equality of the sexes and so on, but at the time it was pretty grim.'

'It must have been horrible for you. What ghastly people!' said Antonia vehemently.

'They felt they'd nurtured a viper in the bosom of the family.'

'It takes two!'

'Well, to be fair, they weren't frightfully pleased with their son, either!'

'So what happened next?'

The young Diana, devastated by her experience, was utterly shattered to find she was pregnant. And when her elderly, ultra-respectable parents proved so outraged and lacking in support she fled back to Janet.

'But didn't he even try to contact you?' asked Antonia.

'Actually he did. But I never knew at the time. When I ran off my parents refused to have anything more to do with me, but when they died a packet of letters addressed to me came to me with the legacy and various other effects. Some of the letters were from—him, still unopened.'

Antonia sat forward in her chair. 'Did you read them?'

'Oh yes, I read them. They were passionate outpourings that tore me to pieces even all those years afterwards. There weren't many. After a while he gave up when he heard nothing in return. I assume he married his eligible fiancée in due course, and went into the family business, as expected.' A shadow crossed Diana's face. 'And all the time I was breaking my heart in the house where you were born a few months later. Then, to finish me off completely, I had to go through the agony of parting with you.'

What happened after that was less dramatic. Diana Moore went to London and got work as a waitress by day, and learned to type in the evenings. Janet and Lewis Grant lent her the money for the lessons. Eventually she became a secretary in a firm which numbered Brazil among the countries to which it exported goods, and in time rose to the dizzy heights of Personal Assistant to the Managing Director who occasionally took her to Brazil on business trips. During one of these visits they were invited to a party at the British Embassy in Rio de Janeiro.

'And Francisco was there.' Diana smiled. 'The rest you know, more or less. He had been a widower for years; I had been off men altogether since—since my earlier experience. He swept me off my feet, and all of a sudden, instead of being lonely, with no family, I had a husband and two grown-up stepsons, neither of whom, miraculously, resented the new stepmother. The only cloud in the sky was being so far away from you. But one can't have everything in life, my love. I learned that the hard way, early on in my career. It's like a dream come true to have you here with me now at long last.'

Antonia jumped up impulsively and bent down to kiss Diana's cheek, which flushed at once with pleasure. 'I'm glad we've finally made it. But I can't help feeling sorry for that poor young man all those years ago. He never knew about me, then?'

'No. And he never will, I suppose.'

'And you're not going to tell me his name.'

Diana looked at her thoughtfully. 'I've never told *anyone* his name, and now after all these years there seems no point.'

'I've read books where all sorts of complications have arisen in these circumstances,' said Antonia, to lighten the atmosphere a little. 'I might even have fallen in love with my brother, or something gruesome like that.'

'In which case I would have stepped in pretty sharpish.' Diana smiled demurely. 'Of course, where your stepbrothers are concerned there's no consanguinity involved.'

'My, my,' said Antonia, refusing to rise to the little dig. 'What long words you use, little mother!'

The truth about her father was a great relief to Antonia. Ever since learning about Diana her imagination had run riot on the subject, and it was reassuring to learn that the unknown young man had at least been a lover—and even of respectable background of some kind, despite Diana's deliberate vagueness on the subject. As she lay watching the stars through the window Antonia wove little fantasies about some young Spanish *hidalgo* with a passionate, romantic face—then she frowned. One thing she *did* know about the gentleman, now she came to think of it. Whoever, or whatever that unknown father had been, he had unwittingly begotten a daughter who resembled him very closely, because Diana had said so. And there *were* fair Spaniards, in plenty; the King of Spain himself, Juan Carlos, for one.

'Have you decided to go sailing?' asked Diana the next day, when the three of them returned to lunch after their morning ride.

Antonia shrugged. 'I don't know.'

'Can I come?' demanded Marisa.

'You know you're only allowed out on the lake with Jaime or Mario,' said Diana firmly, and Marisa looked mutinous.

'Why can Antonia go on her own, then?'

'Because Vasco has asked her to go with him. And besides, Antonia's a big girl.'

'Don't like Vasco,' said Marisa moodily.

'Why not?' asked Antonia.

Marisa thought it over. 'He says nasty things to me—calls me "*bichinho feio*". That means ugly little insect, I think.'

'Not at all polite,' agreed Antonia gravely. 'If he says things like that to me I shall dive overboard and swim back straight away.'

Diana gave her a whimsical look. 'Highly unlikely, I'd say. And, incidentally, I shouldn't recommend swimming in the lake. It shelves very deeply, and there are treacherous currents out in the middle.' Her large grey eyes were deadly serious, and Antonia nodded.

'Of course I won't—look, I won't go if you'd rather. I made no firm promise, and I'm really not all that enthusiastic.'

'Nonsense, of course you must go. It's a lovely day and heaven knows, you must find it very quiet here. Bring Vasco back for a drink afterwards. He can stay to dinner if he likes, and amuse us with tales of the glamorous race-track.'

When Antonia strolled down the path to the lake after lunch the *Paraiso* was already moored there, and Vasco lay flat on the boards of the jetty, his face turned up to the sun. Stealthily Antonia negotiated the last few feet, her sneakers noiseless on the red earth. Vasco suddenly came alive to the fact that she was there and jumped to his feet, a broad grin on his face.

'*Como vai*, Antonia? You came after all!'

'Hello. Diana vouched for your respectability, so I decided to chance it.'

He laid a hand on his heart theatrically. 'Then I am eternally in Dona Diana's debt. Let me help you with the life-jacket.'

After much playful adjusting of buckles Vasco handed Antonia into the dinghy, which seemed alarmingly frail at close quarters, and overfull once Vasco joined her in it after casting off. At once life became very hectic, with much dodging about as the boom swung over when they tacked into the wind, which was much stronger now they were out on the lake. Antonia's previous experiences on the water had been confined to a punt on the river at college and the cross channel ferry to Jersey, and the athleticism and ultra-quick reactions necessary to act as Vasco's crew came as something of a shock. The sailing commands were unfamiliar to her, for one thing, doubly so when shouted in a pronounced foreign accent, and it took her a while to come to terms with them. She had expected a serene glide over the water with the sun on her face, with no need for anything more energetic than to look as decorative as possible, exchanging repartee with the engaging Vasco, and after half an hour or so shouted as much to him, grinning, during a few relatively calm minutes as they flew across the water. To her surprise there was no answering grin on his face as he cast an anxious eye on the sky from his post at the helm. Antonia swivelled to follow his gaze and gulped as she saw a bank of purple clouds advancing behind them, dragging in its wake a solid wall of rain.

Oh boy, she thought, and bit down hard on a gush of panic as a squall of wind hit them. From then on her entire energies were concentrated on trying to follow Vasco's yelled instructions, most of which were carried away on the wind. Then the rain reached them and blotted out everything but the immediate lashing waves. Antonia let out a screech of fright and tried to duck out of the way of the boom, but it struck her head with a sickening crack and everything went black.

When Antonia opened her eyes again she thought for a moment she was in the shower, except that the floor was bumping about madly. Then she became aware of the roar of an engine and the smell of diesel oil and struggled to sit up, but a hand thrust her down and she flopped back on the bucking deck of a rubber inflatable. She peered up groggily at the figure at the controls, wondering if she was dreaming when she saw it was Jaime, with his hair and clothes plastered to his body by the driving rain. Antonia turned her head gingerly to see Vasco bending over her, his face wild with anxiety.

'Antonia, *fala comigo, por favor!*' He chafed her hands violently until she protested, and his eyes lit up with relief as the craft reached the shore. He was elbowed summarily out of the way as Jaime de Almeida bent to pick Antonia up, his face black with fury as he strode along the jetty of the yacht club, with Vasco pouring a voluble stream of impassioned Portuguese in his cousin's ears as he ran alongside. Then Diana was flying towards them and Antonia struggled in Jaime's arms and he set her on her feet so she could let Diana hold her close. Several men were milling around, the rain was still sheeting down and everyone was soaked to the skin and arguing loudly, making Antonia's aching head throb abominably.

Suddenly Diana rounded on everyone with a few cutting words, and Jaime, with a swift word of apology to his stepmother, scooped Antonia up once more and followed after Diana to the car parked near the clubhouse. Antonia tried to protest that she was fine, she could walk, but Jaime gave her a withering look and said tersely, *'fica quieta'.* Rightly assuming he meant her to shut up and stay still, she did so.

'Will you drive my car, Diana?' asked Jaime, and Diana nodded, her face strained.

'You hold Antonia,' she instructed, and Jaime slid carefully into the passenger seat with his sodden burden in his arms. They arrived at the house to uproar as Maria and Pascoa exclaimed over Antonia, then went rushing to run hot baths, make coffee, all the while demanding an account of Antonia's adventure from Diana, and in no time at all Antonia was warm and dry in bed, where she was ordered to stay until the doctor arrived.

'But I'm not ill,' protested Antonia, who felt completely normal by this time, apart from the lump on her head. Diana, dressed in warm jersey and trousers, sat down by the bed to share the coffee Maria had brought, and heaved a heartfelt sigh of relief.

'Maybe you're not, but until Dr Ferreira arrives from Campo d'Ouro, my lovely, you can just stay put. You might have concussion for all we know. Jaime agrees with me.'

'Ah yes, Jaime.' Antonia kept her face carefully blank as she drank her coffee. 'Where did he spring from?'

It appeared that Jaime had decided to start the weekend early, and arrived at Lagoa del Rey while Antonia was out in the *Paraiso* with his cousin Vasco.

'He wasn't terribly pleased to hear you'd gone in the first place,' said Diana drily. 'Then when the weather turned we drove back to the clubhouse and he got out the rescue boat. I was very worried,' she added quietly.

'It wasn't much fun,' admitted Antonia. 'Not my idea of entertainment at all. Where's Marisa, by the way?'

'Zelia took her over to Sabino's house to his son's birthday party. Thank God she was out of the way.' Diana got up as someone knocked on the door, and went over to let in Jaime. He'd changed his clothes but not his mood, from the look on his face, and Antonia slid further down beneath the covers, not sure she felt up to his company in his present state of mind.

'I have told Vasco he is never to take you sailing again,' he said without preliminaries.

'Jaime——' began Diana warningly, but he took no notice.

'He may be a boy wonder in a racing car, but in a boat he is an amateur,' he went on brusquely. 'In future, Antonia, if you wish to go out on the lake you will go with me.'

The well-being derived from the hot bath and Diana's cosseting evaporated abruptly. Antonia's head throbbed as she looked up at Jaime's angry face. Why *was* he so angry? she wondered. And in any case he had no right to be laying down the law so trenchantly. She hadn't done anything wrong—and it was *her* head that had received the crack, not his.

'My enthusiasm for having anything at all to do with the lake has waned,' she said with an effort, and tried to smile at Diana. 'I'll just look at it from now on, preferably from a safe distance.'

Jaime came to the edge of the bed, thrusting a hand through his damp hair. 'You look ill,' he said, frowning.

'I've felt better—but I'll mend.'

Diana jumped up again at the sound of voices in the hall, and opened the door to Dr Ferreira from Campo d'Ouro, and Jaime left them together after greeting the doctor, while Diana explained what had happened. After a few questions it took Dr Ferreira very little time to pronounce his young patient perfectly well, apart from the sore head, and to compliment her on the fine head of hair that had probably saved her from concussion. A couple of hours' sleep would be the best medication, he assured Diana, but left some mild pain-killers in case Antonia's headache persisted, then went off to have a chat and a drink with Jaime before returning home.

'I'm so sorry, Diana,' said Antonia penitently. 'I had no idea my little outing would cause so much bother.'

'It wouldn't have if Vasco had kept an eye on the

weather. No doubt he was too busy chatting you up to notice the squall coming straight at you.' Diana touched a hand to Antonia's. 'Try to sleep. I'll let Marisa stay up a little later since Jaime's here. She'll be bursting to see you. I'll pop in later on to check on you.'

'I bet you never thought a daughter of my age would cause more trouble than your five-year-old,' said Antonia drowsily.

Diana smiled. 'I admit I was a bit het up there for a while, but it wasn't your fault. See you later.'

Dr Ferreira was right. A few hours' rest worked wonders and Antonia was able to join the others in the study later, feeling remarkably normal. Marisa was wild with curiosity about the incident, and sat close to Antonia on a sofa, bombarding her with questions while Jaime poured drinks and Diana sat quiet, looking drawn and tired.

'Did you fall in the water? Were you frightened? Did Vasco rescue you?' Marisa asked excitedly.

'I don't know, poppet. I didn't have much time to be frightened. I was so busy trying to do what I was told.' Antonia looked at the others. '*Did* I fall in the water?'

Jaime nodded, his face grim as he handed her a drink. 'You flew rather than fell, just as I was bringing the rescue boat alongside. I was able to fish you out almost at once, with Vasco's help. *De certeza* he dived in after you, at which point the *Paraiso* capsized and everything became rather—chaotic, I think you say.'

Diana shuddered. 'I couldn't see a thing because the rain was coming down like spears. It was nerve-racking waiting in the clubhouse until I heard the inflatable's engine and eventually saw there were three of you on board.'

'It certainly knows how to rain here, doesn't it?' asked Antonia cheerfully. 'When I saw that wall of water coming towards us I bitterly regretted ever setting foot in Vasco's boat, I can tell you! What happened to it, by the way?'

'It is wrecked, I imagine,' said Jaime with indifference. 'Which will matter little to Vasco. Tia Caçilda will buy her darling son a new one, I've no doubt.'

Oops, thought Antonia, as she caught Diana's amused
eye. Despite the amusement Diana was looking distinctly
fragile this evening, and Antonia felt deep remorse, since it
was obvious that the afternoon's trauma had been the
cause. Jaime had put some Vivaldi on the stereo, and with
the curtains drawn against the rain outside Antonia was
lulled by a feeling of security and warmth as she listened
dreamily to Diana and Jaime discussing arrangements for
the party the following week, while Marisa cuddled up to
Antonia and changed her doll into its nightdress. Antonia
smiled a little, then pulled a face as she tasted her drink,
finding there was no gin with the tonic water. Jaime caught
her eye and shrugged in apology.

'No alcohol for you tonight, I regret, Antonia. Dr
Ferreira's instructions.'

'I don't mind. Alcohol's not one of my weaknesses.'

'May we know what they are?'

Antonia laughed and squeezed Marisa. 'Oh, chocolate,
and coffee ice-cream, and little girls called Marisa.'

'Is your head too sore to read to me tonight, Tonia?'
asked the little girl anxiously.

'No, of course not. I'm right as rain.' Antonia groaned.
'Only I'd rather not think about rain for a while.'

'I'll read to her tonight,' said Diana, but Jaime
intervened.

'*I* shall be the story-teller,' he said firmly and Marisa
beamed, kissing Antonia and her mother goodnight before
skipping off happily with Jaime, prattling away as they
went hand in hand from the room.

'Well?' asked Diana, when they were alone. 'Are you
really as right as rain?'

'Yes. Honestly. I must have a very thick skull!'

Later, when dinner was over, and they were sitting over
coffee in the study, Diana began to look very tired, Antonia
noted uneasily.

'Why don't you go to bed?' she suggested. 'I had such a
long nap I'm still wide awake, but there's no reason for you
to stay up.'

Diana looked doubtful, but Jaime added his own persuasion, promising that he would lock up and see to the fire.

'Please, Diana,' he said with quiet emphasis.

She capitulated gracefully, reminded Antonia that the pain-killers from Dr Ferreira were on her bedside table should she need them, then kissed both of them goodnight and left them together.

'Diana looks utterly shattered,' commented Antonia and Jaime shot her a sombre glance as he sat down.

'It is no great surprise, Antonia.'

She sighed. 'I'm very sorry for all the drama this afternoon. It obviously shook her badly.'

'It was more than that, I fear.' Something in his voice made her look at him closely.

'What do you mean?'

'I mean that it must have been very hard for Diana to see you go out on the lake at all, even without the added shock of the storm and your accident. But you are adult—she cannot tell you what you must, or must not do.'

'But I really wasn't all that keen,' Antonia assured him. 'I told her I wouldn't go if she thought it was a bad idea.'

'I know. Diana told me. But she thought it would amuse you to go sailing. She worries that it must be boring here for you.'

'Boring!' Antonia laughed. 'Who could be bored in such a beautiful place—besides, I'm very glad of the peace and quiet. Life was quiet enough for me in England just before I came, I admit, but very lonely. I'm very lucky to be given such a wonderful holiday here.'

Their eyes met and for several moments they looked at each other steadily, then Jaime rose and crossed the room to sit beside Antonia on the sofa.

'Diana said I must not tell you this, but I am certain it is better that you know.'

Antonia's eyes widened apprehensively. 'Know what, exactly?'

He looked away into the fire. 'My father died in the lake

in an accident very much like the one you had today. But he was alone, and no rescue boat turned up in time to help him. He suffered a blow on the head and drowned. It was two months before Marisa was due to be born. Diana went into—how do you say—early labour?'

'Premature,' said Antonia, her face stricken.

'*Está certo. Então*, Marisa arrived early in the world, but too late for her father to see her.' The pain on Jaime's face affected Antonia deeply and she laid her hand on his arm. 'How utterly tragic for all of you. Believe me, if I'd known I'd never have set foot in Vasco's wretched boat.'

'Dinghy,' corrected Jaime, his face softening. He covered her hand with his. 'If you come sailing with me I promise you will be safe, Antonia.'

She grimaced. 'At this particular moment the thought of sailing anywhere with anyone holds no charm at all. And why should I be safer with you than Vasco, if the weather can change so suddenly like that?'

He smiled loftily. 'Because I am expert. And because anyone who knows the lake as Mario and I do would never take a craft out with an inexperienced crew with a weather forecast like today.'

Antonia frowned. 'Then how did your father's accident happen? Presumably he knew the lake well.'

'He was not sailing—he was fishing. He was no great distance from the shore when the wind rose, and it was not even bad like today. Diana was on the veranda watching for him through the binoculars. He tried to start the outboard engine on the dinghy, which was an old one Mario and I had as children. Diana saw him slip and hit his head on the engine as he pulled the starting cord. She ran for Geraldo and Sabino, but by the time they reached the jetty and set off in the other boat it was too late. He had fallen overboard unconscious and drowned.' Jaime's clasp on her hand tightened convulsively, and Antonia looked up at him appalled, the gold glints in her eyes highlighted by the flicker of the fire.

'Poor Diana,' she said unsteadily. 'And poor you, too.'

Jaime didn't appear to be listening as he gazed down at her in silence, his eyes very intent. 'You know it is very strange, Antonia—sometimes I have this feeling I have met you before.'

She attempted a chuckle, to lighten the sombre atmosphere. 'Now that, Senhor de Almeida, is the corniest line in the book.'

He shook his head, his eyes gleaming. 'No, no—please credit me with more subtlety than that, which is what men say who need an opening to—get to know a woman.'

'You mean pick them up!'

'Do I?' Jaime shrugged. 'But I have the good fortune to know you already. Perhaps this feeling is what the French call *déjà vu*.'

'Maybe we met in a former incarnation,' suggested Antonia, very conscious, by this time, of the warmth of his hand on hers.

'And what would we have been in a former life, you think?' Jaime followed her lead instantly. 'Were we friends, or brother and sister—or lovers, perhaps?'

His voice dropped several notes on the last word, and a *frisson* of reaction to it ran up Antonia's spine, startling her. She moved away a little, and he laughed softly.

'I promised you would be safe with me, *carinha*—remember?'

'You said in a boat. Nothing about elsewhere.'

'You do not trust me?'

Antonia turned to look at him, her eyes speculative. 'Well, put it this way, I think you'd upset Diana by trying to seduce her daughter under her own roof.'

'You think I should wait until we are on neutral territory?' he said, poker-faced.

'No, I do not!' she snapped, then lapsed unwillingly into a laugh. 'You're teasing me, Senhor Stepbrother!'

'Is that how you think of me—as your stepbrother?'

'No.' The moment she said it Antonia realised how true it was. Mario, who had seemed so breathtaking at first sight was far easier to look on as a brother than Jaime, for some reason.

Jaime watched the changing expressions on her face and smiled, that rare, tender smile of his that transformed his hard, imperious features, and caused erratic changes in Antonia's pulse-rate.

'I am glad,' he said quietly, and reached out a hand to touch her hair. 'And how is the bump on your head? May I see for myself?'

Antonia bent forward, pointing out the exact place, and Jaime's fingers touched it delicately, then she froze as his lips touched the nape of her neck where her hair parted and swung forward, and she breathed in sharply, suddenly tense. His lips lingered, then moved sideways until they reached the hollow of her ear. Afraid to move, both astonished by and acutely aware of Jaime's touch, Antonia sat perfectly still, her face hidden by her hair, until his lips lifted and she relaxed, only to tense again as, very gently, he slid his arm round her waist and put his free hand under her chin to turn her face up to his.

'I was kissing it better,' he said gravely. 'As I do with Marisa.'

'Not quite as you do with Marisa.'

'No,' he agreed, and kissed her mouth.

The moment Antonia's lips met his she was filled with startled acknowledgement of the sheer inevitability of the caress; that she had been, unknown even to herself, unconsciously waiting for him to do just this since the first moment of their meeting, when Jaime de Almeida had looked on her with such cold suspicion in his dark eyes. Even as her senses were swimming with the ravishing physical pleasure of contact with his lips she made a little sound deep in her throat at the thought, and he raised his head.

'I frightened you?'

Antonia shook her head slowly, her eyes locked with his. 'I was surprised.'

'Because I kissed you, *carinha*?' Jaime's arm tightened about her waist, and his free hand smoothed away the hair from her face.

'No. Just how—how inevitable it seemed.'

'You mean you knew from the start I wished to make love to you.'

'I did not! You were pretty foul to me in the beginning.'

'Only because I thought Mario had found you first.'

'And you minded?'

'*Sim, senhora*—I *minded*.' Jaime laughed softly. '*Que lingua sensato*!'

'Are you being rude?'

'No. It is only that this English language of yours is so—so down-to-earth, I think you say. No passion. I not only *minded*, Antonia, I was filled with such *ciúme*—such jealousy I insulted you next morning from sheer *maldade*. I felt evil towards Diana's beautiful daughter, who preferred my brother to me.' He frowned suddenly. 'But this inevitability of yours—was it that you felt the same way?' Light flared in his eyes as she nodded silently, and his mouth found hers again.

Jaime de Almeida was a man with much experience in the art of making love. Antonia recognised this by instinct as his mouth coaxed very gently at first, but with an assurance that refused to acknowledge any possibility of her denial. Very gradually his kisses deepened, grew more demanding, and she answered the demand without hesitation. Her breathing quickened and grew uneven as his tongue found hers and began a seduction of its own, and eyes closed, utterly lost to everything, Antonia gave herself up to Jaime's lovemaking with an abandon she would be surprised at later. But not now. For the moment she was entirely taken over by the sensations in her own body as it responded to the long, drugging kisses that were beginning to drive her wild. Somewhere in the back of her mind she knew she should be making at least some sort of token protest, but for the moment her body had the upper hand,

and astonished her with its fierce response to this man she
had thought she disliked. In the end she was saved from
begging him for more by the bump on her head, which
suddenly made its presence felt with a sudden sharp pain,
and she gave an involuntary moan. Instantly Jaime drew
away, his face dark with self-condemnation.

'*Querida*,' he groaned. '*Perdone me—tem dor de cabeça*? Your
head hurts?'

'A little,' she admitted, and smiled shakily. 'It must have
been my blood pounding about like that.'

Jaime groaned and held her close. '*Desculpe-me*, Antonia.
I am a fool to—to behave like that when you are wounded.'

'I'm not wounded,' she protested breathlessly.

'Even so, I should not have been so—*urgente, carinha*.'

'It was my fault as much as yours.' Antonia's eyes
dropped at the look in his. 'I can't pretend I didn't like
being kissed, because I did very much.'

For answer Jaime bent and gathered her up so that she
lay across his knees, secure in his arms, her head on his
shoulder. 'It pleases me to hear you say so. And it would
please—no, *delight* me to continue kissing you all night if
that were possible. But it is not.'

Antonia lay relaxed in his embrace, utterly at peace,
oblivious of the throb in her head, or of anything but this
delicious security—which was not quite security. 'Why?'
she asked.

Jaime shook her very gently. 'You know very well, I
think Antonia. For one thing you are not yet completely
recovered, and for another we must leave this room very
soon and retire to our regrettably separate beds. And last,
but not least, I can no longer go on kissing you without
wanting to take off these clothes of yours that are so
ridiculously like mine and worship every inch of your
beautiful body that is so different—so exquisitely different.
I do not need to tell you what would happen after that.'

The picture Jaime's words conjured up rendered
Antonia dumb, her mouth dry and her heart thumping

again, and held close to his chest as she was it was all too
clear that the man holding her cruelly tight felt the same. In
tense silence they lay together until Antonia felt Jaime's
iron grip relax a little and the tension receded from his
hard, muscular body. She shivered slightly and he dropped
a kiss on her hair before getting up to set her gently on her
feet.

'Are you well now, Antonia?' he asked.

'Yes. At least, my head has stopped throbbing.' She gave
him a crooked little smile. 'It's just that I feel all at sea.'

He frowned. 'All at sea? What is that?'

'Uncertain how I feel. I was convinced I didn't like you
very much.'

'And have you changed your mind?'

'It seems I must have. I don't usually behave like that
with people I dislike, you know!'

'Do you "behave like that" with many people?' Jaime
asked swiftly, his face deadly serious.

Antonia opened her mouth to say something cutting,
then changed her mind as something in his eyes prompted
her to honesty. 'No,' she admitted quietly. 'I don't.'

His face relaxed and he held out his hand. 'Come, *carinha*.
There are shadows beneath those beautiful eyes. You need
rest.'

Antonia put her hand in his, and he turned off the
solitary lamp burning in the room and very quietly they
went out into the hall and turned down the corridor to her
bedroom. At the door Jaime lifted each of her hands in turn
to press a kiss on her palms, then he said softly,

'*Boa noite*, Antonia. *Dorme bem.*'

'Goodnight, Jaime,' she whispered. 'I hope you sleep
well, too.'

His eyes danced as he grinned down at her. 'So do I,
devoutly, *carinha*, but I fear it will not be easy tonight!' And
he bent swiftly to kiss her hard before leaving her standing
in her doorway, her fingers clenched tightly over her warm
palms where his lips had been.

CHAPTER SIX

THE following morning Antonia felt wonderful. The sun was shining and cocks were crowing and she felt like crowing with them. God was in his heaven, and all was exactly right with her world. Not even the lump on her head did more than remind her of its existence a little when she brushed her hair. From her mirror her eyes glowed back at her in her tanned face as she stuck out her tongue at her reflection, then rummaged in the jacaranda wardrobe for yellow trousers and a white T-shirt, adding an oversized yellow shirt with white spots before she hurried to the veranda to join Diana and Marisa for breakfast as usual, hoping Jaime would be there with them.

He was. As she came through the door he jumped to his feet, looking quite devastating, she thought, in a white shirt and khaki trousers, his feet in dusty riding boots. Diana and Marisa looked up smiling, and Antonia bent to kiss them both, assuring them of her return to normal in response to their enquiries.

'Aren't you going to kiss Jaime, too?' demanded Marisa, as she returned to her boiled egg, and Antonia laughed.

'Why not?' she said and reached up to kiss his newly shaved jaw.

'*Muito obrigad*', Antonia.' He held her chair for her. 'You are obviously feeling better today.'

Diana poured coffee, her lips twitching. 'Better hardly seems the word for it.'

'Ah, but English is such a down-to-earth language,' Antonia informed her slyly. 'Not given much to superlatives.'

'What are soup—those things?' asked Marisa.

'Words which describe how pretty all three of you ladies look this morning,' said Jaime, grinning.

Antonia avoided his eyes and applied herself to her dish of chilled *mamão*, which Jaime informed her was known as papaya in other countries.

'I went riding very early,' he added, 'because for some reason I could not sleep last night.'

Fortunately at that moment Pascoa brought in a platter of omelettes, which diverted attention from the sudden colour in Antonia's cheeks.

'I thought your intention in arriving early for the weekend, Jaime, was to get some rest,' said Diana admonishingly.

'Whereas I arrived just in time to fish Antonia from the lake.' Jaime attacked his omelette with enthusiasm.

'I'm not sure I even thanked you properly,' said Antonia.

He looked up into her eyes. 'Oh, but you did, Antonia. Besides—if I had not been there one of the others at the club would have done as well. Or perhaps Vasco could have atoned for his lack of skill in sailing by his expertise at life-saving.'

'I'm glad he wasn't obliged to find out,' said Diana, her eyes shadowed, and Antonia changed the subject quickly, asking Jaime how preparations were going for the party. Quick to respond, Jaime soon had them laughing over his description of the activities of the married couple, Diva and Joachim, who kept house for him. Everything in the house, it seemed, including the terrace, had been scrubbed and polished within an inch of its life already.

'Nothing escapes Diva,' he said, sighing. 'Even the leaves on the house-plants have been polished. I dare not stand still for fear she attacks even me with her duster and brush.'

Marisa thought this exquisitely funny, and climbed on Jaime's knee once breakfast was over. 'I wish I could come to the party, Jaime. When I'm a big girl will you have a party for me?'

'*Sem falta, chica*, of course I will.' He gave her a hug. 'But you will be there at my house for this one, remember. Perhaps we can coax *Mamãe* to let you stay up long enough to see the visitors arrive.'

Diana nodded, resigned. 'But only from the landing, Marisa.'

Jaime rubbed his cheek against Marisa's curly head. 'I wondered, Diana, if you ladies might not like to go back with me to Boa Vista on Monday morning?'

Diana looked surprised. 'You mean, spend the entire week before the party at Casa Madrugada?'

Jaime's eyes met Antonia's questioningly. 'Would you care for a few days in Boa Vista, Antonia? You could go shopping, or to the cinema, and at least you would be in little danger there from inexpert dinghy sailors!'

Antonia chuckled, then looked at Diana, who nodded, pleased.

'That's a very nice idea, Jaime. Thank you. You'd like that, Antonia, wouldn't you? It's only an hour's ride by car.'

If it meant seeing Jaime every day, Antonia discovered, she would have been quite happy to row up the Amazon. 'I would, very much. Only won't it put your Diva out, Jaime, if she's already prepared the house for the party?'

'*N'importa*. She will be delighted. For some reason she adores this little monkey here.' Jaime pulled Marisa's curls. 'And I know she is very curious to meet the unknown daughter of Dona Diana.'

'How many guests will be coming?' asked Diana.

Jaime shrugged. 'I am no longer sure. Some of the people I invited have visitors staying with them and wish to bring them also. *Não tem problema*. The house is suitable for a large number, and I am glad of the opportunity to repay hospitality to many people.' He set Marisa on her feet and jumped up. '*Muito bem*, that is settled then. So now we shall go to the club and I shall take Antonia sailing.'

Antonia looked at him aghast, and Diana shot to her feet in alarm.

'Jaime! Are you mad? The poor girl got knocked unconscious and half drowned on the lake yesterday and you want her to risk it *again*?'

'She will risk neither of those things with me.' Jaime turned to Antonia. 'If you do not go out again at once you will always be afraid. And I would very much like you to enjoy sailing.'

Since her vocal chords appeared temporarily paralysed Antonia merely nodded her assent feebly, and Jaime's brilliant smile was her reward.

'*Otimo!*' He smiled reassuringly at Diana. 'Do not upset yourself, *cara.* Today the weather forecast is perfect, and *we* shall go out in the old Heron.'

Diana's face cleared. 'Oh well, in that case—I thought you meant to have Antonia hanging out of that Flying Dutchman of yours by her toenails.'

Jaime laughed and explained that the Heron was a more pedestrian dinghy: as safe as putting out in a *baçia*—a basin. It could even be used as a fishing-boat with an outboard motor, when required, but today they would use sails.

'I shall give you ten minutes to change,' he told Antonia, consulting his watch. 'Then we shall all drive to the clubhouse and ask Virgilio to have lunch ready there for us when Antonia and I get back from our little voyage.'

'Marisa and I will follow on later,' said Diana quickly.

'Because you have a better view from the veranda here, no doubt!' Jaime put an arm round her comfortingly. 'Do not worry, *cara.* I promise that not only will she be safe, she will enjoy it.'

To Antonia's surprise he was entirely right. At the clubhouse, which was very modern and luxurious, Jaime provided her with a life-jacket to wear over her shorts and sweater, and introduced her to the manager of the club, Virgilio Diaz, a thick-set, pleasant-looking man who sympathised with her volubly on her mishap of the day before in heavily accented English, obviously very much impressed by her courage in going out on the lake so soon after the accident.

'But with the *Patrão* you need not fear,' he said, as Jaime secured the buckles on her yellow life-jacket. 'Jaime is *campeão*—champion, *não é?*'

Jaime took Antonia down to the array of boats moored along the edge of the lake, coming to a halt at a more modest craft than any of the others. The dinghy looked a lot wider and much less dangerous than Vasco's Hornet, and Antonia began to feel happier.

'I think I may enjoy this after all,' she said, and Jaime lifted her into the dinghy, which was rigged ready, the sails flapping only slightly in the gentle little breeze.

He cast off and leapt lightly on board, and right from the first everything was totally different from the day before. This man had no need to impress. Every move he made demonstrated all too clearly his casual, confident expertise. He settled Antonia at the tiller, and showed her how to helm, while he did any necessary dodging about with the boom as she had done so disastrously the day before. This time, once she got the hang of it, she enjoyed playing helmsman, and was able to sit quite serenely with her hair blowing in the breeze, enjoying the beauty of the sun on the water in its setting of mountain peaks. Soon she could see the house at Lagoa del Rey in the distance, in its sheltering trees, and raised an arm in triumphant greeting, knowing Diana would be monitoring the Heron's progress through her binoculars.

'Well?' shouted Jaime, as he saw her wave. 'Is this not better, *carinha*?'

Antonia smiled blissfully. 'It's wonderful!'

His answering smile gave her a great glow of happiness, and as they glided over the water she looked up towards the great blue bowl of the sky, wondering if somewhere, somehow, Janet knew what she was doing and was happy. I hope so, thought Antonia fervently, because I am. Her eyes lingered on Jaime's athletic figure as he hauled on the sheets and shouted instructions to her as he brought the dinghy about to begin making back to the shore. It seemed utterly incredible that only a short time ago she had never set eyes on him, yet now she wanted nothing better than to be here with him, or anywhere else if it came to that. A slight shadow dimmed her happiness as she remembered how soon she would have to fly home and leave all this, and Jaime, behind. She shrugged off the thought quickly, determined to let nothing mar the day. If there was repining to be done she would leave it until the day came. For now there was all this sunshine and crystalline air, and not even immediate parting from Jaime after the weekend to worry about.

When they were back at the shore Jaime showed Antonia how to help him take down the sails and rigging and stow everything neatly away, giving her a new insight on the word 'shipshape'. She toiled willingly, very warm by the time they were done.

'Well?' Jaime demanded, as they walked up to the clubhouse afterwards. 'Was I not right, Antonia?'

'You were indeed,' she agreed blithely. 'I'm utterly hooked.'

Jaime paused to look down at her. 'What is "hooked"?'

'Captured, fascinated——'

'Then so am I hooked, Antonia.' His eyes blazed down into hers for a moment, taking her breath away, then there was a screech of tyres as the Lagoa del Rey estate car drew up and Diana and Marisa tumbled out of it, leaving a grinning Sabino at the wheel to return to the house.

'We saw you! We saw you!' called Marisa, launching herself towards them like a little arrow. Jaime fielded her neatly and swung her up in his arms.

'You see, *chica*? We came back safe and sound.'

Diana reached them only slightly less precipitously, her face alight with a smile of relief.

'*Mamãe tive medo, mais eu não,*' said Marisa loftily.

'Speak English, you little savage,' said Diana severely. 'And I was merely apprehensive, not frightened.'

'After the first few minutes I thoroughly enjoyed it,' said Antonia, 'and now I'm absolutely starving.'

'Then we shall all go and eat a large lunch of *bifes* and *batatas fritas* and *salada misto*——' began Jaime, but Marisa interrupted him loftily.

'You must speak English or you are a savage!'

'No, I am not,' he said promptly, and turned a wicked grin on Antonia. 'When treated correctly I am very tame.'

Diana watched, riveted, as black eyes turned to meet

gold and Antonia's cheeks, already flushed with triumph
and fresh air, coloured even more as she excused herself to
wash before the meal. Lunch was very lively and light-
hearted, interrupted from time to time by introductions as
people began to arrive for the weekend's sailing and came
over to meet the new arrival at Lagoa del Rey. The meal
grew very protracted and Marisa dozed on Antonia's lap
eventually, as more wine was brought and several people
joined their table.

'Shall I take her?' asked Jaime quietly, under cover of the
general conversation, but Antonia shook her head.

'I'm perfectly happy.'

'I am glad. That you are happy,' he added. '*Eu também.*'

'That means "me too",' said Marisa sleepily, waking up
as the other two laughed. Not long afterwards Mario
arrived on the scene, complaining loudly of the lack of
welcome at the house, and how such a hard-working
member of the de Almeida family should be better treated
when frivolous brothers like his took time off to take such a
charming companion sailing.

'You had the pleasure of bringing Antonia from
England,' said Jaime lightly. 'Now, *rapaz*, it is my turn, *não
é?*'

Mario looked taken aback for a moment, then the
familiar smile lit up his handsome face, and he touched his
brother fleetingly on the shoulder. *Sim, senhor,*' he agreed.
'*Perfeitamente!*'

The luncheon party was the start of a hectic weekend,
which was the occasion of the annual regatta at the yacht
club. Antonia enjoyed herself enormously, meeting a great
many people and deriving immense satisfaction from
watching Jaime and Mario sweep the board in the races in
their particular class. Jaime's Flying Dutchman, the
Esperança, looked light and small to Antonia's lay eye. She
was apprehensive to learn that the dinghy itself weighed
less than the combined weight of the two brothers, and held
her breath as she watched Jaime balanced precariously on
the trapeze as they soared across the lake to cross the
finishing line in the best time over and over again.

Diana stayed with Antonia most of the time, as they watched from the observation balcony of the clubhouse, and quite evidently enjoyed herself too, as numerous people came up to chat and exclaim on how good it was to see her there, and ask why they to seldom had the pleasure of her company. It was gratifying to Antonia to see Diana blossom under the attention, also to note that she was quite obviously serenely unruffled at introducing Antonia as her child of a former marriage. Everyone seemed to take this for granted, and accepted Antonia with a casual warmth that she much appreciated. The Cardosos were there to race in their Hornet, the *Borboleta*, Isilda very smart in her all-in-one black sailing suit. At first she was a trifle cool with Antonia, but when Jaime and Mario joined them to watch other dinghy classes race her shrewd dark eyes picked up the change in Jaime's attitude towards Antonia almost immediately. He lounged alongside Antonia, laughing and talking with the crowd of people at their table, seldom actually saying anything directly to her, but with his arm casually along the back of her seat, in a way that plainly reassured Isilda enormously. Diana left at one stage to see how Marisa was faring under Zelia's watchful eye with a group of other children, and Isilda slid into Diana's place by Antonia to ask about the accident with Vasco. Antonia made light of it, treating it as a joke, but Jaime picked up what she was saying and interrupted, shaking an admonishing finger at Antonia.

'I have told her that in future she is to sail only with people who know what they are doing, not an idiot like Vasco.'

'It was certainly a lot different going out with Jaime yesterday,' conceded Antonia.

'You went out *yesterday*—after a bump on the head from the *Paraiso's* boom?' said Isilda with respect. 'You were brave.'

'Not really. I didn't have much choice. Jaime more or less dragged me by the hair!'

'You were honoured,' exclaimed Isilda. '*Geralmente*, no

one but Mario is allowed in the *Esperança* with him.'

'*Deus*, Isilda,' protested Jaime. 'I did not take her out in *that*. We went for a nice, quiet little sail in the old Heron. You know very well that Mario is the only one with the correct weight to combine with mine for the *Esperança*.' He grinned across at his brother. '*De por enquanto*, that is. Doubtless he will grow too fat in time.'

Mario protested indignantly, and then Diana came back with Marisa, and Isilda gave up her place, looking much happier as she and Janio went off to rig their Hornet ready for the next race. In the evening there was to be a buffet dinner and dance. Diana needed much persuading to return to the clubhouse with Antonia and the two men for this, but since Marisa was dead to the world after a long day in the open air she finally gave in, aware that Antonia's pleasure in the evening would be lessened otherwise. She advised Antonia to wear something casual since a lot of the women would be in trousers, but after deliberation Antonia rejected trousers in favour of an ankle-length white jersey skirt, narrow and slit from ankle to knee at one side, worn with a man's collarless shirt belted in at the waist, in a dull china blue. She added a gold Victorian locket on a heavy gold chain and put flat white leather pumps on her feet, then went to join the others, finding Jaime alone when she arrived on the veranda. It was their first time alone together since the evening of the accident and Antonia felt absurdly shy as she enquired whether she was suitably dressed for the occasion. Jaime had been standing at the rail, smoking a thin cigar, which he threw into the garden below as he turned to see her in the doorway.

'*Beleza!*' he said, and started forward to take her hands, kissing them lingeringly. 'You look delicious, but——' He laughed as he straightened, and waved a hand towards his own white sailcloth trousers and dark blue shirt. 'Once again it seems we have similar taste, *não é*? Does it extend to all things, *carinha*?'

Antonia pretended to think it over. 'I know we both like

Vivaldi, and Diana and Marisa and dogs—and now sailing——'

'But we like other things too, I think,' he said softly, and drew her towards him, but she pulled away, flushing bright red as footsteps sounded on the polished floor of the hall. The next moment Mario was with them, dressed in tight white trousers and blue denim shirt. Jaime groaned.

'*Deus me livre*—we look like a pop group. Shall we take bets on what Diana chooses to wear?'

Mario grinned, unconcerned. '*Não faz mal*—it is easy to tell which one is Antonia! Ah, Diana, *graças a Deus*, you are in black.'

Diana laughed as she looked from one to another. 'At least I shan't lose my family in the crowd!'

Antonia had a wonderful time all evening at the Festa de Regatta, where a lot of the faces were familiar by this time. There was a delicious cold supper of king-sized prawns, crayfish, smoked salmon and chicken; savoury little fried pasties stuffed with meat or fish, called *pasteis de vento, empadinhas*, which were little pies with fillings hot with peppers, and salads made from enormous tomatoes and *palmito*, the white edible heart of palm. Jaime insisted on serving Antonia with a little of everything, and she sat with him enjoying the food and the local wine, which was excellent. At one stage, in the midst of the animated chatter going on around her, with the sophisticated music playing in the background, she was struck forcibly by the fact that only a short time before she had felt so utterly alone in the world without Janet. Jaime noticed her fingering her locket, and bent close to ask the identity of the photograph inside.

'Is it some man—a former lover in England, perhaps?' A smile curved his lips, but something in his eyes belied it.

'No, it's not a man.' She hesitated, rather reluctant to open the locket, when Diana put out a hand to touch hers.

'If you're asking about the locket, Jaime, I'm fairly sure I know whose pictures are in it.' And with a word of permission from Antonia she snapped open the two halves

of the locket to reveal the dark, humorous features of Janet
Grant and the lined, delicate face of her husband Lewis,
who was only a vague memory to Antonia.

'My adoptive parents,' said Antonia, and Jaime's hand
crushed one of hers.

'I am sorry,' he said at once. 'Their faces are very kind—
muitos simpáticos.'

'They were,' Diana assured him. 'The best in the world.
Now—why don't you two dance?'

Jaime shot to his feet with alacrity and led Antonia into
the crowd on the small dance floor, where it was hardly
possible to do more than move slightly to the rhythm
played by the three men on guitar, piano and drums. Jaime
linked his arms loosely round Antonia's waist, smiling
down at her.

'You put your arms around my neck, *carinha.*'

Antonia cast a look about her, but everyone seemed to be
doing the same, so obediently she did as he said. 'I feel
conspicuous like this,' she told him.

'Because you are accustomed to dance alone, I suppose,
with no contact with your partner.' His clasp tightened. 'I
prefer this.'

Antonia's face grew hot, but no one noticed in the dim
light, and after a while she relaxed, moving to the music in
time with Jaime. It came as no real surprise to find his sense
of rhythm as good as his skill at sailing, and once her first
diffidence subsided Antonia gave herself up to the sheer
pleasure of the music and the contact with Jaime's fit, hard
body. Suddenly the tempo changed, whistles were blown,
the lights went up and there were shouts from all corners of
the room as the strains of a carnival *marcha* sent everyone
into the stiff-kneed, samba-like rhythm, hands waving, and
Jaime laughed as Mario and Isilda came running to join
them, all three showing Antonia what to do as they chanted
the words of a medley of carnival tunes, some of them
dating back to their parents' generation.

'*Eu vou para Maracangalha, eu vou,*' yelled everyone. '*Eu vou
convidar Analha, eu vou.*'

It was almost half an hour later before Antonia was allowed to return to the table, where she flopped down alongside Diana, laughing and out of breath, her cheeks poppy-red. 'They've nearly killed me!' she gasped. 'Where do they get the energy from at this altitude?'

'You are young to complain,' protested Mario. 'You should be able to dance all night. Never mind, *chica*, in a few minutes you shall dance something nice and slow with me.'

'I think she'd do better to sit quietly here for a while,' said Diana firmly, and Jaime agreed, sitting down next to Antonia.

'You must save your energy for next week's party,' he said, sliding an arm along the back of her chair.

Mario turned to Isilda as the *conjunto* began to play a *bossa nova*. 'You will dance with me then, *cara, por favor.*'

'*Pois é*,' she said readily, her smile brilliant as they went to join the other dancers on the floor. Diana became engaged in conversation with another couple at the table, Don and Nancy Ericson, an American couple who lived in Boa Vista, and Antonia and Jaime were left to sit in silence together, watching the dancing. Antonia felt perfectly content. There was no constraint in their lack of conversation, only a rapport that stemmed from the contact of his arm behind her shoulder, and the touch of his thigh against hers, and after a while she sighed, her eyes dreamy.

'What are you thinking?' asked Jaime, his breath warm against her ear.

'Just—how much I'm enjoying all this. How kind everyone's been to me.'

'I was not—at first.'

'But you changed.'

'*Sim*. I changed. I will not change again.'

Antonia twisted her head to look up at him, and what she saw in his eyes made her tremble. His arm tightened along her shoulders and his head bent towards hers involuntarily, then he blinked rapidly and thrust a hand through his hair.

'Will you have more wine, *carinha*?' he asked unsteadily.

'I'm thirsty, Jaime. I'd like a soft drink, please.'

At once Jaime got to his feet, pressing the others at the table to more drinks, and while he was away at the bar Diana smiled tenderly at Antonia.

'Are you having a good time, love?'

'Wonderful. Thank you so much for asking me here to Lagoa del Rey.'

'You don't have to thank me for doing exactly what I've wanted to do for more than twenty years, love!'

Jaime's return prevented further conversation, and he was followed closely by a waiter with a tray of drinks, and then Isilda and Mario, with Janio hot on their heels.

'Dona Diana,' asked the young Brazilian punctiliously. 'May I ask Antonia to dance?'

Isilda and the Ericsons laughed as Jaime and Mario said '*Não!*' in unison, but Diana smiled kindly at the boy.

'Antonia had a bump on the head a couple of days ago, Janio. She should rest a bit.'

'Then will *you* do me the honour, Dona Diana?' he asked gallantly, and Diana looked nonplussed for a moment. She gave a hesitant look at Jaime and Mario, then smiled and went with Janio to the dance floor. Jaime and Mario exchanged surprised glances, and Isilda explained quietly to Antonia that on the rare occasions Diana had been to parties since Francisco de Almeida had died she had always refused to dance.

'Perhaps she didn't want to hurt Janio's feelings,' said Antonia, and looked at Jaime and Mario challengingly. 'But I'd have you know I'm perfectly capable of answering for myself, when someone is kind enough to ask *me* to dance.'

'*I* was refused,' said Mario instantly, aggrieved. 'So why should Janio have the honour? I am your brother, *mais ou menos.*'

'And how about you, *amigo?*' Isilda smiled at Jaime, who was back in his former seat close to Antonia. 'Did you succeed in dancing with Antonia first because you are her elder brother?'

'I am Diana's stepson, but no relative of Antonia's, *graças a Deus!'* Jaime grinned and Antonia eyed him warily.

'That doesn't sound very complimentary,' she commented, then yawned involuntarily, to her mortification. 'Heavens, sorry, everyone. Not boredom, I assure you—just too much fresh air, I suppose.'

'Don't worry, honey,' said Don Ericson kindly. 'We're all the same at first. You get used to the altitude after a while.'

His pretty wife agreed ruefully. 'When we first came I kept falling asleep any old time of the day—just like my grandma. Just the same, dear, you do look a little weary.'

'That makes two of us,' said Diana breathlessly, as she returned with Janio. 'I'm sadly out of practice, but thank you, Janio, that was lovely.'

'*De nada*, Dona Diana.' Janio eyed Antonia hopefully, but Jaime dashed his hopes by getting to his feet briskly.

'I think I shall take my two ladies home. Mario, you stay—but not too long. I do not want my crew too tired to win tomorrow.'

Mario groaned, vowing he would try to put on weight as quickly as possible, to disqualify himself as Jaime's partner in the *Esperança*, but goodnaturedly saw the other three to the car after a round of leave-taking, and promised to be home at a reasonable hour.

'Not that Mario's idea of a reasonable hour is quite the same as mine,' said Diana with a chuckle as they drove back to the house. 'I hope you didn't mind coming away so early, Antonia?'

Antonia was able to reassure her quite truthfully that she didn't. On the contrary she was tense with anticipation, certain that Jaime's idea in going home early was to snatch a few moments alone with her after Diana was in bed. Squeezed between Diana and Jaime on the front seat of the car, her hip close against his, she longed for further contact with him, for him to kiss her as he had done two nights ago, to do more than kiss her—her cheeks burned as she clamped down on her thoughts, and her descent from the car after Diana was rather hurried. While Jaime put the car

away to an accompaniment of barking from the dogs,
Diana made herself a pot of tea in the kitchen and gave
Antonia the glass of fruit juice she requested.

'I shall take my tray to my room and read for a while,'
Diana said as Jaime came in through the kitchen door. 'I
presume you'll smoke a cigar on the veranda as usual,
Jaime. Perhaps Antonia will keep you company. Goodnight, love. Sleep well.' She kissed them both, and Jaime
carried her tray to her room for her, leaving Antonia to
wander out on the veranda to look at the stars, and the faint
glow in the sky from the clubhouse. Suddenly the glass was
taken from her hand and her cry of surprise stifled as Jaime
spun her round in his arms in the darkness and kissed her
with the air of a man at the end of his patience.

'I have not done that for far too long,' he muttered
against her lips. 'I could exist no longer without having you
in my arms and feeling your mouth tremble under mine.
Why does it tremble, *querida?*'

'I don't know. I'm not afraid. At least, not of you.'

His arms tightened and he rubbed his cheek against hers.
'Then of what, Antonia? I will not harm you.'

'I know,' she said with certainty. 'But I'm nervous of the
way you make me feel.'

A tremor ran through his body. 'And how is that, *linda
flor?*'

'You know very well, Jaime,' she said breathlessly, and
reached up to bring his head down to hers. His mouth
crushed hers fiercely and his arms tightened about her like
steel bands, then he picked her up and crossed to the sofa,
sitting down with her across his knees, his mouth never
leaving hers. Antonia clung to him, giving him back all the
response that no one had ever ignited in her before. At last
Jaime lifted his head a little.

'You have been kissed much?' His voice sounded
strained, harsh and more strongly accented than usual.

'Some.'

'*Poise é.* How could it be otherwise? You are so sweet,
such a *tentação——*' And he fell to kissing her closed eyes,

her cheeks, her chin, then his mouth feathered a line of kisses down her throat to the place where her shirt was fastened. His head grew heavy against her breasts, his face burning through the thin cotton, and she felt, rather than heard him say. 'You truly have no one—there in England?'

'Yes.'

'But you have had, how do you say, boyfriends?'

'Yes.'

'Did you love any of them?'

'No.'

'And did their kisses make you tremble like so?' And Jaime de Almeida raised his head and took possession of her mouth with such finality Antonia was afraid; afraid of her own body and the blatant clamouring of her senses she thought he must surely feel through their clothes as he held her hard against him.

'*Eu te quero*, Antonia,' he said hoarsely against her mouth, and undid the buttons of her shirt with shaking fingers, his hands sliding beneath it to find her breasts. They seemed to rise to his touch, answering his fingers and lips with a life of their own, and Antonia ground her teeth together to keep from crying out. Her fingers closed convulsively in Jaime's thick hair as she felt his teeth graze and tug first one nipple then the other, rousing them to such a degree of sensitivity that her breath hurt in her chest as she writhed helplessly beneath his touch.

'*Deus*—I shall go insane!' Jaime gasped at last and sat up.

Antonia's eyes opened to stare up into his taut face, which was just visible in the dim light filtering through from the hall. 'Please——' she said, almost sobbing.

He crushed her against him. '*Perdone-me, querida*,' he said thickly. 'I did not mean—I intended only to kiss you. Most of the day I have been close to you, but never close enough, and I could not endure it a moment longer, which is why I brought you home.'

Antonia clung to him, hot tears of frustration soaking through his shirt, and Jaime cursed softly in Portuguese and stroked her hair, making soothing noises as though she were Marisa.

'I am a fool,' he said bitterly, 'but not so lost to all reason that I can seduce Diana's daughter under her own roof. I should not have come to you, but I could not help myself.'

Antonia pushed him away gently and began to button her shirt with unsteady fingers. Jaime watched, his body communicating its tension to her even across the distance separating them. 'If you hadn't I'd have come looking for you,' she said matter-of-factly, and he drew in his breath sharply.

'Antonia——' he said hoarsely, and moved to take her in his arms, then stopped short at the sound of an outboard motor coming up from the lake.

'What's that?' asked Antonia quickly.

'It is Mario returning,' he answered tersely, and caught her by the shoulders, kissing her fiercely. '*Boa noite, querida.* Go to bed, *por favor.* I shall go down to meet Mario. I do not wish him to see you.'

'Why?' But Antonia knew very well. Before Mario joined them the veranda light must be turned on, and even the dimmest of lights would show only too plainly to what extent she had been turned on herself—and Jaime, too, if appearances were anything to go by.

'Because the way you look now is for me alone,' said Jaime softly, and Antonia backed away, her mouth dry at the look in his eyes, and fled to her room in unashamed retreat.

CHAPTER SEVEN

THE exodus from Lagoa del Rey early on the Monday morning had the air of a royal progress.

'All we lack is Queen Elizabeth's bath,' said Antonia as she helped Marisa pile Jaime's car with the toys and books apparently indispensable for even a few days away from home.

Marisa frowned. 'There are lots of baths in Jaime's house. We don't have to take one.'

Antonia grinned as she ran up the veranda steps with Marisa to fetch the rest of her belongings. 'In Queen Elizbabeth's day people didn't have bathrooms,' she explained, 'so she took a wooden tub with her everywhere—it was the responsibility of the Master of Horse.'

'*Engraçado!*' pronounced Marisa and ran up to Jaime who stood at the head of the steps, smiling.

'Are you ready, *chica?*' he asked, picking her up. His eyes met Antonia's over the dark curls. 'I am informed that this solitary suitcase is all you wish to take?'

'That's right. I didn't think I'd need all I possessed for just a few days.' She smiled at him diffidently, thinking how dark his face looked after his weekend of sun and wind on the water. Against the bronze of his skin his shirt collar looked dazzlingly white, and she marvelled inwardly that she could ever have thought of Mario as the more attractive. Or perhaps her vision was clouded by—by what? Her smile faded. Was it love? Or something far less cerebral?

'What is it?' asked Jaime swiftly, and set Marisa on her feet. 'Tell *Mamãe* we are almost ready,' he told the child and she ran off importantly.

'I was just thinking how tanned you look.' Which was partly the truth.

Jaime leaned against the veranda rail, close beside her, his arm touching hers. 'So do you, Antonia. You gleam like gold, all of you, hair, eyes, skin—*moça de ouro*, my golden girl.'

Antonia turned to look up at him steadily. 'I don't think you should say things like that, Jaime.'

'*Porquê?*' His face was suddenly arrogant.

'Because we hardly know each other.'

'I must wait until we are old before I say how beautiful you are?'

She looked away, staring blindly at the roses in the bed below them, wishing Diana and Mario would put in an appearance.

'Is that why you avoided being alone with me all day yesterday?' he went on relentlessly, his mouth close to her ear. 'Were you afraid I would forget my scruples and abuse my privilege as your so-called stepbrother?'

It was true that Antonia *had* kept out of his way all of Sunday, after the shock of those self-revelatory moments in Jaime's arms the night before. Her night had been restless, and daylight had brought not sanity exactly, but a shyness never before experienced by Antonia Luisa Grant in her entire life. She had gone to the yacht club with the others, and watched the second day's races, and contrived to surround herself with other people all the time so that Jaime, in between races, was never close enough to touch her. She had avoided his baffled eyes and kept close to Diana, who had looked thoughtful now and then, but made no comment. Afterwards, at the house, when the regatta was over and they were eating a belated cold supper left for them by Maria, Antonia had been very quiet. As soon as she could, once the meal was over, she had excused herself, pleading an overdose of fresh air and a yearning for sleep. But now, this morning, Jaime was here beside her, his arm burning hers where it touched it, and for the moment there was no escape.

'I wasn't afraid of what *you* might do, Jaime,' she said carefully. 'More of my own reactions. I'm not used to—to feeling like that. And there's no point in it, is there? I'll be gone again soon. Back to England and the real world.'

Jaime caught her wrist and jerked her round to face him. 'So I must keep my distance, pretend there is nothing between us but the courtesy due to relatives?' His eyes blazed down into hers. 'But I am a Brazilian, Antonia, a Latin, and I cannot switch off my emotions like you Anglo-Saxons.' And he pulled her close and kissed her with a starving, desperate sort of fury that left her shaking as he thrust her from him seconds before Diana joined them, looking cool and elegant in a dark blue linen dress, with Marisa running behind, issuing a multitude of instructions to the patient Zelia.

'Right then, you two,' said Diana briskly, apparently unaware of the tension crackling in the air. 'Mario's just ready. Shall we go?'

When she saw Jaime's car, piled high with Marisa's belongings, Diana laughed at her sombre stepson. 'I think Marisa and I had better travel with Mario, darling. There's just enough room for you to take Antonia with you, I think.'

Jaime's face lightened and he swung open his passenger door with alacrity. 'An excellent idea, Diana.' He grinned as Mario sprinted down the steps towards them. 'Mario— you take Diana, Marisa and Zelia, *por favor*. Antonia—and all Marisa's worldly goods—travel with me.'

Mario smiled and lowered an eyelid, then sighed theatrically. 'Whatever you say, *capitão*! See you later at the house.' And with his usual good grace he set about installing his passengers comfortably, and eventually, with much waving of farewells, the little convoy moved off.

'We shall arrive there much sooner than the others,' said Jaime as they began the long circular detour around the lake. 'Marisa becomes *enjoada*—sick—if one drives fast.' He glanced at her. 'Do you?'

Antonia laughed, suddenly light-hearted. 'No. I love it. And I'm sorry I upset you just now.'

'Upset!' He cast his eyes heavenwards. 'This language of yours! But do not worry, *carinha*, I will not distress you by my——' He paused, frowning. 'Attentions? Is that right?'

'Probably.'

'For this week at my house I will behave like the perfect host, I promise. No more kisses or—or anything likely to cause you distress.'

Antonia's smile was wry. 'I don't know whether to be glad or sorry.'

Jaime sent her a gleaming sidelong glance. 'But only for these few days at Casa Madrugada, *compreende*! After that *vamos ver*—we shall see.'

Uncertain what he meant, Antonia decided to forget her misgivings, reminding herself that Jaime had to be at his office that day, his brief holiday over, and this journey together might be the only time alone with him all week.

They left the lake behind and began the steep, ascending journey through the spectacular countryside, where at times she could see the road for miles in the distance, winding like a red ribbon around the high green waists of the mountains. The gentian blue of the sky was decorated here and there with fat white puffs of cloud, as regular as a child's crayon drawing above the endless mountain peaks, and Antonia sighed with satisfaction, enjoying the journey, secure in Jaime's skill as he handled the powerful Audi in the same relaxed, controlled way he helmed the *Esperança*. She felt deep exhilaration as they flew along the rare straight stretches, her eyes glittering as Jaime negotiated the swooping curves. In places it was possible to look straight down at sheer drops to the valley floor far below; in others the hillside sloped away more gently, threaded through with a criss-cross pattern of muletracks.

'You are not nervous?' asked Jaime. 'I will drive more slowly if you wish.'

'No, no—I love it.' Suddenly Antonia remembered something. 'Did you hear any more from Vasco, by the way? I never gave him a thought afterwards, and he wasn't at the regatta, poor boy.'

'He rang to ask how you were, and to say he had a cold.' Jaime chuckled evilly. 'He is fortunate his sufferings are so slight. If I had not been so anxious to get you home I would have been less lenient with him, I assure you.'

'Poor Vasco! It wasn't his fault a storm came up.'

'You waste your sympathy. My cousin is a reckless fool.' Jaime's teeth clenched. 'You could have drowned!'

'But I didn't, because you were there to rescue me,' she said placatingly, and smiled at him as he met her eyes. His face relaxed and they changed the subject by tacit consent, discussing the party and the various things Antonia could do to pass the time during the day while she was at Casa Madrugada.

'I can take care of the evenings,' he said, 'but no doubt Diana will be able to suggest diversions for daytime.'

'When two women are gathered together, Senhor de Almeida, the first thought is shopping!' she assured him, laughing.

Soon they reached the main highway to Boa Vista, leaving the wild, beautiful terrain behind them as the car shot down the metalled road like an arrow let loose from a bow. In what seemed like seconds the city came into view in the distance, its tall, white geometric shapes gleaming against the skyline. Jaime slackened speed as they came to the scattered small houses and shops in the outskirts of the town, and soon they were driving through roads lined with red-roofed, white-walled houses with small gardens and dusty palm trees here and there, and the occasional small church with twin bell towers. Then the road widened and branched off into tree-shaded avenues of larger, more luxurious houses with velvet lawns and flowering shrubs in secluded gardens. Jaime drove slowly, to give Antonia time to gaze about her before he finally turned into a private road that ended in high metal gates and white walls, and a plaque that bore the name 'Casa Madrugada'.

'We've arrived then,' she said quietly, trying not to look over-awed.

'*Sim, senhora*. This is my home.' Jaime hooted on the horn and a man appeared, smiling, to open the gates to let them through. Jaime pressed a button to open his car window and leaned out, calling, '*Como vai*, Joachim? *Tudo bem*?'

'*Tudo bem, 'brigado*, Senhor Jaime.' Joachim was heavily built, with thick dark hair and a broad smile on his face as he welcomed them. Antonia smiled back readily, but privately decided Joachim looked like someone to reckon with, equal to all eventualities.

'*Posso appresentar-lhe Dona Antonia, a filha de Dona Diana*,' said Jaime formally, as they got out of the car, and Antonia offered her hand to the man.

'*Muito prazer*, Senhor Joachim,' she said, and glanced at Jaime for confirmation. He nodded, pleased, and Joachim positively beamed with pleasure.

'*Muito prazer também*, Dona Antonia.' He began to unload the car as Jaime took Antonia's hand and led her along a short drive through lawns fringed with palm trees and studded with beds of roses, towards a very different house from the one at Lagoa del Rey. The house at the lake, for all its size and spaciousness, had something rustic about its appeal. Casa Madrugada, on the other hand, was comparatively new, and had an indefinably urban sophistication. It was on two floors, the upper one ornamented by a balcony with white wrought-iron railings fashioned in a pattern of sunbursts, the same pattern echoed in the iron grille protecting the slab of smoked glass which served as front door.

'Very impressive!' said Antonia, then drew in a deep breath as Jaime opened the heavy door and ushered her down three shallow marble steps directly into an enormous reception-room, furnished starkly with long couches covered in off-white linen. Gilt porcelain lamps stood on the dark carved tables scattered over the carpet, which was ivory, like the walls. These were bare, except for a dramatic painting of boats driven before a storm on an ink-blue sea, a collection of beaten copper plaques, and a pair of shelves which held a bronze head of a young girl and a blue-green porcelain vase. The only note of warmth came from the maize-coloured raw silk which hung from ceiling to floor at the windows which formed the two outer walls of the room.

Jaime stood just inside the door, looking at Antonia's face. 'Do you approve?' he asked.

She spread her hands in an eloquent little gesture. 'It's very beautiful and—and *very* perfect.'

Jaime went across to double jacaranda doors and threw them open to reveal a central hall, part of which was used as dining area. At the far end a stairway curved up in a graceful sweep to a gallery above, with doors leading off to what were presumably bedrooms. Beneath it an archway led to the kitchen, visible in all its modern, gadgeted glory through a half-open door, and beyond to the left another flight of stairs led surprisingly downwards.

'Your cellar?' asked Antonia.

Jaime shook his head, smiling, and held out his hand. 'Come.' He led her down a spiral curve of stairs into a large basement living-room. The land behind the house dropped steeply, so that the extra room extended the full width of the house, but went back for only half its depth with a front wall of patio windows giving access to the garden, which descended a portion of hillside in a series of terraces, giving a breathtaking view of mountains in the distance, and the city of Boa Vista in panorama spread out below.

The view took Antonia's attention at first, but then she turned to look round the room, which was not exactly untidy, but had a much more lived-in look than the cool, uncluttered beauty of the drawing-room upstairs. There were odd chairs and sofas, covered in leather and tweed and chintz, a warm russet carpet, curtains in the same shade, printed with great sprawling flowers in cream and gold. One wall was lined with shelves packed with books and videos and records, a television stood in one corner, a stereo system in another, with speakers at points round the room. Framed photographs of boats of varying kinds hung on the walls, alongside photographs of Marisa, Diana and Mario, and Francisco de Almeida, so like his elder son it was easy to see how Jaime would look in middle age.

'I prefer this room to the one upstairs,' confessed Antonia, and Jaime laughed.

'Upstairs I impress business associates; down here I entertain family and friends.'

And what happens in those other rooms on the top floor? wondered Antonia in secret. Who do you entertain up there, Jaime de Almeida?

'What is going on in that brain?' he asked, and looked at her searchingly. 'When your eyes take on a certain expression I am reminded of Diana. She has a trick of looking inward, and so do you. Otherwise you do not resemble her at all.'

'She says I look like my father.'

Jaime's eyebrows rose. 'And did Diana tell you who he was?'

'Not exactly. Only the circumstances of my birth. But it seems he was respectable enough, which was something of a comfort, to be honest.'

'You did not relish the thought of a father of humble background?'

Antonia's eyes flashed. 'I didn't care a damn about that! But I knew Diana had come back from a holiday pregnant, and I couldn't help wondering if I was the result of—well, of rape.'

'*Meu Deus!*' Jaime crossed the room swiftly and tried to take her in his arms, but Antonia resisted, still smarting from his remark.

'You promised to keep your distance here,' she reminded him tartly.

Jaime's eyes narrowed. '*Pois é.* My intention was comfort only, I assure you.' He turned as footsteps sounded on the stairs and a woman bustled into the room voluble with apology, her face wreathed in smiles as she greeted Antonia.

'This is Diva,' said Jaime. 'She is very sorry that she was out doing the marketing when you arrived.'

Antonia greeted the woman warmly, then a small figure hurtled precipitately down the stairs and Diva held out her arms to Marisa with loud exclamations of welcome, embracing her rapturously, and smiling at Diana, who was following more decorously behind. At once Diva went off to organise coffee, Marisa at her heels chattering nineteen to the dozen, and Diana flopped down on one of the sofas gratefully.

'Thank the lord! We just about made it. Mario drove like an angel, but Marisa was firmly convinced she felt sick for the last few kilometres.'

'She looks full of beans now!' said Antonia.

'She's fine once she's out of the car. Oh, Jaime,' added Diana, 'Mario went straight to the office once he dropped us off.'

Jaime looked at his watch. '*Nossa senhora*—is that the time? I must go too, I have a meeting in half an hour.' He turned to Antonia. 'Diana will show you your room. I hope very much you will be comfortable—and happy—here.'

'I'm sure I shall,' she said serenely.

'I shall see you tonight. Perhaps not early, but in time for dinner.' Jaime bent to kiss Diana's cheek, then after a moment's hesitation raised Antonia's hand to his lips. '*Até logo*,' he said, looking into her eyes, then took the stairs two at a time, shouting goodbye to Diva and Marisa as he went.

Antonia gazed at the view for a time after he'd gone, while Diana gazed at Antonia.

'Well?' asked Diana at last.

Antonia started slightly, then smiled a little sheepishly. 'I'm sorry, what did you say? I'm afraid I was miles away.'

'I didn't actually say anything,' said Diana drily. 'Come and sit down.'

Antonia left her post at the window and sat down beside Diana as Diva arrived with a tray of coffee and some toast and preserves. Marisa, it appeared, was having her mid-morning *merenda* upstairs in the kitchen with the servants.

'Who will let her have black coffee and all the biscuits she can eat,' said Diana, resigned, when Diva had gone. 'Incidentally the toast is in your honour. Diva's convinced that we English live on the stuff.'

'It's very kind of her. Have she and Joachim been with Jaime long?'

'She started work as a very young girl with Jaime's mother. Joachim had a spell in the army, then came to work here and married Diva. His work is chauffeuring Jaime and seeing to security rather than things domestic. Diva has a girl in to help in the house.' Diana looked up from pouring the coffee. 'What is it? You look dazed, Antonia.'

'I am. I was pretty impressed with Lagoa del Rey. This——' Antonia waved a hand ruefully. 'This is smaller, of course, but even more impressive, somehow.'

'And that bothers you?'

'Well, it's a far cry from a shabby semi-detached house in Bristol, Diana!'

'A good thing Janet can't hear you say that.' Diana buttered a piece of toast and pushed it across to Antonia. 'Here, eat that, for heaven's sake, or Diva will be mortally wounded.'

Antonia nibbled without enthusiasm, oddly depressed, and not sure why.

'I thought you and Jaime were getting on quite well,' remarked Diana casually. 'You seemed to avoid him a bit yesterday, but I didn't get the impression you'd quarrelled. You can tell me to mind my own business, of course.'

'But I *am* your business, aren't I? So's Jaime.' Antonia sighed, her face troubled. 'Diana——'

'Yes?'

'Does Jaime have any attachments?'

'Like a fiancée or girlfriend, you mean?'

'Exactly. I mean both he and Mario must be top of the poll in the marriage stakes, surely? Rich, handsome——'

'So you think Jaime's handsome, then?' said Diana, amused. 'Most people consider Mario the real catch, you know. Jaime's appeal is a shade on the abrasive side for some women.'

'It's true I thought Mario was the handsomest man I'd ever seen when I first met him. I still do. But Jaime——' Antonia halted, flushing.

'Jaime's the one who strikes the spark,' offered Diana helpfully.

'Is it so obvious?'

'No. But I know Jaime very well. Before you arrived he had pretty strong reservations about this grown-up stepsister I'd sprung on him out of the blue, I can tell you.'

'So he told me!'

Diana chuckled. 'Didn't take him long to change his mind, though, did it? In fact, my love, I'd bet my boots my stepson has become very, very partial to my elder daughter already. How do you feel about him?'

Antonia slid to the floor and leaned her head against Diana's knee. 'Bowled over,' she said frankly. 'That's why I stuck to you like glue all day yesterday. I was afraid I'd give myself away to the entire world if he so much as touched me.'

Diana was silent for some time as she stroked the downbent head, her hand smoothing the thick, curling hair. 'You mean you're in love with him, or do you just want him to *make* love to you?' she asked at last, and Antonia's head shot up, her eyes wide.

'That's very straight from the shoulder, little mother!'

'Well?'

Antonia shrugged, her eyes dropping from Diana's clear grey gaze. 'Both, I suppose. The two usually go hand in hand, don't they?'

'Not necessarily. When I was a working girl my female colleagues used to leap in and out of various beds with great enthusiasm until they found the one they wanted to stay in permanently and legally.'

'But you didn't.'

'It was different for me. I'd never had any sort of boyfriend when—when I met your father. I, too, was bowled over, as you put it. And afterwards, to me sex was synonymous with pregnancy and grief, so I steered clear until I met Francisco.'

Antonia jumped to her feet suddenly, her face clearing. 'Why on earth am I worrying about it? I should be thanking my lucky stars I'm here in this lovely house having the holiday of a lifetime, instead of indulging in the vapours. After all, a kiss or two won't hurt me, will they?'

'Not if you stick to just kissing, no,' agreed Diana drily. 'Probably you're made of sterner stuff than I was at the same age.'

'Rubbish! Besides, you never played around afterwards, did you? So you can't have been too weak-willed in that department.'

'It's easy to resist doing something you don't want to do, love!'

They laughed and went up to collect Marisa from the kitchen so she could have the pleasure of showing Antonia to her bedroom, where Zelia had already unpacked. The room was large and airy, with large glass double doors giving on to a balcony overlooking the back garden. While Diana took Marisa away to wash Antonia stood on the balcony, leaning on the rail as she looked down, her eyes shining as she saw the gleam of a pool far below, with a tennis court near by. Jaime had neglected to mention this, she thought, amused, when he spoke of ways to pass the time—probably took them for granted, like the rest of his lifestyle, which was quite a bit different, one way and another, from her own. Antonia turned back into the room briskly. Since there was no point in dwelling on the differences between Jaime and herself the sensible thing to do was relax and do her best to enjoy the rest of her stay to the full.

CHAPTER EIGHT

Boa Vista was a town of vivid colours and contrasts, and entirely modern, with a central *avenida* of shops and hotels shaded by trees trained to grow in an arch of shade under the sun which beat down on all the dazzling whiteness. The brilliance made Antonia dive for her sunglasses as Joachim set her down on the *avenida* with Diana and Marisa on that first afternoon.

Marisa was ecstatic as she trotted along between her mother and Antonia, exclaiming in rapture as she spotted tempting things for sale in the shops.

'Shops aren't exactly thick on the ground in Lagoa del Rey,' chuckled Diana, as she gave in to her little daughter's plea for ice-cream, which they ate in a café where they could watch the passing scene while they enjoyed delicious confections flavoured with coffee and chocolate. The rest of the time was spent in window-shopping until they met Joachim at the appointed hour and went back to Casa Madrugada, where Antonia was glad of a long soak in the bath after the heat of the city. Later, when Jaime came home they all sat on the terrace watching one of the spectacular sunsets for which the city was famous and later still, when Marisa was in bed, the three of them ate dinner together in a harmony which made Antonia's doubts of the morning seem silly. Jaime, in fact, seemed bent on reassuring her that while she was his guest she had nothing to fear from him, yet somehow, cleverly, his eyes made it plain that the respite was strictly temporary, that his feelings towards her, while banked down for the moment by the social obligations of his position, were none the less unchanged, that he desired her as much as ever. Antonia smiled serenely at him across the candles in the heavy silver candelabra in the centre of the table, and Diana saw the smile and relaxed as Jaime told them Mario had been asked to join them but had a previous engagement to take Isilda Cardoso to the cinema. He sent his apologies and hoped the ladies were settling in comfortably.

'Perhaps you might like to go to the cinema yourselves tomorrow night,' Jaime went on, as he helped himself to Queijo Estepe, a local cheese which Antonia had enjoyed at lunch time. 'The new Meryl Streep film is showing.'

'I'd love to,' said Antonia at once, then looked at Diana. 'If *you* would, that is?'

'Lovely,' Diana nodded, then remarked casually, 'and in the morning I thought we'd pop round to Guillerme Moreira, Jaime, if it's all right for Joachim to drive us.'

'*Pose é.*' Jaime smiled at her tenderly. 'You have no need to ask, *cara.*'

'Thank you, darling. Let's go downstairs for our coffee, shall we?'

The three of them sat talking for the rest of the evening, to the accompaniment of music from Jaime's stereo, and

Antonia curled up in a corner of a sofa, her eyes on Jaime's face at times, at others on the lights of the city far below, feeling utterly at peace, and she smiled a little, attracting Jaime's attention.

'What amuses you?' he asked.

'I was just reflecting on the fact that just a short time ago I didn't know either of you even existed, yet here we are together like this, and I feel as though I've known you both all my life.'

Diana's eyes glowed, and she leaned across to touch Antonia's hand. 'Thank you,' she said simply. 'It means a lot to me to hear you say that.'

Jaime said nothing, but the look he sent Antonia dispensed with the need for words. Later he escorted both of them to their respective doors, kissing Diana on the cheek, then hesitating a little before saluting Antonia in the same way. '*Boa noite, dorme bem,*' he said huskily, and she smiled and took in a deep breath.

'*É voce também,*' she said carefully, to his amusement.

'Who taught you that?'

'Marisa, who else?'

Antonia slept dreamlessly in Jaime's guest-room, and woke next morning to see the view from her balcony veiled in mist.

'Mountain mist,' explained Diana at breakfast. 'It usually clears quickly, then we'll have a really hot day—by your standards, anyway. Winter here is just about over and the hot season nearly on us.'

Marisa was running about in the garden with Zelia in hot pursuit, and the child's shrieks rose in the still air to the ground-floor room, where a small table had been laid for breakfast near the window.

'I didn't think you'd want to eat formally in the dining-room,' said Diana, as she poured coffee.

'It's lovely right here. Look!' Antonia pointed to patches of blue sky, where the mist was clearing rapidly to display mountain peaks and the tops of the tallest buildings down below in the city. 'Before it gets hot, how about a game of tennis?' she asked eagerly.

Diana pulled a face. 'Heavens—I haven't played for years, but I'm game if you'll make allowances for an elderly lady!'

Antonia hooted at the description, and later, when they were on the tennis court, both in shorts, suntops and sneakers, from a distance no one would have thought them mother and daughter until Diana called for mercy at the end of the first set, panting as she flopped down on a garden chair, fanning herself with a sunhat. Marisa, who had been watching excitedly as her mother played, clamoured to take her place, but Antonia explained that the racquet was too heavy for her to hold.

'I'll buy you a special one when we go out shopping,' she promised, then jumped up, holding out her hand to the little girl. 'How about a swim instead, while Mummy has a rest? I'll help you change.'

The morning passed so quickly Antonia forgot Diana had intended going somewhere in the car.

'Sorry,' she said remorsefully over lunch. 'Why didn't you remind me, Diana?'

'No rush, we can go this afternoon. It's not very far from here.'

Later, as they set off without Marisa, who had elected to stay behind, Antonia examined Diana's face closely as Joachim drove them away from the city. 'You overdid it this morning, you look terribly pale.'

'A slight headache, that's all.'

Eventually they stopped outside a house in a quiet, tree-shaded road and Joachim went to ring the bell before assisting his passengers from the car. An elderly woman let the two women into a dim, shuttered room.

Antonia looked at Diana in surprise when they were left alone. 'Where are we?'

'You'll see in a moment.'

A man came in swiftly, profuse in his apologies at keeping the ladies waiting, and Diana introduced Antonia to Guillerme Moreira, who spoke English with a strong

American accent and welcomed her to his house with great formality. He was slight and dark and wore black-rimmed glasses with thick lenses, and over the coffee he insisted they drink he explained to Antonia that he was a gemologist. He smiled at her baffled look.

'Come,' he said, rising. 'I will show you what I mean.' He led the way along a dark, windowless corridor to the type of steel door found in bank vaults. He unlocked it and ushered them into a room which made Antonia gasp as he switched on lights to reveal walls lined with shelves bearing great chunks of quartz and every kind of mineral, some in its raw, untreated form, others cut and polished to give the room the look of Aladdin's cave.

Guillerme Moreira waved his guests to a leather couch with a glass-topped table in front of it. 'Now, Senhora de Almeida,' he said. 'What do you wish to see? Or shall I just display some of my wares and let you choose?'

'That would be lovely, Senhor Guillerme,' said Diana, and watched Antonia's face with anticipation as the man opened a safe and took out some velvet pouches. With ceremony he laid several pieces of black velvet on the table, then spilled the contents of the pouches one by one on each square. Antonia stared speechlessly at the heaps of stones in front of her, all glittering and darting fire in profligate splendour. There were amethysts and aquamarines, topazes, garnets, tourmalines and still more whose names were unfamiliar to her.

'Glory,' she said in awe. 'What a sight! I've never seen anything like it in my life.'

The man smiled, gratified. 'So now it is a little more easy to explain my calling. I cut and polish the stones, you understand. My customers choose the ones they desire, also what design, and I send the stones to the goldsmith, who makes them up into the finished pieces.'

'So which do you like best?' asked Diana.

Antonia looked at them all in turn, her eyes rapt. 'I don't know—they're all beautiful; such colour and brilliance.' She smiled radiantly at Senhor Guillerme. 'Thank you so much for showing them to me.'

He looked amused. '*De nada*, Dona Antonia.' He scrutinised her closely, peering at her face, lingering on her eyes as she looked back at him uncertainly. 'Senhora de Almeïda,' he said at last, taking a last look at Antonia's hair. 'I believe I have the perfect stones.'

'I was sure you would,' said Diana and smiled at Antonia's puzzled face as the man returned to his safe to search for a small pouch which he produced with a beam of triumph. Reverently he laid two small oblong stones on a black velvet square and stood back. At first sight they seemed less remarkable than the heaps of glittering, glowing colour on the other squares. They were pale, almost the colour of a yellow diamond, but as Antonia leaned closer she saw a streak of fire in the centre of each stone.

'Imperial topazes,' breathed Diana. 'How clever you are, Senhor Guillerme. Do you like them, Antonia?'

'Who wouldn't!' Antonia looked assessingly at Diana, then back at the stones. 'I don't know that they're exactly right for you, though, if that's what you mean?'

'They'd look nothing at all on me, love, but against your skin and eyes I think they'll be sensational.'

Antonia's jaw dropped inelegantly. 'But——'

'But nothing,' said Diana with energy. 'Surely a mother is entitled to give her daughter a twenty-first birthday present, even if it *is* belated.' She brushed aside all Antonia's protests and Guillerme Moreira put his glowing heaps of stones away in the safe and brought out a large book with illustrations of pieces of jewellery for Antonia to choose the way the ear-rings should be made up, eventually suggesting the stones should be suspended from a tiny diamond stud in the earlobe, and Antonia nodded, too dazed by this time to do anything but agree.

'*And*, Senhor Guillerme,' went on Diana, gently relentless. 'I want them by Saturday.'

'*Sábado?*' he repeated, blenching.

'*Sábado qui vem, sem falta*,' she confirmed and smiled her

luminous, irresistible smile. 'You will not disappoint me, I know.'

He spread his hands in defeat, saying it would need a miracle from God, but he would do his best, and Diana patted his hand and assured him she could ask no better than Guillerme Moreira's best, after which they were obliged to drink yet more coffee in his stifling little *sala* before they were able to emerge into the blinding afternoon sunlight and the waiting car, which Joachim had parked strategically in the shade of a tree.

'Diana,' began Antonia urgently, as they drove back. 'I'm sure those stones are horribly expensive—you never even mentioned money with Senhor Moreira.'

'Please.' Diana laid a hand on hers. 'Don't deny me the pleasure of buying you a present, love. I know I paid for some of your school fees, but that was a cold, impersonal sort of thing. When you were little I could never buy you so much as a doll. It hurt.'

'I'm sorry. I don't mean to be ungrateful.'

'I know. Just as I always knew Janet gave you everything a child could need, especially love, which was the most important thing of all.'

Antonia looked at Diana closely. 'You look very pale, you know. Are you all right?'

'My headache's a bit worse,' admitted Diana. 'It's always so stuffy and hot at Guillerme's. I'll be fine once I've had some tea.'

She was wrong. By the time they arrived back at the house Diana obviously felt very unwell indeed and Antonia took charge firmly.

'Bed!' she ordered, and Diva came rushing to exclaim over the pallor of Dona Diana's face, while Marisa looked on anxiously, her lower lip trembling.

'Just one of my headaches, darling.' Diana smiled, white to the lips. 'I'll be fine in a couple of hours, you'll see.'

'Let's help Mummy upstairs,' suggested Antonia, and took Diana by the elbow, holding out her other hand to Marisa. Very slowly the three of them negotiated the curving stair, then once in her mother's room Marisa drew the curtains importantly and fetched handkerchiefs while Antonia helped Diana undress and get into bed.

'Shall I turn on the air conditioning?' asked Antonia, worried by the beads of perspiration on Diana's paper-white forehead.

'No, love, it's cool in here—like heaven after Guillerme's strong-room. Don't worry, I get migraines from time to time.' Diana smiled wanly at Marisa. 'Thank you for helping, sweetheart.'

Marisa planted a moist kiss on her mother's cheek. '*Está doendo, Mamãe?*'

'No, it's not hurting *very* much.'

'Come on then, chicken,' said Antonia cheerfully. 'Let's have our swim and leave Mummy to sleep. Ah, splendid, here's Zelia with a tea tray.'

After Diana had been provided with pain-killers and a cup of tea, Antonia took Marisa off for a swim, and afterwards played ball with her and the willing Zelia until it was time for the child's supper. A silent visit to Diana's room confirmed that she was deeply asleep. Joachim, apparently, had gone to fetch Jaime. To distract Marisa's attention from her mother's illness Antonia demanded a Portuguese lesson, and a lively half-hour passed as the maids joined in with enthusiasm, teaching her the names of all the kitchen equipment, and the various items of food Diva was preparing for dinner. Marisa's face was flushed with importance as she translated for Antonia, and after a while insisted on subjecting the student to a test to see if she remembered what she had learned. Antonia pretended to hesitate over some words to give the child the opportunity to prompt her, and each time Marisa scolded her and told her to pay attention, and Diva and Zelia laughed behind their aprons as Antonia winked at them conspiratorially.

'So this is where everyone is hiding!' a voice interrupted them mockingly. 'Not a living soul to welcome me after a hard day earning *cruzados* to feed my family!'

'Jaime!' Marisa hurled herself at the tall figure in the

doorway, and Antonia's heart turned over as his eyes met hers above his little half-sister's curly dark head.

'Good evening,' she said breathlessly. 'Have you had a good day?'

'Boring,' he said succinctly, and tossed Marisa in the air. 'And what have you been doing, *bichinha*?'

Marisa told him about Diana's headache solemnly, giving him all the details. 'And Tonia and me put *Mamãe* to bed, and Diva made her tea, and Tonia gave her pills and now she's sleeping,' she finished in a rush.

'*Que pena!*' Jaime looked concerned as they went downstairs to the garden-room. 'Poor Diana suffers from the migraine occasionally. *Geralmente* the only cure is rest and sleep.'

'It's all my fault,' said Antonia in remorse. 'I made her play tennis with me this morning and tired her out. She had a headache before we went to Senhor Moreira's, then his house was like an oven, and we spent a long time in his strong-room, and by the time we came out Diana looked white as a sheet.'

'It's *not* your fault, Tonia.' Marisa scrambled on Antonia's lap and put her arms round her neck fiercely. '*Mamãe does* get headaches, really truly, like Jaime said. Please don't cry!'

'I'm not crying,' protested Antonia, laughing, though she came very close to doing so as Marisa hugged her tight.

Jaime's eyes were tender as he watched them. 'I think we all deserve a drink,' he suggested, and Marisa assented eagerly, sliding down on the sofa beside Antonia.

'*Tem suco de maracujá*, Jaime? *Faz favor?*'

'*Tenho.*' Jaime poured fruit juice and ice into a glass and handed it to the child. 'Antonia, what may I give you?'

'The same as Marisa, please; it looks delicious.'

Jaime grinned. 'With perhaps a dash of gin, since it is almost dinner time?'

Privately Antonia doubted very much she needed the added lift of alcohol now Jaime was home. Just to have him near was stimulation enough! 'I don't know that I should——'

'Just a little,' he said firmly and handed her a tall glass before making himself a gin and tonic. He took off the jacket of his fawn suit and tossed it on a chair, pulling off his tie. 'You permit?' he asked belatedly, as he sat down next to Marisa.

'Of course.' Antonia tasted her drink and smiled at him. 'Why was your day so boring?'

'How could it not have been when I was obliged to spend it with metallurgists and mining engineers instead of with three charming ladies?'

'We had a lovely day,' Marisa said with satisfaction, and gave him an account of her swimming and games with Antonia. 'And Tonia's going to buy me a tennis racquet tomorrow!'

'Is she so? *Que* Antonia *bondosa!*' Jaime looked suitably impressed.

'But not if Mummy's still poorly,' warned Antonia.

'You can if you wish,' said Jaime casually, 'as long as Joachim and Zelia accompany you, of course.'

Antonia's eyebrows rose. 'Such formality!'

He nodded, his face suddenly serious. 'I would prefer it so.'

Marisa looked hopeful. 'Can we, please, Antonia? Please? Then *Mamãe* can stay in bed.'

Antonia laughed and ruffled her curls. 'OK! Now it's time you and I went up for a bath, madam. And when Zelia's finished scrubbing you I'll read you a story.'

Marisa could see no reason why she needed a bath at all after her swim, but Antonia ignored her protests cheerfully and jumped up, holding out her hand. 'Come on, poppet. Kiss Jaime goodnight.'

Marisa obeyed with enthusiasm, then ran up the stairs to look for Zelia. Antonia smiled at Jaime a little shyly. 'I'll see you at dinner then.'

He rose to his feet, stretching a little, and smiled at her lazily. 'Shall we ask Diva to set a table for us down here, since we are only two tonight?'

Antonia very much doubted the wisdom of this. In the dining-room they were within earshot of the kitchen, but down here they were entirely cut off from the rest of the house.

'Do not worry,' he added, reading her mind with ease. 'I promise to eat only my dinner, not my guest!'

'Oh well, in that case,' she countered lightly, 'why not?'

Diana was still sleeping soundly when Antonia went to check on her. After a swift shower Antonia put on the green crêpe dress and took extra care with her face and hair before reading Marisa the promised story.

'You look all sparkly,' the child informed her when the story was finished.

'I *feel* sparkly,' said Antonia, smiling. 'Goodnight, poppet. Sleep well.'

'G'night, Tonia.' Marisa yawned widely. 'Tell Jaime to come and kiss me goodnight—please.'

'I am here already.' Jaime came in quietly and bent to kiss the rosy cheek. '*Mamãe* is fast asleep, Marisa, which means she will be well again by morning when you wake up. *Dorme bem, chica, boa noite.*'

'*Boa noite,*' mumbled the child, and turned her face into her pillow with a sigh.

Jaime took Antonia's hand and silently they went down to the garden-room, where the great expanse of glass let in the beauty of the starlit night.

'Now,' said Jaime briskly. 'May I give you another drink, Antonia?'

'Yes, please. I liked whatever it was you gave me earlier.' Antonia looked at him, troubled. 'Jaime, does Diana often get these headaches?'

'No, not very often. But of late her emotions have been very much overtaxed. Come,' Jaime handed her a glass, 'let us sit out on the terrace for a while. It is not cold, I think.'

'Far from it!' Antonia laughed a little as he sat down beside her on a cushioned cane sofa. 'This is a hot summer's night to a Brit like me—but go on about Diana, please.'

'First she was much grieved to hear of your adopted mother's death, after which I think she felt much guilt about her eagerness to hear your response to her invitation. She grew even more tense when she knew you were coming.' Jaime's voice softened. 'She both longed and dreaded to meet you, I think.'

'It was the same for me in a way. I can understand how she felt,' said Antonia, nodding.

'Then came the relief of actually seeing you and finding you were—*simpática*. And in the wake of the release of tension comes the migraine. I am not really surprised.' Jaime touched her hand. 'Do not worry. Diana has some medication from Dr Ferreira. It simply sends her to sleep for several hours and afterwards all is usually well.'

At that moment Diva and Zelia arrived with the dinner, and Antonia went inside with Jaime to enjoy melon and *prosciutto*, followed by fillets of *garoupa*, a white fish served with tomato and pepper sauce garnished with prawns.

'Would you still care to go to the cinema?' asked Jaime during the meal.

'Should we?' Antonia looked at him doubtfully.

'Diva or Zelia will look after Diana, who will doubtless sleep for hours yet.' Jaime smiled at her crookedly. 'And I assure you it is perfectly acceptable to go alone with me, because we are related.'

The thought of an evening out alone with Jaime was infinitely alluring. Antonia thought about it at length, wondering if it would be more sensible to refuse, then reminded herself that this was likely to be a one-off in her life. An evening out with Jaime de Almeida would be something to look back on when she was in England and down to earth once more, if nothing else. She smiled suddenly, thinking how casually she would have accepted an invitation to the cinema back home.

'You will come?' asked Jaime, seeing the smile.

'Yes. Thank you, I'd like to very much.'

'Then drink your coffee quickly. The film starts in half an hour.'

Joachim drove them to a cinema in the suburbs. It was small, but ultra-modern, with a brightly lit foyer packed with people for the final performance of the day. Jaime had booked their seats and they were soon side by side in the darkness inside the theatre, watching the credits roll past as the film began.

Afterwards Antonia was never sure what the film was about, since the moment they sat down Jaime took her hand in his and leaned as close as the arm of the seat allowed. From then on her attention was centred solely on the touch of his fingers, the warmth of his thigh and shoulder against hers, and each time she stole a look at him she found him gazing down at her face, not even making a pretence of watching the screen. Heat rose inside her, and she watched the screen blindly, aware only of Jaime's presence in the intimate darkness. When the lights went up Antonia left her seat like a sleepwalker, responsive only to the touch of Jaime's hand beneath her elbow as he ushered her into the bright lights and noisy hubbub of voices as the audience left the theatre. Antonia shrank close to Jaime's side and his arm tightened about her protectively, then she heard him exclaim as he directed her towards a woman standing a little apart near the entrance.

'Senhora Andrade!' he called, and the woman turned in pleased surprise. She was in her late thirties, Antonia estimated, with fair hair elegantly knotted on top of her head, her olive-skinned face beautifully made up.

'Senhor de Almeida,' she said, smiling, and held out her hand. *'Como vai?'*

Jaime took her hand and kissed it, then drew Antonia forward.

'May I present my stepsister, Miss Antonia Grant,' he said. 'Antonia, this is Senhora Isabel Andrade, who has only very recently come to live in Boa Vista.'

'How do you do?' Antonia smiled warmly, and the other woman returned the smile, her eyes oddly surprised.

'It is a pleasure to meet you, Miss Grant.'

'You are surely not here alone, Dona Isabel?' asked Jaime. 'If so, may we take you home?'

'No, no, you are so kind, but Luis has just gone to fetch the car.' Isabel Andrade laughed. 'I am so lazy—I did not wish to walk because my shoes are new.' She turned to Antonia. 'I look forward very much to seeing you again at the party on Saturday, Miss Grant—ah, there is the car, I must go. *Boa noite; até sábado.*'

Antonia joined with Jaime in saying goodnight as the elegant woman hurried to a waiting car.

'Come,' said Jaime peremptorily. 'Here is Joachim with our car.' He handed her inside and got in beside her, sliding an arm around her waist as the car moved off. With Joachim in the front seat it seemed pointless to protest and Antonia relaxed against Jaime, her head on his shoulder, his cheek against her hair, both of them silent for the short journey home. Home! Antonia checked her thoughts sharply. Home was a very long way from Boa Vista, and she would do well to keep it firmly in mind.

When they arrived at the house Diva informed them Dona Diana had woken briefly for a cool drink, but had gone back to sleep again almost immediately.

'You will need to see for yourself, I know,' said Jaime indulgently. 'I shall be in the garden-room when you come back.'

Anyone with any sense would go straight to bed, thought Antonia, as she stood watching a deeply sleeping Diana. She dismissed the thought and hurried back down to Jaime as fast as her feet would carry her, finding him at the open door of the garden-room, which was lit only by a lamp or two. He closed the door as she came slowly down the last few steps into the room, and fetched two glasses from the drinks tray.

'I anticipated your wish,' he said quietly, and held out one of the glasses to her.

Antonia thanked him and drank deeply, her mouth dry at the look in his eyes. He led her to a couch and sat down beside her, his legs stretched out in front of him as he stared down into his glass.

'It is strange that we should meet Isabel Andrade tonight,' he said. 'It solved a little mystery for me.'

Antonia finished her drink and set her glass down on the table beside her. 'Mystery? It sounds intriguing. Though oddly enough she seemed vaguely familiar—which is silly; I can't possibly have met her before.'

Jaime turned a little to look down into her face. 'You remember that I felt you were familiar at first, that I had met you before? Yes? Isabel Andrade was the reason. You are somewhat like her to look at, Antonia.'

She looked taken aback. 'Really? How odd! Do you know her well?'

'No, not well. Her husband is a heart consultant at the hospital here. He took up the appointment only a few months ago, but I have met them on several occasions at the houses of friends, you understand, and invited them here to the party on Saturday.' Jaime's eyebrows rose. 'I think Isabel could see the likeness also, no?'

Antonia nodded slowly. 'Now you mention it, I suppose that's why she looked so taken aback. I thought——' She stopped, annoyed with herself.

'What exactly did you think?' Jaime put a finger under her chin and turned her face up to his. Her eyelids dropped defensively and she tried to move away, but his other arm slid round her waist, holding her fast. 'Tell me, *carinha*. What was this thought you had?'

Antonia's face looked mutinous. 'I thought she was surprised to see me with you. In short, that she was jealous.'

'Ah!' He pulled her close. 'You thought she was my *amante, não é?*'

'Even if she were, it was nothing to do with me,' she said, sounding rather strangled, and he chuckled.

'Was it not, *querida? Mentirosa!* You are lying. You know very well that we had just spent almost two hours together in the darkness of that cinema, touching a little, but in no way enough. Enough only to send me mad for you.'

Antonia's eyes opened wide as they met Jaime's, which were eloquent with the feelings he was fighting to keep in check. Suddenly Antonia didn't want him to hold them in check. She wanted his mouth on hers, and his hands on her body. 'Did you enjoy the film?' she asked, in an odd, gruff tone.

'I saw nothing of the film!' He slid his fingers into her hair, his eyes holding hers. 'You will need to tell Diana the plot.'

'I can't,' she said flatly. 'I've no idea what it was about either.' And abruptly she got her wish. Jaime's mouth came down on hers hungrily, his arm tightened about her waist and his free hand left her hair to run over her shoulders and down her spine then upward to cup her breast through the thin crêpe. Antonia's arms closed convulsively round his neck and her mouth opened to his, her body melting bonelessly against him. Jaime made an inarticulate sound deep in his throat and then they were lying full length on the couch, bodies pressed desperately together as Antonia's fingers dug into the muscles of his shoulders, her nails pricking him like dagger-tips through the fine cotton of his shirt. Jaime tore his mouth away, rubbing his cheek blindly against hers.

'I said I would not,' he groaned. 'You are Diana's daughter, a guest in my house, my stepsister—*meu Deus*, I would go against every principle I possess if I make love to you. But I want you so much—you do not realise——'

'Do I not?' she said fiercely. '*I* want *you*—now. Please, Jaime—I'm on fire. I don't care if Brazilian girls don't say these things, I just want you to make love to me—I think I'll die if you don't.'

At her words Jaime de Almeida, for the first time in the thirty-three years of his life, utterly lost control. He pulled Antonia to her feet, sliding down the zip of her dress with shaking fingers, lifting her clear of the clinging crêpe and removing her remaining brief garments almost in one movement. In seconds his own clothes were stripped off and he lifted her high against his chest, his eyes burning with a question she answered by laying her mouth against his shoulder and running the tip of her tongue over his skin. Then there were no more questions, or answers, only the coming together of two bodies that could no longer exist disparately. Antonia, utterly overcome by urges never dreamed of before, gave herself up to Jaime without reserve, exulting in his possession from the first sharp pang of pain to the final cataclysm of feeling she had never believed really happened. Afterwards they lay very still for a long time, limbs still tangled, until at last Jaime very slowly lifted his head to look down into her face, his dark eyes brilliant with mingled triumph and guilt.

'*Querida, perdoneme*——'

Antonia touched a finger to his lips. '*Mea culpa* too, Jaime.' Her eyes were drowsy with wonder. 'It was—miraculous. I just didn't know——'

'But I did, *meu amor*.' Jaime's eyes closed, as though he were in pain. 'I should not have lost my head like a stupid schoolboy.'

Antonia sat up and reached for her clothes. 'You regret it, then?'

'Regret!' Jaime sprang up to dress hurriedly. 'How could I regret such—such rapture! It is not a common thing. But I did not know—dared not hope it would be a new experience for you.'

Antonia slid her dress over her head and yanked up the zip, suddenly cold. 'You mean you thought it was a fairly routine sort of thing for me.'

Jaime turned on her like a panther, shaking her mercilessly. 'I mean that you are so beautiful, so tempting, I could not believe you had never—that I was——'

'The first,' she said flatly, and met his eyes, shrugging. 'Well, you were. But no big deal. I won't hold it against you. I was equally to blame.'

He glared down at her angrily. 'You can dismiss what just happened so very lightly, Antonia? Is this the famous British phlegm? I am Latin, and I cannot.' He shook her less violently. 'Even now at this minute I want you again. I want your body under mine, to feel that skin that is so *sedosa*, so silk-smooth——'

Antonia pulled away, shaken. 'Stop it, Jaime! What happened was—oh, I don't know, an act of nature, sort of elemental, like a storm or a flood. It overtook us. It just happened. But if you made love to me again it would be premeditated, something we intended. I think that's against the rules in our particular case.'

'Rules?' He closed his eyes and stood with legs apart, his hands clenched. '*Deus me livre*! I have already broken all my own rules. I have no more to break, little *stepsister*!'

'If you insist on referring to me like that, one of the rules might be referred to as incest,' she said cruelly.

Jaime winced and she flew to him touching his cheek in instant remorse. He seized her hand and kissed each finger one by one, then touched his lips to her palm, his tongue touching her skin, and she shook and he snatched her against him. 'Do not tremble,' he said unevenly against her hair. 'I shall not make love to you again. At least, not tonight,' he added, and held her away from him to look in her face. 'While you are under my roof I shall be circumspect. Somehow. But after that I make no promises. In the meantime remember this, Antonia Luisa Grant. The gift you gave me this night is for me alone, you understand?'

Her eyes glittered at him in the dim light. 'I'm not sure I know what you mean.'

'I think you do. You are mine. Do not forget it.' And Jaime bent his head and kissed her in a way that underlined his arrogant statement with emphasis. When he raised his head Antonia felt shaken to the core, but determined to ease the dangerous tension between them.

'Perhaps in future I'd better avoid alcohol—or gin, at least,' she said, smiling up at him. 'You must have put too much in the fruit juice for the good of my self-control.'

Jaime's taut face relaxed, and he smiled as he took her hand to go upstairs. 'Perhaps it was not the gin, *meu amor*, but the *suco de maracujá*.'

'Why—what *is suco de maracujá?*'
'The juice of the passion fruit, *carinha!*'

CHAPTER NINE

DIANA appeared at breakfast next morning, still pale, but obviously very much better, to Antonia's great relief. Marisa, it seemed, had eaten earlier with Jaime, who had been later than usual leaving for the office.

'Were you late last night?' asked Diana. 'I'm glad you went to the cinema, by the way. Was it a good film?'

'Yes, very good.' Antonia mentally crossed her fingers. 'I looked in on you after we got back, but you were out for the count.'

'I'm always the same after my knockout drops. Sorry about that.'

'You still look a bit fragile to me, Diana. Jaime says it's all right for me to take Marisa to buy her tennis racquet as long as Joachim and Zelia go along too, so why don't you take it easy this morning while we're out?'

Diana agreed, admitting a quiet morning would be sensible, and later on Antonia set out for the city with an excited Marisa. Zelia, only slightly less excited, confessed, via Marisa, that she would be grateful to do a little shopping herself, a birthday present for her mother in Campo d'Ouro. Joachim saw them safely inside a large department store where they could make all their purchases under one roof, and promised to return for them later. Marisa was very quickly in possession of a child's tennis racquet, with the bonus of a new pair of white shorts to go with it. Zelia went off on her own with instructions to return to the *sorvetaria* on the second floor half an hour later, and Marisa took Antonia on a tour of the store, delighted to be asked for help in choosing a present for Antonia's friend Jane at home in England. A crocodile belt was eventually found, also a beautifully embroidered handkerchief to take home for Diana.

'Now let's have ice-cream,' said Marisa triumphantly, and Antonia laughed, letting the child tug her towards the *sorvetaria* where Zelia was waiting patiently for them, clutching the little china figurine purchased for her mother. Marisa ordered ice-cream for herself and Zelia and coffee for Antonia, who had less appetite than usual. She chatted brightly to Marisa, and even to Zelia with the odd words of Portuguese she knew, and they were all laughing together at her mistakes when someone stopped at their table and said '*Bom dia.*'

Antonia looked up in surprise to see Isabel Andrade smiling at them and greeted her warmly, introducing Marisa and the instantly shy Zelia.

'Won't you join us, Senhora Andrade?' asked Antonia.

'Why, thank you, how kind.' Isabel Andrade settled herself next to Marisa while fresh coffee was brought, and quickly won the child's approbation by admiring the tennis racquet extravagantly, and a very pleasant half-hour was passed before Isabel said regretfully that she must leave to go home to lunch with her brother who was staying with her on a short visit to Boa Vista.

'He has never been here before,' she said, getting up. 'So I must not let him get too lonely.'

Antonia got up. 'It was so nice to meet you again. I'll look forward to seeing you on Saturday, Senhora Andrade.'

The other woman hesitated, glancing at Marisa, who was engrossed in conversation with Zelia for the moment. 'Senhor de Almeida—Jaime—introduced you as his stepsister last night. Forgive my curiosity, but how can that be?'

'My mother is his father's second wife—well, widow now, unfortunately.' Antonia could feel tell-tale colour in her cheeks. 'I'm not actually related to—to Mario and Jaime.'

Isabel Andrade's face cleared. 'Ah, I see. You are the child of a previous marriage.' Impulsively she took

Antonia's hand in hers, gesturing towards the mirror that lined one wall of the coffee-shop. 'It amazes me that we look so much alike.'

Seen at a distance the girl in pink trousers and white shirt bore a quite decided resemblance to the elegant woman in the expensively simple black linen dress.

'You could be my daughter,' said the latter.

Antonia laughed and shook her head. 'No way. You're much too young.'

Isabel Andrade patted her cheek. 'How kind. But I have two sons at the *universidade*, and a daughter in school, you know.' She glanced at her watch and sighed. 'I must go. But I would so much like the opportunity to talk to you again alone. Would your mother permit you to have lunch with me tomorrow?'

Antonia looked blank. 'Why—yes, I imagine so.'

'Then perhaps Jaime's chauffeur could bring you to the Restaurante Alba Mar at one o'clock. Will that suit?'

'Yes, fine. Thank you, Senhora Andrade.'

'Call me Isabel, Antonia.' Isabel bent to say goodbye to Marisa, and with a little wave went off, leaving Antonia surprised but quite definitely pleased that the charming Brazilian lady seemed so anxious to get to know her better.

Diana was pleased, too, when the shopping expedition arrived home. She was waiting for them on the terrace looking very much more rested, and eager for company.

'Diva's up to her ears in preparations for the party and quite obviously wants me well out of the way,' she said ruefully, 'so I'd be very glad of some interesting conversation, please, girls.'

Marisa was only too ready to oblige, showing her new racquet and shorts, and chattering away like a magpie about the pretty lady they had met. Antonia explained about the encounter with Isabel at the cinema, and that after their meeting today Isabel wanted Antonia to lunch with her the following day.

'But only if it's all right with you, Diana,' added Antonia.

'Of course. You'll enjoy lunch at the Alba Mar, and a rest

from us all for an hour or two will do you good.' Diana
shooed Marisa off to wash her hands ready for lunch, and
when they were alone looked questioningly at Antonia.
'Did you survive an evening alone with Jaime without too
much trouble, darling?'

Antonia gave an odd, strangled little laugh. 'It all
depends, as someone used to say, on what exactly you define
as trouble——'

She was saved from explaining by the return of Marisa,
now arrayed in the new shorts, ready for her tennis lesson
after lunch. Glad of the diversion, Antonia produced the
little gift she'd bought for Diana, which turned the latter's
attention very successfully from a subject her daughter was
by no means keen to discuss.

The afternoon passed very pleasantly with the promised
tennis lesson followed by a swim in the pool, while Diana
sat in a garden chair under an umbrella, content to watch
her daughters at play. When Zelia brought out a tray of
cool drinks later in the afternoon she was pressed into
service to take over the task of entertaining Marisa for a
time, giving Antonia a respite. The sun was still hot on her
skin, a great deal of which was exposed to it in her brief
white bikini, and she lay back in a reclining chair with a
tall, clinking glass of orange juice in her hand, her eyes
dreamy.

'Mario's coming to dinner tonight,' said Diana. 'He rang
while you were out, with apologies for not coming last
night. He had some business do to attend, I gather; Jaime's
pigeon really, but he dumped it on to Mario instead.'

Antonia thought about the last remark a lot while she
was playing with Marisa again in the pool, wondering
whether she was glad or not that Jaime had delegated his
obligations to spend the evening with her. If he *had* gone to
his business dinner there would have been no trip to the
cinema, and, more important, no explosive love scene
afterwards.

'Are you coming?' called Diana, as Zelia helped Marisa
out of the pool. 'We're off to have baths before dinner, but

there's plenty of time if you want to stay for a proper swim on your own.'

'I think I will—it's so lovely out here.' Antonia shook the water out of her eyes and smiled. 'I'll be in soon.'

Alone she struck out in the stylish crawl taught her at school, and swam several lengths of the pool as fast as she could, trying to quell the thoughts milling around in her brain. Head low, she cut through the water at a fair speed until gradually she began to tire and decided one more length was her limit. Before she could reach the end of the pool two arms seized her in an iron-hard grip and she let out a little scream that was silenced instantly by Jaime's mouth in a way that sent her entire body limp.

'You should not be swimming here alone like this,' he muttered as he raised his head. He began towing her to the shallow end of the pool until he could stand upright and hold her against him, and Antonia's face flamed as she realised he was naked.

'Jaime!' she gasped. 'We'll be seen!'

He laughed and pushed back her wet hair, kissing her with little nibbling kisses all over her face. 'The pool is visible from two rooms only—yours and mine. Diana sent me with your robe, but when I saw you there in the water I could not resist joining you, *carinha*.' And he kissed her again, full on her mouth, and Antonia abandoned all pretence of resistance and kissed him back, her damp breasts pushing against his chest, the nipples standing erect through the wet white fabric. Without taking his mouth from hers Jaime released the catch of her top and drew it off, then her breasts were in his hands, and her mouth opened wide, gasping under his until he raised his head a little to move his lips down her throat and down again. The graze of his strong white teeth was unbearable, beautiful anguish as he nuzzled first one breast and then the other until Antonia's knees buckled abruptly and he picked her up, walking up the shallow steps with her to the place where he had dropped her robe and then his clothes. He wrapped her in her robe, breathing hard, then dried himself roughly with her towel and dragged on trousers and shirt. All the time his dark eyes never left hers and Antonia gazed back at him, mesmerised, her body yielding to his as he put his arm around her and held her close against him, hip to hip and thigh to thigh as they went slowly up through the terraces towards the garden-room.

'It has been a long, long day, Antonia,' he said huskily, his breath warm against her ear. 'All day when my mind should have been on other things all I could think of was your body beneath mine, so sweet, so—ah, *querida*, I could not wait to get home to be with you again.'

'You did say you wouldn't make love to me again under your roof,' she reminded him, as they reached the terrace outside the garden-room.

'I will not——' he began, then checked, laughing, his eyes gleaming into hers. 'No more than I have just done, I promise. Come.' He led her along the terrace to a small door Antonia had never noticed before. When he opened it she blinked, surprised, to see a white-painted spiral stair. 'It leads directly into my bathroom,' Jaime informed her. 'With a little luck no one will know I've been swimming. Come.'

'Not on your life!' said Antonia. 'You go that way and I'll go separately through the garden-room. See you later.'

At the foot of the stairs in the hall she met Diana, already dressed for dinner. She eyed her damp daughter in surprise.

'Aren't you in yet? I sent Jaime after you some time ago.'

'He came in ahead of me,' said Antonia airily, and ran up the stairs. 'Won't be long, I promise.'

Half an hour later, her hair gleaming after a hasty session with a hot brush, and her skin glowing darkly from her afternoon in the sun, Antonia ran downstairs in a white dress, gold hoops in her ears and her gold locket round her neck, to find Mario waiting in the hall. He looked quite ridiculously handsome in white trousers and a thin dark red shirt, his face alight with a smile of greeting as he saw her.

'Antonia! *Meu Deus*, what a golden girl you are tonight. I need dark glasses just to look at you.' He kissed her cheek and she smiled radiantly at him.

'Lovely to see you, Mario. You know, I'd forgotten just how beautiful you are.'

'Beautiful!' Mario recoiled in disgust as his brother came up the stairs from the garden-room. 'Did you hear, Jaime?'

'I heard,' said Jaime, and raised an eyebrow at Antonia. 'My brother does not care for comments about the face God was pleased to give him, you understand.'

'Oh, I'm sorry, Mario,' said Antonia in contrition, and patted his cheek. 'I won't mention it again.'

'*Bom!*' Mario looked quickly from the girl to Jaime, surprising an expression in his brother's eyes a stranger might have missed. '*Vamanos*, you two, let us join Diana and Marisa, even though my little sister's conversation, I would warn you, is monopolised by the subject of her tennis racquet. I will go first,' he said loudly, but the other two didn't even hear him. Mario shrugged philosophically and went down the stairs, and instantly Jaime took Antonia in his arms, kissing her with a hunger that sent her senses reeling.

'I do not think I am capable of keeping my promise,' he said unsteadily against her mouth, and Antonia smiled and touched a loving hand to his springing dark hair.

'Then I must avoid being alone with you. I'll begin right now.' She reached up to kiss his mouth fleetingly, and dodged his outstretched arms as she sped down the stairs to join the others.

It was an enchanted evening in some indefinable way. On the surface it was just a conventional family dinner, with all four in complete harmony as they talked together. There was much discussion of Saturday's party and the guests that were invited, and Mario gave an account of the film he had taken Isilda to see. Diana smiled blandly and told him she'd heard from Antonia how good it was, and Jaime's eyes held Antonia's as she agreed breathlessly, and the other two watched, fascinated, as the dark, intent man and the the fair, glowing girl gazed in silence at each other and never even seemed to realise that the conversation had come to a full stop.

Diva's arrival with the cheeseboard and a bowl of fresh fruit started things in motion again, since it was necessary for everyone to reassure the apologetic woman that such a sketchy meal was no reflection on her culinary skill.

'She and Joachim have been chopping meat up all afternoon into suitable portions for the *churrasco*,' explained Diana. 'So Zelia made the fruit salad and I insisted Diva give us something cold so she wouldn't be trying to do a hundred and one things at once.'

'I think you made the hollandaise sauce for the fish,' said Jaime, shaking his head. 'I thought you were to rest today, Diana.'

'I did! I was bored silly by the time the girls came in from shopping. And this afternoon all I did was laze by the pool and watch Marisa and Antonia swim.'

'I wish I had been with you,' said Mario fervently. 'Does Antonia swim well?'

'Oh yes,' Diana smiled seraphically at Jaime. 'She does, doesn't she, Jaime?'

Mario literally goggled as his normally imperturbable brother looked distinctly uncomfortable, a rare hint of colour creeping along his cheekbones.

'Yes, she does,' said Jaime, and presssed Antonia to more cheese, which she accepted obediently, then sat looking at the sliver of cheese on her plate as though wondering how it got there.

Diana showed mercy at that point by suggesting they had their coffee downstairs to give Diva the opportunity to clear away.

'What *is* a *churrasco*, by the way?' asked Antonia, and sat down by Diana on a sofa.

'Barbecue,' said Jaime, and went over to a tall chair near the window, where he could look at Antonia unobserved, well out of range of the glow cast by the lamps.

'Jaime has a barbecue pit in the garden,' explained Mario.

'And that was the meat Diva was preparing today,' added Diana. 'Portions of chicken, pork, steaks, that type of thing. They're all stacked in the freezer now, ready to take out on Saturday.'

Antonia bit her lip as she wondered what on earth was suitable dress for a barbecue in Boa Vista. The few she'd been to at home had been simple affairs, bonfire night with sausages and jacket potatoes at a neighbour's house, or on the beach during a rare seaside holiday with Janet, when jeans and sweaters had been the accepted garb. Diana guessed at the way her mind was working and smiled reassuringly.

'Are you wondering what to wear? One dresses for a *churrasco* here at night in much the same way as any other party, darling.' She cast a look at her two stepsons. 'Jaime and Mario will probably wear something similar to the clothes they have on tonight, but the ladies are likely to dress up a bit.'

'Trousers?' asked Antonia.

'If you like. I generally wear a dress, but then I'm getting on a bit.'

'And you seldom grace us with your presence anyway,' pointed out Jaime. 'It is some time since you have even consented to pay a visit to Casa Madrugada at all, Diana.'

'I've become a bit of stick-in-the-mud, haven't I?' she agreed ruefully.

Mario laughed at the expression and asked Jaime to put some music on the stereo. 'Put us in the mood for Saturday,' he said, as his brother searched through the records on one of the shelves. 'No Vivaldi tonight, *por favor*.'

'*Pagão!*' said Jaime, as some lively samba rhythms began.

'Not everyone who dislikes Vivaldi is a heathen,' protested Mario, and jumped to his feet, holding out his hands to Antonia. 'Come, little sister. Dance with me.'

She cast a doubtful glance in Jaime's direction, but he smiled at her indulgently then pulled Diana to her feet, ignoring her laughing protests as they joined in. Mario was an even better dancer than his brother and under his guidance Antonia learned just what the samba can be when danced by a Brazilian with rhythm in his very bones, as most of his countrymen have.

After a few minutes Mario released Antonia and neatly detached Diana from Jaime, who took Antonia is his arms just as the tempo of the music slowed to a dreamy sensuous rhythm. They moved together in silence, barely touching, yet Antonia was so acutely aware of him that when the music stopped it was an effort to move away. She resumed her place by Diana as Jaime mixed drinks for all of them, and as he gave Antonia hers he smiled down into her eyes.

'Orange juice only tonight, Antonia.'

Her answering grin was mischievous. 'Spoilsport!'

Antonia felt it best not to risk more time alone with Jaime that night. When Mario went home she went upstairs with Diana, after a single chaste kiss on her cheek from Jaime. The light caress made her pulse race just the same, and she went to bed wishing he was there beside her, his arms holding her close, instead of in another bed in another room. The only glimmer of consolation she had to keep her company during the restless night was the certainty that Jaime was wishing the same thing on the other side of the bedroom wall.

Antonia woke early and flew out of bed to dress at top speed before running downstairs to the garden-room in the hope of catching Jaime before he left. You're shameless, she told herself, but was fiercely glad of it when Jaime sprang to his feet at the sight of her, his eyes lighting up with undisguised delight as he held out his arms.

'*Querida!*' At once his mouth met hers as he swung her off her feet, holding her up against him.

'I came to say good morning,' she gasped, when her mouth was free, and smiled at him incandescently.

Jaime buried his face in her hair, muttering something unintelligible. She tipped her head back.

'What did you say?' she demanded. He breathed in deeply, then set her down on her feet and took her face gently in both hands, gazing deep into her wide trusting eyes.

'Now that I have seen you, held you in my arms, it is a very good morning,' he said softly, and suddenly Antonia felt a lump in her throat. Her eyes closed quickly, but not soon enough to prevent the tears which trickled from beneath her lids and down her cheeks. She heard his sharp intake of breath as he held her close.

'*Não chora, carinha,* please—I cannot endure your tears!'

Antonia sniffed loudly as she tried to smile. 'I was suddenly so happy, Jaime, that's all.'

His face cleared, and he kissed her on the tip of her nose. 'I must go, *querida.* God knows I do not wish to, but I must. I shall send Joachim back at once and he will take you wherever you want.'

'Just to this restaurant to lunch with Senhora Andrade.'

'Ah yes. Where are you meeting her?'

'At the Alba Mar—is that right? At one o'clock.'

'You shall tell me all about it tonight. *Até logo, carinha.*'

'*Até logo,* Jaime.'

They moved together instinctively for one last kiss, which developed into a series of kisses, until Jaime thrust her from him, groaning.

'*Bruxa*—little witch. I am late.'

At once Antonia put her hands behind her back and moved away, smiling at him demurely. 'I'm not keeping you.'

Jaime picked up his jacket and straightened his tie, looking her up and down with half-closed eyes. 'Are you not, Antonia? Now, this time, I go. *Até logo.*' He sprinted up the stairs and Antonia watched him go with a little smile Eve would have had no trouble in recognising.

Seized by the desire to do something, Antonia took Jaime's coffee tray up to the kitchen, greeting Diva with a beaming smile and a blithe '*Bom dia!*'

'*Bom dia,* Dona Antonia, *mais não faz isso não!*' Diva took the tray from her, scolding, but Antonia only laughed, and insisted on loading it with fresh breakfast things, which she bore off downstairs with the idea of saving Diva's legs a little. She was enjoying her toast and quince jelly in the morning sun by the open patio door when Diana arrived with Marisa, looking amused.

'My goodness, you're early!' she said, kissing Antonia's cheek.

'Did you have breakfast with Jaime?' asked Marisa, climbing on to her chair.

'No. But I did see him for a moment. Then I cleared away his breakfast and brought some down for me. Shall I pop up and get yours?'

'No, no, stay where you are,' said Diana. 'Zelia will bring ours.'

'I'd forgotten Zelia—servants aren't something I'm used to!'

'Can we play tennis again this morning?' asked Marisa eagerly. 'Please!' she added, at a look from her mother.

'Yes, of course.' The way Antonia felt at that particular moment she felt equal to taking on Martina Navratilova.

'But only for an hour or so,' said Diana firmly, 'because later on I'm going into town with Antonia to do some boring grown-up shopping before I drop her at the restaurant to lunch with the nice lady you met yesterday.'

Marisa looked crestfallen, but cheered up at the suggestion that Zelia might like to learn how to play tennis. 'You can give her a lesson while I'm out,' said Antonia, 'and I'll be back later this afternoon.'

The day was hotter than the previous one as Antonia wandered round the shops with Diana, Joachim following behind in the background to carry their parcels. They paused at a pavement café for cold drinks in preference to coffee, and afterwards Diana visited the dark, cool interior of a delicatessen, which sold wonderful cheeses, smoked sausages of every description, and the succulent ham which was the speciality of the house. Joachim was soon loaded with purchases and sent back to the car with them while Diana took Antonia into a shop selling fabrics of every description from home-grown cotton to *seda pura*, pure silk imported from Japan.

'I thought I'd buy a couple of dress lengths,' Diana said. 'I make quite a few things myself, especially for Marisa.'

Antonia was impressed. 'Really? I'm no good at that sort of thing at all.'

'I enjoy it—and of course, I only make dresses. I'm no good at the sort of tailoring you'd need for winter clothes in England.' Diana darted suddenly to the rear of the shop, beckoning to the attentive male assistant. 'Look, Antonia! What do you think of this?'

The man extracted a bolt of cloth from a stack of others and shook out a length of gauzy, drifting material in a muted shade of brown, spattered here and there with a drift of gilt dots.

'What the French call *feuille-morte*,' said Diana ecstatically.

'Dead leaf?' Antonia touched the delicate fabric doubtfully, surprised to find it was lawn, not chiffon. 'It's unusual—but——'

'Oh, it's not for me!' Diana spoke to the assistant, who draped a length of the fabric near Antonia, nodding enthusiastically at the effect.

'*Perfeito!*' he agreed.

Antonia laughed and shook her head. 'Where would I wear something like that?'

'To the party on Saturday, of course. I'll make it up for you,' said Diana airily.

'You will *not*! It's Wednesday today, for heaven's sake. I'm not having you go down with a migraine just so I can have a dress.' Antonia pushed the material away and the man's face fell.

'I shan't have a migraine,' said Diana firmly. 'Sabino can bring my sewing machine in today and bring Pascoa with it. She sews beautifully—so does Zelia, if it comes to that. Between us all we can achieve a dress in not much more than a day, I assure you.'

Nothing would move her. She brushed away Antonia's

protests and bought several metres of the gold-dusted material, also two lengths of printed cotton for Marisa and another for herself.

'Do stop arguing, Antonia,' she said at last, as they rejoined the waiting Joachim. 'Indulge me, please!'

It was Antonia's first encounter with the gentle obduracy Diana was capable of on occasion, and she climbed in the car defeated.

'All right, you win. But heaven knows what Jaime will say.'

'And does what Jaime says matter so much to you, my love?'

'I'm not frightfully keen on his thinking I'm wearing you out for the sake of a dress. I showed you the green affair I had for the summer ball. Wouldn't that do?'

'Not quite right for a *churrasco*.' Diana tapped the parcel. 'This will be.'

Antonia was balked from further argument by their arrival at the Restaurante Alba Mar, which was in a quiet side road leading off the main *avenida*. Diana gave her a quick kiss, then remained in the car while Joachim escorted Antonia inside the restaurant where Isabel Andrade was already waiting. She greeted Antonia warmly, had a quick word with Joachim, who nodded and bade Antonia goodbye, then Isabel summoned a hovering waiter, who led them to a table screened by potted greenery at the rear of the room.

'It is so kind of you to come,' said Isabel after they'd ordered. 'I can drive you back afterwards myself, at whatever time you wish.'

Antonia thanked her, very much drawn to this charming, friendly woman, finding it very easy to talk to her on all kinds of subjects over the sole meunière and the strawberries topped with crème Chantilly that followed. When Isabel laughed over the Gallic flavour of their meal, and promised something more ethnic next time they ate together, Antonia smiled regretfully, and told her companion her holiday would soon be over.

'Holiday?' Isabel's large dark eyes were searching. 'You do not live here?'

Antonia felt a little awkward. It was difficult to explain her situation without revealing details that were very personal to Diana.

'You have been brought up by your father's family perhaps?' said Isabel tactfully. 'Do not be concerned. I have no wish to, how do you say, pry?'

'It's not that exactly.' Antonia fiddled absently with her coffee spoon. 'I've been in college in England and I've just got my BA, my degree. And soon I must go back to my life over there.' She felt very uncomfortable. Everything she said was only making things worse.

'It is difficult in matters of divorce, I know. No doubt you divide your time between your parents,' said Isabel with sympathy. 'How sad.'

Antonia made a sudden decision. 'Senhora—Isabel, I mean. It isn't like that at all. But I'm not free to give you any details because they concern Diana—my mother.'

'Diana?' Isabel went very still, her eyes holding Antonia's. 'Your mother's name is Diana?'

Antonia nodded warily. 'Yes. Why?'

Isabel took a handkerchief from her handbag and touched it to her upper lip. She looked at Antonia uncertainly, as though trying to find the right words to say. At last she leaned across and grasped Antonia's hand. 'Cara,' she said very gently. 'Tell me your mother's name before she married. Was it by any miracle Moore?'

Antonia's eyes opened wide. 'Why yes, it was. But—but how on earth?' Her face cleared. 'You met her here when she came to Rio perhaps.'

'No, Antonia. I met her long before that, if she is the Diana Moore who was at your Univeristy of Bristol; a very pretty girl, with big grey eyes and long fair hair.'

'Yes, that's right. Did you know her in college, then?'

Isabel Andrade shook her head, dazed, like someone in shock. 'Let us have more coffee.' After the waiter had brought it she took a deep breath. 'The name alone should have been enough to confirm the coincidence of such a resemblance,' she said. 'Antonia, I am not Brazilian, I am Spanish, my family are wine exporters. Diana Moore came to live with us one summer to improve the English of my sisters and me, and to gain fluency herself in Spanish. My brother came home from abroad after she had been with us for a time, and fell in love with her at first sight. My parents did not realise it, but Rosa and I knew only too well, young though we were. They were so romantic to us schoolgirls, like Romeo and Juliet, and we tried our best to help keep their secret.'

'But you didn't manage it,' said Antonia hollowly. Her mouth felt dry and her heart was pounding in her chest. She gulped down some coffee, regardless of its heat, feeling distinctly shaken. 'What happened to—to your brother?' she asked with difficulty.

Isabel gave her a strange little smile. 'I mentioned him yesterday, *cara*, remember? He is at home in our house on the Rua Tupinambas at this very moment.'

Antonia stared dumbly at Isabel. She saw tears start in the other woman's beautiful dark eyes and blinked fiercely as they threatened in her own.

'Is his wife with him?' she asked gruffly.

Isabel shook her head, drying her eyes. 'He is *solteiro*—bachelor, *cara*. He has never married. For a long time he was very angry and bitter towards my parents for separating him from Diana. He spent much time in England trying to find her, but her parents said she had left home and they had no idea where she was. The university said she had left, also. He was a very different person when he returned home; older and harder, and concerned only with the business. He told my father he would work in it as expected, but he refused to marry his *noiva*, the girl he had been betrothed to since a boy, and has never shown any signs of marrying ever since.' Isabel cleared her throat. 'But Diana married twice, then?'

'No. Only once. She married Francisco de Almeida twelve years ago. I was adopted by Janet and Lewis Grant

soon after I was born. Diana lodged with them when she
was in college. I didn't know anything about her until
my—my adoptive mother died recently.' Antonia explained about Diana's struggle to help support the child she
had been forced to give away.

'*Meu Deus*,' whispered Isabel, stricken. '*Que tragédia!*' Her
attractive face looked drawn, and suddenly older. 'I would
so like to meet Diana again. I loved her too, so did Rosa. We
were heartbroken when she was sent away, but no one
knew about—that Diana——'

'Was pregnant,' finished Antonia. 'Not even Diana did
for a while.'

'And she had been told my brother must marry someone
else.' Isabel sighed deeply.

'And just to top things off, Diana's own parents more or
less threw her out when she gave them the glad news.'

'*Nossa Senhora!*' Isabel was silent for a while, lost in her
own thoughts, then suddenly she stood up. '*Desculpe-me*,
Antonia, I must bathe my eyes. I shall be swift.'

Antonia sat alone at the table, staring blindly at the
screen of plants concealing her from the rest of the crowded
restaurant. All the other people there were just eating and
enjoying themselves, she thought, doing business over the
lunch table, or perhaps even keeping assignations, while
she felt as if she'd been run over by a truck. Her father—she
drew in a shaky breath at the very thought of the word—
was actually here in Boa Vista. And so was Diana. What in
the world should she do now? Keep quiet about it, or rush
to Casa Madrugada gaily calling, 'Guess what I heard
today?' And what would Jaime think of it all? Jaime. The
mere thought of him had a steadying effect. She wished
fervently he was here right now, so she could throw herself
into his arms and let him shoulder her problem. She looked
up as Isabel returned, and smiled.

'Do you feel better now?' she asked sympathetically.

'Yes, *cara*. It is not so very unpleasant to find I have a
beautiful new niece, you know.' Isabel held out her hand.
'Come. Let us go.'

Outside the afternoon was very warm, and Antonia was glad when Isabel's car was moving so that the air conditioning could function efficiently.

'I haven't thanked you properly for my lunch,' said Antonia, as Isabel drove off. 'It was delicious.'

'In spite of the mutual shock of our discoveries!' Isabel drove very expertly and Antonia, unused to the roads of Boa Vista, failed to notice at first that they were heading in a different direction from Casa Madrugada. It was only when Isabel stopped the car in front of a strange house in a quiet cul-de-sac that Antonia woke to the fact that they must be outside the Andrade home. 'This is where I live,' said Isabel and looked beseechingly at Antonia. 'I entreat you, *cara*, to come inside and meet my brother. I confess I rang him from the Alba Mar. He—he wanted very much to jump in a taxi and come to us right away, which is most unlike him. I persuaded him it was better to wait until I brought you home.'

Antonia felt panic rise inside her like steam in a kettle. 'Isabel—I don't know that I can face him right now. It's too sudden—I need time!'

'But how else can you meet him? I am sure Diana does not allow you out alone—and he so badly wants to see you.'

Antonia gave up. Life had been throwing so many things at her lately, of one kind and another; one more seemed unlikely to make much difference. She got out of the car, wishing her knees would stop shaking, and followed Isabel through a small formal garden to the door. Isabel pushed her in front of her as she opened it.

'Go through to the *sala* at the back. He is waiting there. I shall join you later.'

Antonia had no eyes for her surroundings when she entered the room. All her attention was centred on the slim figure of the man waiting by the french windows opening into the garden. He stood like a statue as Antonia went hesitantly towards him. He was of medium height, and certainly no dark *hidalgo*. His curly fair hair was greying a little at the temples, but otherwise his darkly tanned skin and gold-flecked hazel eyes were identical to her own. He was very attractive, despite the faint lines at the corners of his eyes and mouth, and could easily have been taken for a man several years younger than the age she knew he must be. They looked at each other in silence that lengthened and grew unbearable, until suddenly the man's eyes closed tightly and his hands clenched at his sides. Slowly his eyes opened again and he crossed the space between them, taking her by the shoulders.

'*Minha filha,*' he said, in a quiet voice husky with suppressed emotion. '*Nunca na minha vida*——'

Antonia shook her head, and smiled shakily. 'I'm sorry. I know it's ridiculous, but I don't speak Portuguese.'

His face relaxed and his mouth curved in a delighted smile, his eyes lighting up, and suddenly he hugged her tight. 'No, little English miss, I do not suppose you do! Antonia, Antonia, you cannot imagine how happy I am to meet you. Little daughter——' And he turned her face up to his and kissed her on both cheeks.

It was too much. Antonia began to cry. She laid her head on his shoulder and sobbed like a child, drenching the elegant linen jacket of this total stranger who, by some miracle, was in reality her father. He held her close and patted her shoulder, murmuring words of comfort into the hair that was so like his own. The words were foreign to Antonia, but their meaning was crystal clear. He rocked her in his arms and let her cry away all the shock and tension until at last she pulled away, accepting the handkerchief he offered her, mopping her eyes and blowing her nose.

'I think it is time I introduced myself,' he said, when she was more composed. He smiled at her, his eyes twinkling as he swept her a graceful bow. 'Antonio Luis de Freitas, at your service.'

'Snap,' said Antonia, grinning.

'*Como?*' He looked puzzled.

She bobbed him a little curtsy. 'I'm Antonia Luisa—but my other name is Grant.'

He ran a slim brown hand through his hair, his eyes full of sudden pain. 'Diana named you for me? Even after all that happened?'

'It seems she did. But until this moment I didn't know it.'

'And the name Grant?'

Antonia gave him a brief account of Diana's story after she was sent back in disgrace to England and Antonio de Freitas sank on to a sofa, drawing his daughter down beside him. The lines in his face deepened as he learned the circumstances of her birth and adoption, and of the secret financial support by Diana over the years. Antonia poured it all out, telling him how smooth and uneventful life had been for her in the years between Lewis' death and Janet's, how wonderful a mother Janet Grant had been.

'And now I have Diana,' said Antonia very distinctly, and looked at her father's face.

'While I do not,' he answered sombrely. 'This Francisco de Almeida she married has given her all those things I should have done.'

'I think you should know I have a little stepsister too,' added Antonia with care. 'Marisa is five.'

Antonio de Freitas winced. 'Is there more family?'

'Only Jaime and Mario de Almeida—Francisco's sons from a previous marriage.'

'Then she is well protected,' he said and met Antonia's eyes searchingly. 'Tell me, please *cara*, how is she? Has she changed? Is she still beautiful?'

'I don't know how much she's changed, because I've only just met her myself. But she *is* beautiful.'

Antonio de Freitas stared down at his hands blindly. 'She will not wish to see me. It would be too much to expect after all that has happened.'

'Do *you* want to see *her*?'

'More than anything in the world. I had given up hope of ever finding her again, Antonia, but never did I stop thinking of her—and grieving.'

'Then come to Casa Madrugada. Or would you like me to tell her?'

'*Não! Não, filinha.*' He touched a hand to her cheek. 'When I see her it must be unannounced so that her—what is the word? Reaction? This will be one of instinct, and I shall know if she still—still has any trace of affection left for me.'

Privately Antonia had few doubts on this score herself, but thought it wisest to keep her own counsel. Strong as her rapport was with Diana already, it would be rash to speak for her on a matter as important as this.

Later on Isabel came into the room hesitantly, to receive an affectionate welcome from her brother, so affectionate that she dissolved into tears, the result of half an hour spent pacing up and down her bedroom, wondering what was happening in her *sala*. Antonia joined in with the soothing, then saw with dismay that it was very late and Diana might well be worried.

Antonio de Freitas insisted on driving her back, stopping the car a short way from the gates of Casa Madrugada. He turned in his seat to look at his new-found daughter, his eyes still full of wonder and disbelief as they rested on her face. 'My deep desire is to go into the house with you, Antonia, and meet Diana at this very moment, but I am no longer the headstrong fool of my youth. Unfortunately I must fly to São Paulo tonight on the business which has brought me to this country, and I shall not return until Saturday. Somehow I must hold myself in check, practise patience, until then. So do not inform anyone, Diana most of all, of my presence yet, I beg. As soon as I return I shall come here to visit her.'

'I think we're here until Sunday, but after that we go back to Lagoa del Rey where Diana lives. This is Jaime de Almeida's house.'

'I see. Then I shall come before then.' He sat looking at her, still bemused. '*Que milagre*—to think God has sent me a daughter—such a beautiful daughter.'

Antonia grinned mischievously. 'Careful—Diana says I look just like you.'

His eyes glowed. 'She does? Then she must still care for me a little. Only the eyes of love could see your face in this battered visage of mine.'

'But you weren't so battered, as you call it, when she saw you last!'

He groaned and ruffled her hair. 'You do not comfort your poor old father!' He hugged her close and kissed her on both cheeks. 'I shall see you when I return, *minha filha*. Go now, or Diana will be worried for you. *Adeus, cara.*'

'Bye.' Suddenly Antonia was close to tears, and she slid out of the car, running to the gate without turning round, not wanting him to see her cry as she rang the bell for Joachim.

Diana was waiting on the terrace with a very bored Marisa. The child flew at Antonia, scolding her for being late and pulling at her urgently with demands to play tennis. Diana restrained her and commandeered Antonia herself first to take measurements, asking details of the lunch as she noted down the figures. It took immense effort for Antonia to behave normally, as though the meeting with Antonio de Freitas had never taken place. Some of her feelings obviously seeped through the composure she was struggling to maintain, since Diana assured her there was no need to rush around the tennis court if she was too tired.

'You look drained, love. Is the heat beginning to get to you a bit, perhaps?' Diana asked as she finished.

'Too much food and not enough exercise,' said Antonia, feeling so horribly guilty she was glad to go off with Marisa while the newly arrived Pascoa helped Diana cut out the dress on the dining-table before Diva wanted the latter laid for dinner.

Jaime was very late getting home, for which Antonia was deeply thankful at first. By the time she'd played with Marisa, had a swim, then a leisurely bath, she felt more able to cope with concealing the secret she felt at first must be branded on her face for all the world to see, and she devoutly hoped Jaime wouldn't suspect she was inwardly consumed with excitement. When she joined Diana in the garden-room for a drink before dinner Diva had apparently already been down twice to see if there were any news of Jaime's arrival, since Joachim had not been required to pick him up from the office. He was coming home by taxi.

'Strange,' said Diana, frowning. 'He always rings if he's going to be late. Anyway, Marisa, it's high time you were in bed. Jaime can kiss you goodnight when he comes in.'

Soon afterwards Marisa was tucked up in bed and Diana and Antonia were alone in the garden-room chatting desultorily, neither of them anxious to communicate the worry both of them felt. Antonia talked about the lunch with Isabel Andrade and Diana discussed the style of the new dress, deep relief on her face when a door banged upstairs and Jaime's voice sounded in the hall.

Antonia forgot all about the meeting with her father as she jumped to her feet, watching the stairs. After a minute or so Jaime came down slowly into the room, stumbling a little over the last couple of steps, and Diana stared at him in astonishment. Antonia's heart sank as she took in the crooked smile, the dark shadow along Jaime's jaw, and the tie dangling loose from his open shirt collar. His jacket hung by its loop from one finger as he swept a grandiose bow to them both, a slight stagger somewhat spoiling the effect.

'*Como vai, madrasta?*' he said to Diana, then turned to stare at Antonia from narrowed, bloodshot eyes. 'And you, little *sister.* How are you tonight?'

'I'm not really qualified to judge, of course,' said Diana crisply, 'because I've never seen you in this condition before, but unless I'm much mistaken, Jaime de Almeida, you are drunk.'

He shook his head vigorously. '*Não, senhora. Um poucinho embriagado só.* Not drunk.'

Antonia looked at him unhappily. Something was wrong. Drunk or not, Jaime was an entirely different man from the one who'd kissed her with such tenderness in this very room only this morning. The eyes boring into her were angry and hostile and she retreated, stricken. Diana came close and put her arm round her.

'I beg to differ, Jaime,' she said cuttingly. 'Go and take a cold shower and come down to dinner as quickly as you can. Diva is performing miracles in the kitchen to keep the meal edible, so perhaps you might hurry.'

Jaime shrugged and spread his hands in a mocking gesture that was very Latin, and, to Antonia, very alien.

'*Pois é.* I shall be with you in seconds, I promise, *Madrasta*! I would not wish to dish—distress *Diva*! I go at once. *Desculpe-me!*' And he lurched up the stairs unsteadily, leaving a very fraught silence behind him.

CHAPTER TEN

ONE look at her daughter's face was enough to tighten Diana's lips. She led Antonia to the sofa. 'Let's sit down and finish our drinks while Jaime sobers up,' she said calmly. 'Don't be upset. That was the drink talking, not Jaime. Lord knows how much he must have knocked back to get him in that state—normally he has a head like a rock.'

Antonia tried to smile. 'Entertaining business associates, perhaps?'

'I sincerely hope not, in that condition.' Diana hesitated. 'Have you had a little quarrel or something, darling? I wouldn't have thought so. You seemed on top of the world this morning.'

'I was,' said Antonia bitterly. 'Jaime seems to have undergone something of a sea-change since then, though.'

'I rather thought you two were getting on like a house on fire. In fact, last night I was firmly convinced——' Diana stopped, frowning worriedly.

'Convinced he fancied me?' Antonia shrugged. 'Oddly,

enough, so was I. This morning even more so, even in the clear light of day.'

'I confess I'd hoped you two were falling in love.'

'You're a romantic, Diana!' Antonia jumped up, suddenly brisk. 'Come on, let's go up to the dining-room. I'm sure Jaime won't be long.'

She was right. He came down the staircase as they reached the dining-table, and gave them a small formal bow before seating himself at the head of it.

'My apologies, ladies, for allowing you to see me in such a condition earlier. A cold shower has effected the necessary sobriety, as you see.'

Antonia felt sobriety was a mere understatement as she looked at his sombre, brooding face. Jaime's hair was wet from the shower and shone slickly under the overhead light and, presumably in keeping with his mood, he was dressed in black. His thin cotton shirt was open at the neck, but with no red silk scarf knotted there this evening. His sombre mood was contagious, and Diana battled valiantly to introduce various topics of conversation, but without much success. Antonia pushed her chicken around her plate, but ate very little of it, as her mind worked at a furious rate, trying vainly to fathom the reason for the change in Jaime, since he volunteered no reason for his drunken state earlier, and none was asked. At one stage Diana mentioned the fabric bought in the town, and told him Pascoa had been imported from Lagoa del Rey to help her make a dress for Antonia to wear at the party. Jaime smiled at Antonia, with an expression in his eyes that chilled her to the soul.

'How very fortunate you are, little sister. A party given in your honour, jewels bought to heighten your beauty, and now a new dress to complete the effect. What more could you desire?'

A real smile from you for one thing, thought Antonia, and looked him in the eye, her chin up. 'Since you ask, *stepbrother*, I think the new dress calls for gold sandals to make it perfect. I thought to go into town in the morning to look for some. But please don't worry too much, because I can pay for these myself,' she added cuttingly.

Jaime's face looked grim. 'I prefer that you stay here in the house,' he said flatly.

'Jaime!' Diana looked at him appalled. 'What's got into you tonight? Why shouldn't Antonia go shopping if she wishes?'

'Alone? I forbid it. Besides, I need Joachim.'

The gold sandals had been sheer childish invention, to needle him further, but at Jaime's arrogant 'forbid' Antonia straightened in her chair, her eyes bright with a militant glitter Janet Grant would have recognised with misgiving. From the expression on Diana's face she recognised it too, and tried to interrupt, but Antonia smiled at her brilliantly.

'Don't worry, Diana. If transport's a problem I'll just ring for a taxi.'

Jaime got to his feet, pushing back his chair with a grinding noise on the polished floor. He stared at Antonia with eyes like flint and without looking in his stepmother's direction said very quietly, 'Leave us, Diana.'

Diana sprang up, going to Antonia protectively. 'I will not. I don't know what this is all about, but Antonia is my daughter, and I won't allow you to upset her.'

'Upset!' Jaime said with violence. '*Deus*, how I detest that word!' He breathed in and fought visibly for self-control.

Diana capitulated abruptly. 'Very well, if you are to do battle, Jaime,' she said in a deadly soft tone, 'grant me the courtesy of removing to the garden-room. I shall go upstairs for ten minutes exactly while Diva clears away. In that time you may say to Antonia whatever it is you feel you must. But I'm warning you, Jaime de Almeida—hurt Antonia and you hurt me.'

'I do not wish that, Diana——'

'Then take care!' Diana kissed Antonia, patted her shoulder, then made for the stairs. 'Ten minutes,' she repeated over her shoulder.

Without looking at him Antonia preceded Jaime in silence down the short flight of stairs to the garden-room and went over to the open patio door, leaning there as she looked out at the stars. Jaime followed and stood beside her, his eyes on her face. She turned to meet them steadily, her nerves strained to breaking point as she tried to see behind the cold, clinical gaze.'

'Well?' she asked at last, unable to bear the sombre scrutiny any longer.

'*Cara de santa!*' he said, in a tone which cut her to ribbons. 'How can such a beautiful face hide such a wanton little soul?'

Antonia shrank away from him in horror. 'What—what do you mean?'

'Do not plead innocence,' he sneered. 'This morning, here in this room, I felt I held paradise in my arms. I would have sworn you felt the same. Then this afternoon, like a lovesick fool, I could endure my office no longer. I took a taxi and rushed home early—just to be with you. I paid off the driver at the end of the road and began to run towards the gate.' Suddenly he struck his forehead with the palm of his hand. '*Deus me livre*, what a fool!' He took her by the shoulders and shook her. 'And there you were—outside my very gate in a car, in the arms of another man. I could not believe my eyes. I saw him kiss you and I turned and ran. I ran away, Antonia, because if I had stayed I would have killed him.'

Antonia stared at him, appalled. 'Jaime, please, it was nothing like that!' She felt no compunction in breaking her promise to her father, this was too serious to bother about scruples. 'Please, I can explain——'

Jaime clapped a hand over her mouth, glaring down into her outraged eyes. 'Explain? *Que demência!* What is there to explain? I told you that what was mine was not for any other man. It is different, no doubt, in your liberated society in England, but for me I want no woman still warm from another man's arms. The lunch with Isabel Andrade was all *mentira, não é*? You lied! God knows how you met another man—perhaps when you had Marisa with you— an innocent child!'

Antonia freed herself violently. 'I was the idiot, Senhor de Almeida, not you!' Her eyes blazed at him. 'There is an explanation—one I promised faithfully to keep secret for a few days, yet I was all too ready to break my promise just to tell you—and you only, I might add. But to hell with that! What's the point if that's the way you think of me even after—after——' She swallowed an angry sob and ran for the stairs.

'Antonia——' Jaime sprang after her, catching her by the arm, but she struck his hand away, then, as he tried to hold her back, hit out wildly, catching him on his mouth. His head flew back, his hair lifting with the force of the blow and Antonia watched, exulting, as he touched a hand to the blood oozing from his split lip.

'Time up,' said a voice above them, and Antonia looked up into Diana's face and sagged like a rag doll.

'Yes, Diana,' she agreed dully. 'I rather think it is.' Blindly she brushed past her mother and ran upstairs to her room to throw herself down on the bed. I ought to be crying, she thought, but where are the tears? She lay dry-eyed, stiff with misery, suddenly homesick for Bristol and shaken by a longing for Janet Grant's brisk comfort. It seemed a very long time before Diana came to see how she was, and Antonia sat up, blinking as she turned on the bedside lamp.

'Are you all in one piece? No black eyes or any other injuries?' enquired Diana.

Nothing that shows, thought Antonia, and tried to reassure Diana with a smile. As reassurance it was obviously a failure, since Diana shook her head, sighing as she sat on the end of the bed.

'Jaime's bloody but unbowed, and he won't say a word. Will you?'

Antonia was torn, but after a moment's thought shook her head. 'It's nothing—really. Stupid misunderstanding, that's all.'

Diana looked sceptical. 'And now Jaime's gone to bed with a bottle of *cachaça*, God help him, and you look terrible.

Can't you two sort it out, for heaven's sake?'

'I tried—hard. But he wouldn't listen.'

'What's got into the man?'

Antonia shrugged dispiritedly. 'I'm past caring for now—sort of numb.'

'Would you like to go home?'

'Home? To England?' Antonia looked startled.

Diana smiled and leaned forward to brush the tangled curls from Antonia's forehead. 'No, darling. To Lagoa del Rey.'

'Oh yes! Please!' Antonia threw her arms round Diana convulsively. 'I can't bear to stay here now.'

'We'll have to come back for the party,' warned Diana.

'Party? Oh no!' Antonia shuddered. 'Surely Jaime could cancel it or something.'

'No chance, love. Too many people involved—and it isn't solely for your benefit, you know. It's Jaime's way of repaying hospitality. I'm afraid the show must go on—and you have to be there.'

Next morning Sabino arrived to take them back to the peaceful house by the lake. Diana had informed Jaime of their departure before he left for the day, and was rather vague about the encounter when she spoke to Antonia at breakfast.

'He wasn't feeling too marvellous this morning,' she said, once Marisa had gone off with Zelia to pack her belongings. 'One way and another Jaime was not at his best. His lip was a mess—very swollen.'

'Sheer fluke,' said Antonia callously. 'It caught against his teeth, that's all.'

'I don't think it's his lip that's making him look so haggard and desperate this morning, love, somehow.'

'No,' agreed Antonia. 'Probably just a hangover.' She looked at Diana diffidently. 'Would it be all right if I rang Isabel Andrade and explained that we'll be away until Saturday, just in case she gets in touch?'

'Yes, of course, darling—a nice thought. Do it now while

I see if Marisa's ready. Sabino arrived ages ago.'

Feeling distinctly furtive, Antonia rang the Andrade number and had a quick word with Isabel to give her the change of plan, and Isabel thanked her affectionately, promising to tell Antonio.

'He was so very happy, yesterday, *cara*—and so am I. I so long to see Diana again.'

After Antonia rang off she stood still by the desk in Jaime's study, just looking sadly round the room, then listlessly she went off to collect her belongings, suddenly desperate to leave this beautiful house and get back to the peace and solitude of Lagoa del Rey.

Despite her bitter hurt over Jaime's attitude, Antonia found the atmosphere of Lagoa del Rey balm to her troubled heart when they arrived, as Maria sailed out majestically to greet them and embrace Marisa, and to shower welcome over Diana and Antonia.

She had expected the time to hang heavy, but Diana asked her to take charge of Marisa during the day so Zelia could be free to help with the sewing, and Antonia was only too glad of something to do. She asked Geraldo, via Marisa, to rig up a net on one of the lawns so they could play tennis, and the child, delighted to have Antonia to herself most of the time, quickly recovered from the disappointment of having her visit to Boa Vista cut short. They swam and rode, with Geraldo in attendance, and played so much with ball and racquet Antonia felt tired each day by the time darkness fell, and able to sleep better than expected, except when thoughts of Jaime and the memory of those moments in his arms kept her wakeful and bitter in her anger towards him.

The new dress was coming on at a tremendous rate, and by the afternoon of Friday was pronounced ready. After time spent in the hot, dry sunshine of Lagoa del Rey Antonia's skin had darkened even more, and when Diana slid the dress over her head at long last, and fastened it and smoothed it into place, she stood looking at her daughter with a curious little smile on her face.

'Well?' demanded Antonia, looking down at herself. 'What do you think?'

'I think I'm rather clever,' said Diana with satisfaction. 'Not one in a hundred could get away with that colour, but against your skin and hair it's—well, sensational. I think it's the gold-dust effect that really makes it. Come and see yourself in the long mirror in my room.'

Antonia stood looking at herself in silence. It seemed like some other girl in the mirror. Diana had cut the bodice of the dress in a deep V to complement the handkerchief points of the hem, and the thin, delicate fabric clung to Antonia's breasts and waist and the skirt floated delicately as she moved. But the real impact came from the illusion that fabric and skin were all one colour, that it was difficult to tell at first glance where one ended and the other began. And by contrast her hair and eyes gleamed, echoing the gilt splattered on the dress.

'And you consider this suitable for a barbecue?' she asked, shaking her head.

'It is for the type Jaime holds——' Diana stopped, biting her lip. 'Sorry, love. It still hurts badly, doesn't it?'

Antonia nodded. 'Yes. But I hope his lip does, too.'

'And not only his lip, at a guess, Antonia.'

'As to that I wouldn't care to say. Now, little mother, what am I going to do about shoes? What do you say to barefoot with a gold chain around my ankle?'

Diana chuckled and gave her a little hug. 'We'll go in to Boa Vista first thing on Saturday and find something, don't worry. I know just the place.' She slid down the zip carefully on the dress and drew it over Antonia's head.

Antonia pulled on her shirt and jeans and frowned suddenly. 'And what are *you* going to wear, by the way?'

Diana opened her wardrobe and took out a silk dress that gleamed in peacock colours of blue shot with green. 'How about this? I made it some time ago, but haven't worn it yet. I was waiting for a special occasion, I suppose. I could wear my aquamarines with it, maybe.'

Antonia whistled softly. 'You're so *clever*, Diana. It's gorgeous!'

And, she thought later, as she lay in the bath, Saturday could surely be described as a very special occasion, one way and another, for Diana at least, if not quite such unallowed bliss for herself, as she had originally thought. Jaime must be regretting his idea of a party pretty violently by now, but since he was the host he had very little option but to carry on with it. How in heaven's name she herself was going to be able to laugh and chat and pretend she was having a great time under the scrutiny of Jaime's hostile black eyes she had no idea, especially when all she really wanted was to stay here in hiding at Lagoa del Rey. But there was her father to think of; he was probably feeling apprehensive about meeting Diana again. After more than twenty years it was quite possible they might just be strangers to each other, with nothing left in common. Except me, Antonia reminded herself wryly. They have me in common. What a shock she must have been to Antonio Luis de Freitas! Particularly since her resemblance to him was so unmistakable. Antonia sighed. She felt terrible in one way about keeping the news from Diana, but this was one secret no one could share until her father came face to face with her mother at last. She would have told Jaime, nevertheless, done anything to rid him of his blind misconception. But he had refused to listen. It was a great pity she was forced to go back to spend another night under his roof under the circumstances. At first she'd considered asking Diana if they could return to Lagoa del Rey immediately after the party, but there was Marisa to consider. Antonia's mouth drooped forlornly. She'd caused enough trouble already without upsetting Marisa on top of it. And Mario would be there, at least. Dear Mario. Why, oh, why couldn't she have fallen in love with *him*? It should have been easy—heaven knew he was attractive enough. But from the moment she'd set eyes on Jaime's hard face, Mario had just faded into the background, a beautiful, gentle copy of his elder brother.

Antonia set off for Boa Vista with Diana and Marisa, in wary mood. Marisa, clutching her beloved tennis racquet, chattered away to Zelia as usual, while Diana talked desultorily to Antonia, who hardly saw the scenery this time in her preoccupation with the prospect of meeting Jaime face to face again. Nerves knotted in her stomach as she tried to respond sensibly to Diana's conversation.

'Try not to be so tense, darling.' Diana smiled at her reassuringly. 'I'm sure Jaime's had time to repent of his sins by now.'

'But as far as he's concerned the sins are all mine,' answered Antonia rashly.

'What possible sins have you had the opportunity to commit in Boa Vista, silly child?'

More than you know, thought Antonia guiltily, and turned away from the questioning grey eyes to promise Marisa a short session on Jaime's tennis court before she got ready for the party.

When they arrived in Boa Vista Diana directed Sabino to the exclusive little *sapataria* where she was sure Antonia would find shoes to go with the dress. In no time a pair of fragile sandals had been found, not in the gold kid originally planned, but in satin of the same shade as the dress, to Antonia's delight.

'Well, well,' said Antonia, when they were in car again. 'Perhaps my luck has changed!'

Casa Madrugada was in utter turmoil when they arrived. Diva was in the kitchen with what seemed like an army of female relatives, all talking at the tops of their voices as they prepared various salads to serve with the *churrasco*, while Joachim supervised the setting up of a bar on the terrace, and electricians suspended lights throughout the garden in strategic places. Of Jaime, to Antonia's relief, there was no sign.

Diva abandoned her busy minions to greet Diana and Antonia and to make as much fuss of Marisa as though it had been months instead of days since she had last seen her.

Senhor Jaime had gone with Senhor Mario to the airport to meet friends from Rio who were putting up at a hotel for the party. He would be home later. In the meantime the ladies were to make themselves comfortable and take tea in the *sala do jardim* downstairs.

'Don't worry about us,' Diana assured her, telling her that Zelia was there to see to them and that they would keep out of the way as much as possible until it was time for the guests to arrive. Once the electricians had finished in the garden Antonia gave Marisa the promised game on the tennis court, strictly limited by Diana to half an hour only. For once Marisa made no protest, and after her bath repaired to the kitchen to hold court like a queen among Diva's admiring relatives, accepting all sorts of delicacies from the food being prepared for the party.

'I can only hope she won't be sick later,' sighed Diana ruefully, as she went upstairs with Antonia. 'Thank goodness Zelia's here to keep an eye on her.'

They separated to take baths and relax a little before the evening proper began, and Antonia sighed with relief as she closed her bedroom door behind her. She had been longing to hide herself away ever since their arrival, her nerves tuned to concert pitch as she waited for Jaime to appear. Now it would be easier. By the time their encounter was unavoidable she would be bathed and scented and in her warpaint, wearing the new dress as armour against the look she dreaded to see in his eyes. As she wrapped herself in a towel a knock sounded on the bedroom door, and her heart raced madly then slowed down again as Diana came in smiling, holding out a small box. 'These arrived this afternoon—do you like them?'

Antonia opened the tiny leather box and looked in silence at the topaz and diamond ear-rings lying inside. Carefully she lifted one out, touching it with a reverent finger. 'I've never seen anything more exquisite—thank you.' She gave Diana a hug. 'I do have a sort of present for you too, but I'm afraid you can't have it just yet.'

'Really? How exciting!' Diana laughed. 'Don't keep me

in suspense too long, please—I love surprises.'

She went out, closing the door carefully behind her, and Antonia caught her breath as she heard Jaime's voice outside making apologies to Diana for his absence. The voices receded as they went away along the landing and Antonia sat down limply at the dressing-table, furious to find her knees trembling. Idiot, she told herself bitingly, and set to on her hair, refusing to let herself think of Jaime, keeping her mind instead on the thought of Diana's suspense. It was nothing to her own. It could hardly be often a daughter gave her mother a long-lost lover as a present! It was to be hoped that Diana would be pleased with her 'present'—always supposing Antonio de Freitas put in an appearance that evening, of course. But Antonia had no doubt that he would, that his intention was to meet Diana in public here tonight and surprise her into an instinctive reaction to him. One way and another the coming evening promised to be highly memorable.

Half an hour later, her make-up a little more vivid than usual, her hair gleaming with natural highlights by courtesy of the sun, Antonia felt rather pleased with her reflection in the mirror. The effect, as Diana had said, *was* arresting, heightened by the fire from the ear-rings as she moved her head back and forth to admire them. As promised, she went first to show herself to Marisa, who was playing snakes and ladders with Zelia in her room. Both the child and the young maid were so whole-hearted in their admiration that Antonia's spirits rose, and she smiled gaily, holding out her skirts as she curtsied to them before going along to Diana's room to find her mother searching frantically through her suitcase.

'I've just laddered my stocking!' she wailed, then looked up, her eyes widening as she saw Antonia. 'Oh, my darling! You look—I can't find the right word!'

'The word isn't "overdone", by any chance?' asked Antonia drily.

Diana got up and drew her to the dressing-table, meeting her eyes in the mirror. 'No—it's "exotic", I think, love.'

'You look pretty tasty yourself this evening, little mother. I'd suggest a fraction more eyeshadow, but otherwise you're a knockout.'

'Thank you for those kind words. Now—I'll change these stockings and put the extra blob of colour on, as instructed, and then I'll be down. Tell Jaime I'm on my way.' Diana raised her eyebrows at the look on Antonia's face. 'Scared to meet him on your own?'

'Out of my wits. But I'll go down.'

'Good girl.'

Antonia left Diana's bedroom and walked towards the stairs. It seemed inevitable that Jaime should be standing in the hall below, exchanging a word with Joachim before the latter retired to man the gates. At the sound of Antonia's heels on the marble stairs Jaime looked up, his face suddenly very still as he gazed at the girl coming down slowly towards him in her drifting dress, her gilt-tipped, curling hair an aureole of light around her vivid face. Jaime wore an ivory linen suit with a silk shirt a shade or two darker and looked devastatingly handsome—and, Antonia saw with a sinking heart, utterly implacable. She faltered for an instant, then her chin lifted and she came down the last few steps, holding out her hand to him formally.

'Good evening.'

Joachim excused himself, and Jaime looked at Antonia's hand for a moment, then touched it briefly, and gave her a formal bow. 'Good evening.' He hesitated, eyeing her warily. 'You are well, Antonia?'

'Never felt better,' she assured him untruthfully.

He looked at her broodingly for some time, then as though he could contain the words no longer he said rapidly. 'After you left for Lagoa del Rey I had much time to think—to hope there *was* some simple explanation for what I witnessed, to wish very much I had let you tell me.' Jaime paused expectantly, but Antonia kept stubbornly silent. He drew in a deep breath. 'What I am trying to say,' he went on, through clenched teeth, 'is that I desire to hear about that day now I am less—less——'

'Objectionable? Drunk?' she suggested sweetly.

Jaime came a step closer, looking suddenly dangerous. 'Tell me who the man was, Antonia—tell me!'

'I can't.'

'*Porquê?*'

'I promised him I wouldn't.' Antonia looked at him steadily, hoping her face showed nothing of the turmoil raging inside her.

Jaime's face hardened into a cold mask. 'Then there is no more to say.' He stepped back deliberately. 'I regret I was unable to be present earlier to welcome you as a guest in my house.'

Antonia smiled at him with irony. 'Cold feet, perhaps?'

The rigid mask slipped a little. 'Cold feet? What is that?'

'It means you were afraid—of meeting me face to face.'

'*Bobagem!*' he snarled, then stopped short as Diana appeared on the landing above. By the time she joined them Jaime had himself well in hand again. 'You look very beautiful tonight, Diana,' he said, ignoring Antonia.

'Thank you, Jaime.' Diana looked from one taut face to the other. 'I think we both do you credit. Don't you think I did a good job on Antonia's dress?'

Antonia felt Jaime's eyes on her like a brand as he looked her up and down with insultingly impersonal deliberation.

'The *dress* is matchless. You have excelled yourself, Diana.' He glanced at his watch. 'Let us drink some champagne before the guests arrive. We have half an hour's grace, I think.'

'Champagne!' commented Diana. 'Are we celebrating something?'

'Why, yes! Perhaps I spoil the surprise a little, but Mario——' He broke off as the doorbell rang, and handed each of them a brimming crystal goblet. 'That will be him now. Let us go through into the drawing-room.'

'Why is Mario ringing the doorbell?' Diana asked Jaime, as Diva went to the door.

'Because tonight is a special occasion. Come.' Jaime

waved them ahead of him into the beautiful, formal room, as Diva ushered in not Mario, as expected but Isabel Andrade, accompanied by a heavily built dark man. As Jaime started forward he missed the look on Diana's face, and Antonia's heart began to pound heavily as the two women confronted each other.

'Isabel?' said Diana incredulously. '*You* are Isabel Andrade?'

Isabel threw her arms around Diana, embracing her convulsively, to Jaime's bewilderment. 'Diana, Diana *que milagre*! You have not changed at all!'

Diana held her at arm's length, looking from her to Antonia, shaking her head in dazed disbelief. 'It was *you* who met Antonia? Then, then——'

Isabel nodded, her eyes glistening with tears, reaching out a hand to the dark, smiling man watching them. '*Meu marido*, Luis.'

Luis Andrade bowed over Diana's trembling hand. '*Encantado*, Senhora de Almeida,' he said. 'My wife has already told me your story. I am very happy to meet you.'

Jaime stood apart, his face questioning, as one of the white-gloved waiters hired for the evening appeared silently with a tray of drinks. Antonia had rescued Diana's glass the moment Isabel appeared, and she set it down on a nearby table to hide the unsteadiness of her own hands as Isabel smiled brilliantly at Jaime, and explained that through Antonia she had discovered Diana was an old friend, adding an apology for their early arrival. At which point the front door opened and Mario came in with Isilda, who looked sensational in a brief black dress sewn all over with glittering silver beads.

'*Como vai*?' said Mario happily, his face alight with his familiar smile. 'Isilda and I found someone outside in the garden, Jaime.' He paused to kiss his dazed stepmother, and then Antonia, while Jaime introduced Isilda to the others. '*Que coisa linda*, Antonia!' he said, looking her up and down. 'You take the breath away tonight.'

Antonia scarcely heard him. All her attention was on

Jaime, who had gone to welcome the man who came in quietly, holding out his hand to his host while Diana, her back to the door, was still trying to come to terms with meeting Isabel. Antonia could see Jaime stiffen as he looked the newcomer in the eye. The latter bowed and said something quietly, but his eyes turned instantly to the slender figure in the brilliant blue dress. Jaime's face darkened as Antonio de Freitas looked back for a moment at Antonia's tense face in reassurance, then Isabel turned Diana gently by the shoulders so that she looked upon the face of Antonio de Freitas again, for the first time in twenty-two years. Antonia registered the thunderstruck looks exchanged by Jaime and Mario, but her full attention was turned on her mother's face, which slowly went paper-white.

'Tonio?' whispered Diana, and swayed slightly. Both Mario and Jaime leapt towards her, but Antonio de Freitas was before them. He caught Diana and held her tight, his eyes closed as his cheek came down on her hair. Antonia watched them dumbly, her heart full, then she turned away, deeply conscious that she was witnessing something intensely private. Isabel and Luis Andrade came to her at once, as did Isilda and Mario, and Antonia went with them down to the garden-room and out on the terrace, to find the garden had become a softly lit fairyland, complete with its own genie in the shape of Ildefonso, a giant black man in a tall chef's hat who was coaxing the glowing charcoal of his *churrasco* fire to the exact degree of perfection required to grill the first batch of meat. Waiters presided over a bar at the end of the terrace against a background of music relayed to a series of loudspeakers from Jaime's stereo, and Mario slid his arm about Antonia's waist and smiled lovingly at her.

'So little sister. At last we know the secret Diana has kept all these years.'

Antonia nodded and sighed deeply, suddenly glad of the fresh glass of champagne she was offered, as Isabel gave the others a brief account of that summer years before in Spain.

'*Meu Deus*, how romantic,' said Isilda, her vivid face warm with sympathy. She slid her arm through Mario's and smiled up at him. 'No one will be interested in our news now, *querido*.'

Mario bent to kiss her and said proudly, 'I am sure they will, *cara*.' He beamed at the others. 'Today Isilda has consented to marry me.'

There were exclamations and congratulations all round, and much commiseration that their announcement had been overshadowed by the dramatic reunion of Diana and Antonio de Freitas. Then other guests began to arrive and soon the terrace became crowded as Mario introduced Antonia to local friends who were new to her, and Isilda discreetly supplied names of the people she had already met at the yacht club at Lagoa del Rey. Antonia chatted and smiled and agreed that Boa Vista was a beautiful place, that she loved Brazil, but all the time she was on edge, wondering what was happening with Diana and her father, and where Jaime was.

Mario rescued her eventually. 'Let us relieve Jaime from his role of welcoming host, Antonia.' As they went up the stairs he squeezed her hand. 'I thought you were looking a little worried, *cara*.'

'I am,' she agreed. 'I'm dying to find out what's happened.'

The drawing-room was crowded with new arrivals, with Jaime in control in his role of host, but no sign of Diana or Antonio de Freitas. As Jaime caught sight of Antonia and Mario he made his way towards them swiftly.

'Antonia was anxious,' said Mario.

'They are in my study,' said Jaime in instant understanding. 'I think they need much time alone yet. Can you direct people downstairs, Mario? I wish to wait here a little longer; Luc Fonseca is late.'

'*Pois é.*' At once Mario went among the guests, shepherding them towards the stairs. Antonia would have gone with him, but Jaime's hand closed on her wrist.

'Stay with me,' he said urgently, and without risking a scene she had little choice but to acquiesce. Before he could say anything further the last of the guests finally arrived and Jaime drew Antonia towards the couple Diva was letting in and, to her surprise, told her the woman was British like herself. Luc Fonseca, the owner of a goldmine in Campo d'Ouro, was Brazilian, but his wife Emily was small and fair and very English-looking, rather in the same way as Diana.

'How lovely to meet you, Antonia,' cried Emily Fonseca warmly. 'What a surprise you are—we had no idea you had a stepsister, Jaime!'

'Antonia is Diana's daughter, not my sister,' said Jaime, with such emphasis Luc Fonseca clapped him on the shoulder, laughing.

'*Ah, sim, compreendo!*' He raised Antonia's hand to his. '*Muito prazer*, Miss Antonia.' He had some grey among his curling dark hair, but his eyes danced as he smiled at her and Antonia returned the smile warmly, thinking he was almost as attractive as Jaime. Emily asked how she liked Brazil, and Antonia sighed regretfully.

'I shan't be here much longer, my holiday will be over soon.' She felt Jaime stiffen by her side, and Emily smiled, her bright blue eyes mischievous as they twinkled up at him.

'Surely you can persuade her to stay a little longer, Jaime! I'm willing to demonstrate how easily tender British plants take root in this rich Brazilian soil of yours.' She turned to Antonia. 'Come over to Campo d'Ouro—as long as you don't mind children. We're knee-deep in them, especially when Claudia Treharne adds her two. She's expecting a third any time, which is why she and Saul are missing tonight. Bring Marisa—she likes it at Casa d'Ouro.'

'Thank you, I'd like to very much, if there's time.' Antonia smiled, pleased, liking Emily Fonseca very much.

'Come then,' said Jaime. 'Let us join everyone in the garden——'

'*Sim, senhor*—I could eat a horse,' said Luc with enthusiasm.

'I hope that's not what I could smell wafting up when we came in,' said Emily. 'Is the famous Ildefonso presiding over the *churrasco*, Jaime?'

They all left the drawing-room, Antonia's wrist still held fast by Jaime's fingers, but she hung back a little.

'I'd like to find Diana,' she said quietly. 'I'll join you later.'

Jaime let her go with reluctance. 'Antonia——' he began urgently, but she shook her head.

'You must see to your guests,' and she walked away from him across the hall to the study door, unable to resist a look over her shoulder to confirm that he was watching her bleakly before he turned away to follow the Fonsecas down to join the party.

Antonia tapped on the door, and after a moment it was thrown open by Antonio de Freitas, who looked so blazingly happy he seemed to have shed ten years. Antonia's eyes went from him to Diana, who sat perched on Jaime's desk, her face flushed and her hair untidy.

'Well, little mother,' said Antonia with a bright smile. 'How did you like your present?'

CHAPTER ELEVEN

THE evening after that was always a blur in Antonia's mind. The party was a great success in more ways than one, the surprise events of the evening providing spice for the sumptuous *churrasco* served to the guests, and serving as unending topic of conversation at dinner-tables for weeks to come, since Diana de Almeida and Antonio de Freitas saw no point in trying to conceal the truth about their former relationship. It would have been fruitless anyway, since the living proof of their love was there, glowing beside

them, looking so like her father it gave rise to much
exclamatory comment. Added to this was the news that
Mario de Almeida, one of the greatest matrimonial prizes
in Minas Gerais, had finally decided to take the plunge.
Antonia watched him with Isilda who, far from looking
triumphant, seemed unable to believe in her own good
fortune, and spent the greater part of the evening gazing up
into her *noivo's* handsome face in a tremulous sort of
disbelief. Antonia warmed to her more and more, finding
the new, rather vulnerable Isilda easier to like than the
hostile beauty she had assumed belonged to Jaime the first
time they met.

'How are things with you?' asked Diana at one stage,
when they went upstairs together to peep at Marisa. 'I wish
I could believe that things were right again between you
and Jaime, but they're not, are they?'

Antonia smiled whimsically. 'Two happy endings out of
three are enough for one evening, little mother, surely!'

Jaime had tried his utmost to get her alone, it was true,
but Antonia had taken infinite pleasure in eluding him for
most of the evening. She stayed with Isabel and Luis and
the Fonsecas, and once the dancing began Janio Cardoso
and Vasco de Almeida vied with each other constantly in
monopolising her as a partner. By the time the first people
began to leave Jaime was having considerable trouble in
keeping a smile in place. Antonia secretly revelled in the
way his eyes followed her as she talked and laughed with
Vasco or Janio, and in between times returned to Diana
and Antonio, to share the happiness radiating from them
both. At last Mario, kind as always, took pity on his
brother, and joined forces with Isilda to bid farewell to
departing guests, and at once Jaime pushed his way
through the crowd still dancing on the terrace to detach
Antonia from her parents' side with an air of purpose that
decided her against any form of resistance. For several
minutes they moved together in time to the music, while
Jaime never said a word. He held Antonia close, looking
down at her averted face in a way that prompted Antonio

de Freitas to turn to Diana with raised eyebrows.

After a while Jaime said shortly, 'Come.' He took Antonia by the hand and drew her towards the end of the terrace where a screen of imported greenery formed a picturesque setting for the bar, also an effective camouflage for the door hidden behind it. Antonia hung back as she realised where he was taking her.

'No!' she said, but he ignored her, thrusting her through the narrow opening and locking the door behind him.

'Go up the stairs,' he said brusquely, and unwillingly she climbed the spiral which seemed to wind upwards for a very long time until it brought her to the clinical brightness of Jaime's bathroom. He propelled her quickly into the dark bedroom, closing the door behind him before he turned on the bedside lamp.

'You have no right to bring me here——' began Antonia, turning on him furiously, but Jaime was in no mood to listen.

'The man in the car,' he said tightly. 'That was Antonio de Freitas?'

'Yes. My father.' Antonia moved away to stand in the shadows at the foot of the bed. 'I had only made his acquaintance a short time before.'

'Why did you not *tell* me?'

'I tried—hard. But you wouldn't listen,' she snapped.

They stared at each other, Antonia aloof, Jaime haggard.

'*Eu te quero*, Antonia,' he said very quietly.

Antonia knew what it meant by this time. 'Then want must be your master. My mother—Janet—used to say that when I was small.'

'Want?' he moved nearer. 'That was not my meaning. I—I *love* you, Antonia.' Jaime clenched his hands, his eyes suddenly desperate. 'You have much right to be angry. But picture that day, Antonia. If you had seen me so in another's arms would *you* not have been hurt? Mad with jealousy?' He seized her wrists, staring down into her eyes. 'Or are you so cold and Anglo-Saxon that you do not experience such things? Perhaps I am mistaken and you care nothing at all for me.'

'I wish I didn't!' she flung at him, then stopped, furious
with herself as triumph gleamed in his eyes.

'So! You *do* love me!'

'*No*, I *don't*!'

'Then why are you trembling?' The sudden caressing
note in his voice took her by surprise. Antonia tried to pull
free, but he was too swift for her. He caught her wrists
together and held them behind her back with one hand.
'The last time we were alone you wounded my lip,' he
whispered, the look in his eyes turning her legs to jelly. 'Is it
not time you kissed it better?'

The touch of his lips on hers was no cure for the shakes,
Antonia found. Her nervous system had taken something of
a beating all evening, and this final assault on them was too
much. She shook in his grasp like a leaf and he released her
hands and picked her up, walking to the bed, where he laid
her down gently. Antonia promptly bounced up again, but
Jaime caught her in his arms and stretched full-length
beside her, stifling her protests with his mouth. She fought
free, struggling for breath.

'My dress——'

'I do not like your dress!'

'But——'

'You will not wear it again. It is too much the same as
your skin——'

'It was Diana's choice.'

'*Não faz mal*—throw it away.'

Antonia snorted. 'I will *not*. Now let me up—Jaime, be
careful—you'll tear it!'

'Then be still.' And he began kissing her with such single-
minded concentration Antonia soon forgot about her dress.
It was such rapture to be in Jaime's arms again that she
forgot everything else as well, returning his kisses with such
fervour that very quickly kisses were no longer enough. It
was Jaime's fingers between her shoulderblades, seeking the
fine concealed zip, which jolted Antonia to her senses and
she pushed him away.

'What are we *doing*? There's a party going on down there,' she panted, trying to elude his seeking mouth.

'I do not care,' he muttered thickly.

'Well, I do—oh, please—Jaime—stop it! Remember I've got a father now!'

'So you have! Let us go and find him.' Jaime abruptly rolled off the bed and stood up, scooping her up on her feet and pulling her to the door.

'Let's go back the other way—besides I must tidy myself—I look a fright. Everyone will know——' Antonia protested in desperation, but he took no notice, throwing open the door on to the gallery. As they emerged from the bedroom several pairs of eyes turned up in their direction and Antonia's cheeks flamed as Jaime pulled her down the stairs by his side.

'*Acabou a festa*, Jaime,' said Mario grinning.

The party was indeed over. The only people left by this time were Isabel and Luis Andrade, Diana, Antonio de Freitas, Mario and Isilda. As Jaime hauled an unwilling Antonia down the staircase the expressions in the eyes on the dishevelled pair were varied. Isabel and Luis looked amused, as did Isilda, while Mario was obviously having trouble in choking back a laugh. Diana's eyes were hard to read, but Antonio de Freitas looked like thunder as he saw the crumpled state of his daughter's dress and eyed her wildly untidy hair. He started towards them furiously, but Diana laid a restraining hand on his arm.

'Tonio. Don't throw a spanner in the works—please.'

He spun round to look down at her in amazement. 'Spanner in the works, *querida*? What is that? *Meu Deus*, Diana, look at the state of her!' He rounded on Jaime fiercely, but Diana's hand held him back.

'Let Jaime say his piece.'

'*Muito obrigad'*, Diana,' said Jaime and turned to Antonio de Freitas, looking him squarely in the eye. 'I appreciate that you have only just found your daughter; nevertheless I wish to take her away from you. I want very much to marry her.'

'Oh, *do* you?' said Antonia, incensed. 'Well, it's *me* you're supposed to ask—not that I mean any offence to you,' she added hastily, smiling at her nonplussed father. 'No—don't go,' she said quickly to Isabel and Luis Andrade, who were obviously of the opinion they should leave at this point.

'Tonio,' said Diana with patience. 'I have been throwing your daughter and my stepson together with unrestrained enthusiasm ever since they laid eyes on each other, in an effort to keep Antonia with me by the happiest means possible all round. Don't spoil all my good work just because you have a fancy to play the heavy father.'

This was entirely too much for Mario, who began to laugh helplessly, Isilda joining in. 'Women!' he said, spluttering.

'Diana!' Antonia stared open-mouthed at her small, fragile-looking mother. 'You mean you deliberately——'

'Yes.' Diana nodded blithely. 'It seemed the best way to keep you here.'

Jaime looked unsurprised. 'Diana would never have left you alone with me otherwise, *meu amor.*'

Antonia flashed him a kindling look. 'With good reason!'

Antonio de Freitas looked from his daughter's flushed face to the determined one of Jaime de Almeida in startled comprehension. 'It is evident I should have arrived sooner—a great deal sooner.'

'Twenty-two years ago, perhaps,' said Jaime significantly, and there was a tense pause as he stared in challenge at the slim, fair man holding Diana's hand.

'That's unfair!' said Antonia, glaring at Jaime.

'But it is also true,' said her father wryly. He looked at Diana with rueful tenderness. 'You are quite happy to give our daughter to this stepson of yours?'

'Blissfully happy.'

'Then I am happy also, *querida.*'

Isabel came to kiss Diana and take her leave with her smiling husband, then looked at her brother uncertainly. 'Are you coming with us, Tonio?'

'*Pois é,*' he said, surprised, and touched Diana's cheek

lovingly. 'Before there is any wedding for our daughter, I think it only proper there should be a wedding for her parents.' He grinned as Mario collapsed again on Isilda's shoulder. 'Antonia and Jaime will need to wait a little, *não é*?'

Jaime looked totally unconvinced on this point and said so in no uncertain terms, but Antonia scowled at him repressively.

'Haven't you overlooked one little detail, Jaime de Almeida? I haven't even said I'll marry you!'

'Then do so!' he ordered.

'You haven't asked me yet!'

They glared at each other like combatants, while Mario howled with mirth and Isilda tried to hush him and Antonio de Freitas stood poised, ready to intervene, then Diana said sharply, 'Antonia!'

Antonia looked at her, startled. 'Yes?'

'Do you love Jaime?'

All eyes turned on the girl in the crumpled dress and she coloured to the roots of her hair. She looked uncertainly at Jaime, who stood tense, waiting for her answer. 'Well, yes,' she admitted, shrugging. 'I suppose I do.'

Jaime pulled her into his arms without ceremony. '*Graças a Deus. Agora——*'

'Speak English,' she said tartly.

'What a shrew you are!' Abruptly he released her and went down on one knee, taking her hand in his. 'In front of all these people as my witnesses, Antonia Luisa, will you honour me by becoming my wife?'

'Oh, for heaven's sake—only if you'll get up at once,' she said, hideously embarrassed.

Jaime sprang up. 'Was that a yes?'

'Yes!'

He swept her into his arms and kissed her very thoroughly, not in the least perturbed by the public nature of their embrace. When Jaime released Antonia at last she was flushed and laughing, and his face shone with triumph. 'Now let us return downstairs and drink more champagne,' he said exuberantly. 'Much more champagne!' And immediately everyone began talking at once in happy relief, though as they went down to the garden-room Mario's voice could be heard above the rest, working out the various relationships that would result from the forthcoming nuptials.

'Jaime,' he said helpfully, 'you will be Diana's son-in-law as well as stepson, Antonia will be your stepsister and also you wife—*meu Deus*, Isilda, is that allowed? *Então*, Senhor de Freitas will gain a little stepdaughter as well as a daughter, also two stepsons, one of whom will also be his son-in-law . . .'

Any further clarifications ended in howls of anguish as Mario fended off retaliation from his elder brother, until the latter was finally persuaded very sweetly by his intended wife to divert his energies to the happier task of popping celebratory champagne corks instead.

Harlequin Romance

Coming Next Month

2929 LOSING BATTLE Kerry Allyne
Adair has good reasons for the way she dresses and looks. She's not about to change because of arrogant Thane Callahan. After all, he's seemingly no different than the men who'd caused her bitter lack of trust.

2930 BLACK SHEEP Susan Fox
Willa Ross returns to her hometown of Cascade, Wyoming, only to discover she's still drawn to the man she'd been love-struck with as a teenager—and he still blames her for the accident that caused his sister's death.

2931 RIDER OF THE HILLS Miriam MacGregor
Janie's only chance of getting an interview with New Zealand's famous polo player, Lance Winter, is to temporarily replace his injured trainer. Once there, however, she finds her prime concern is what Lance will think of her deception!

2932 HEART'S TREASURE Annabel Murray
Jacques Fresnay's involvement in the Peruvian expedition is a surprise to Rylla. Equally surprising is that he seems to be genuinely kind, though he'd ridiculed her father's work. Should she abide by family loyalty, or give in to Jacques's charm?

2933 THE COURSE OF TRUE LOVE Betty Neels
Claribel's current attentive male friends begin to lack interest when consulting surgeon Marc van Borsele arrogantly breaks into her life. Suddenly he's giving her a lift in his Rolls, appearing at work in the London Hospital, standing on her doorstep. Why? Claribel wondered.

2934 SNOWY RIVER MAN Valerie Parv
Gemma's family had been hounded from their hometown because everyone thought her father a thief. Now Gemma wants to clear his name. But the only guide available to help her search for his body and the missing money is Robb Weatherill, whose father had been loudest in denouncing hers....

Available in September wherever paperback books are sold, or through Harlequin Reader Service:

In the U.S.
901 Fuhrmann Blvd.
P.O. Box 1397
Buffalo, N.Y. 14240-1397

In Canada
P.O. Box 603
Fort Erie, Ontario
L2A 5X3

TEMPTATION WILL BE
EVEN HARDER TO RESIST...

In September, Temptation is presenting a sophisticated new face to the world. A fresh look that truly brings Harlequin's most intimate romances into focus.

What's more, all-time favorite authors Barbara Delinsky, Rita Clay Estrada, Jayne Ann Krentz and Vicki Lewis Thompson will join forces to help us celebrate. The result? A very special quartet of Temptations...

- **Four striking covers**
- **Four stellar authors**
- **Four sensual love stories**
- **Four variations on one spellbinding theme**

All in one great month! Give in to Temptation in September.

TDESIGN-1

Shannon OCork

Ice Fall

The voyage of the century...
where fate, love and destiny meet
in the North Atlantic

A magnificent saga of passion, wealth, greed and power set against one of history's most infamous ocean crossings—the *Titanic*.

Available in September at your favorite retail outlet, or reserve your copy for August shipping by sending your name, address, zip or postal code along with a check or money order for $5.25 (includes 75¢ for postage and handling) payable to Worldwide Library:

In the U.S.	In Canada
Worldwide Library	Worldwide Library
901 Fuhrmann Blvd.	P.O. Box 609
Box 1325	Fort Erie, Ontario
Buffalo, NY 14269-1325	L2A 5X3

Please specify book title with your order.

® **WORLDWIDE LIBRARY**

MAS-1

Lynda Ward's TOUCH THE STARS

...the final book in the The Welles Family Trilogy

Lynda Ward's TOUCH THE STARS...the final book in the Welles Family Trilogy. All her life Kate Welles Brock has sought to win the approval of her wealthy and powerful father, even going as far as to marry Burton Welles's handpicked successor to the Corminco Corporation.

Now, with her marriage in tatters behind her, Kate is getting the first taste of what it feels like to really live. Her glorious romance with the elusive Paul Florian is opening up a whole new world to her.... Kate is as determined to win the love of her man as she is to prove to her father that she is the logical choice to succeed him as head of Corminco....

Don't miss TOUCH THE STARS, a Harlequin Superromance coming to you in September.

If you missed the first two books of this exciting trilogy, #317 RACE THE SUN and #321 LEAP THE MOON, and would like to order them, send your name, address and zip or postal code, along with a check or money order for $2.95 for each book ordered (plus $1.00 postage and handling) payable to Harlequin Reader Service to:

In the U.S.	In Canada
901 Fuhrmann Blvd.	P.O. Box 609
Box 1396	Ft. Erie, Ontario
Buffalo, NY 14240-9954	L2A 5X3

LYNDA-1C

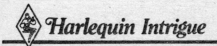

Harlequin Intrigue

Two exciting new stories each month.

Each title mixes a contemporary, sophisticated
romance with the surprising twists and turns of a
puzzler...romance with "something more."

Because romance can be quite an adventure.

Intrg-1

Romance, Suspense and Adventure

ROBERTA GELLIS

Journey across 19th century Europe with her lovers—men and women who struggle with their passionate needs, relentless desires, and tumultuous loves. In five glorious novels that will satisfy your every craving for romance.

_____	THE ENGLISH HEIRESS	12141-8-14	$2.50
_____	THE CORNISH HEIRESS	11515-9-06	3.50
_____	THE KENT HEIRESS	14537-6-12	3.50
_____	FORTUNE'S BRIDE	12685-1-24	3.50
_____	A WOMAN'S ESTATE	........19749-X-23	3.95

At your local bookstore or use this handy coupon for ordering:

DELL READERS SERVICE -Dept. B595C
P.O. BOX 1000, PINE BROOK, N.J. 07058

Please send me the above title(s). I am enclosing $_____ (please add 75¢ per copy to cover postage and handling). Send check or money order—no cash or CODs. Please allow 3-4 weeks for shipment. CANADIAN ORDERS: please submit in U.S. dollars.

Ms./Mrs./Mr._____

Address_____

City/State_____ Zip_____

She rekindles your yearnings
for love, dreams, and
dangerous passions.

Aleen Malcolm

☐ The Daughters of Cameron	12005-5-19	$3.50
☐ Kenlaren	14456-6-27	3.50
☐ Ride Out the Storm	17399-X-04	2.95
☐ The Taming	18510-6-48	3.95

At your local bookstore or use this handy coupon for ordering:

Dell DELL READERS SERVICE-Dept. B595D
P.O. BOX 1000, PINE BROOK, N.J. 07058

Please send me the above title(s). I am enclosing $_____ (please add 75¢ per copy to cover postage and handling.) Send check or money order—no cash or CODs. Please allow up to 8 weeks for shipment.

Name_____

Address_____

City_____ State/Zip_____